TUNNEL VISION

Also by Aric Davis

The Fort
Breaking Point
Rough Men
A Good and Useful Hurt
Nickel Plated

TUNNEL VISION

Aric Davis

THOMAS & MERCER

Published by Thomas & Mercer, Seattle

www.apub.com

Amazon, the Amazon logo, and Thomas & Mercer are trademarks of Amazon.com, Inc., or its affiliates.

ISBN-13: 9781477824955
ISBN-10: 1477824952

Cover design by Cyanotype Book Architects

Library of Congress Control Number: 2014936467

Printed in the United States of America

Dedicated to the memory of Anne Loveland Low

ONE

I have never been so angry in my entire life. I'm traveling south on a bus, with a trail of blood smeared behind me, bodies in my wake, and flashes of violence whenever I close my eyes, but none of it cuts through the rage. There are black marks on my neck, wrists, and ankles, cuts on my face and all over my even-leaner-than-normal body, and a furrow of ruined flesh from a gunshot wound on my left side. Packed gauze and stolen pharmaceuticals aren't the only things keeping me held together. Rage is why I'm alive, and it's carrying me south just as sure as this bus is.

Making your living as a criminal comes with its own list of unique risks, but I never thought that I'd be the one coming down on the wrong side of a setup. Call it naïveté or whatever else you want, but I was sure I had myself in a good place, and the only way I was going to get burned was by someone I trusted. I knew that was possible—there were no illusions for me—but when it happened even my black little soul was caught off guard.

"Sorry," Gary said to me, like that mattered when I was staring down the barrel of a shotgun and getting cuffed and being sent in off the books to a crooked juvenile internment camp.

Gary was my dealer, the loser I'd transformed with money and bags of high-grade marijuana into a kid with confidence. Gary would never betray me—I was sure of it—but I was wrong. The money got bigger and bigger, and that was that. Gary sold me out for a truck full of dope and a connection to move as much as he could harvest in Michigan's Upper Peninsula.

I hope for his sake he enjoyed the money, because his luck is about to change.

In some ways, I should be thanking Gary. Dad always said situations needed to find the right people to emerge as heroes, and I think he's probably right. Even though being a hero is the last thing I am, maybe I needed to end up at the Morton Correctional Camp more than almost anywhere else in the world. Though what I didn't need was to be sent in naked and without a plan.

On the books, Morton functioned as a state-run "camp" to help rehabilitate out-of-control youths. In reality, it was a den of corruption where beatings, rape, and murder were covered up as a matter of routine, and where every day was a savage exercise in squeezing every possible drop of money from the facility and its captive horde of desperate kids.

Gary never could have put me somewhere like that without help, and the help in question came from a man named Spider, who we'd been brokering a deal with up north.

The setup took months, both the part I was involved with and the stuff I found out later, but I'm a lot more concerned with how it ended. Gary and I drove up together in a U-Haul stuffed with baled-up marijuana, but he left alone in an empty truck with a duffel bag full of cash. Spider, as it turned out, wasn't just a white-trash drug dealer. He was also a guard at Morton, and his boss, Reginald Fillmore, was his coconspirator. Getting me out of the way was the plan from the beginning, but I bet they would have put me in the ground if they could do it all over again.

There were two types of people at Morton: those the guards favored and the rest of us. An average day would see us rented out to dig holes, shovel driveways, or perform other menial, usually backbreaking, local maintenance tasks—basically anything Fillmore and Spider could come up with to turn a dime. None of the prisoners were free of that work, but the ones in Spider's favor got better bedding, better food, and the effective right to rape or beat whoever they wanted.

My friend Sam, a shy kid who could draw better than anyone I've ever met, was being abused by an older boy named Tim. When I showed Tim the error of his ways with some of the dirty tricks I'd learned over the years from training with Rhino, Sam and I both found ourselves on Spider's shit list. Things only got worse from there.

Morton had been teetering on the edge of a full-scale rebellion for what felt like forever, and my beatdown of that bastard Tim sent a groundswell of confidence through the boys imprisoned there. But days later, Spider and Fillmore had put up with enough. Sam and I were brought out to the snow, where we were supposed to die. I didn't die, but Sam did. The men who killed him died, too, but that doesn't make up for wasting Sam's life, for his broken body covered by snow and dirt in some anonymous field in Northern Michigan.

Thinking about it as I stare out the window brings the rage back full force. Gary doesn't know I'm coming. He probably thinks I'm dead or locked away forever, but he should know better. Dad taught me to be resourceful and to help others whenever I could, but he also taught me to pay my debts in full. Spider and Fillmore are already dead. I made sure of that as I lay half-naked in the snow over the stock of a stolen M-14, my finger frozen to the trigger guard. But Gary isn't. I ran while Sam bled out in the snow, bullets flying after me, but I came back. Sam's grave was still being cut into the frozen earth, and even though two of Spider's armed flunkies were there, they couldn't kill me.

I smile at my reflection in the window, but my eyes tell the truth. *I'm coming for you, Gary, and I'm going to fucking kill you. Just like Spider and Fillmore.*

They say the first time you sell your body is supposed to be the worst, but they were the same people that told me the first time that you chase the dragon is the best. I think they were wrong on both counts, because selling myself never got better, and heroin never lost its luster, even though all either of them makes me feel anymore is dead inside.

It wasn't supposed to be like this. None of it was supposed to turn out so broken, so fucked-up. I've fucked over literally every person that tried to do right by me. I just didn't realize how much that was going to hurt, or how much those memories would just drive me back to using in the first place. I swear to God, if I could take it all back, I would. I hated being that broken girl at the record store, hated feeling like I was never going to escape my father's house. I hated everything. I'd give anything to have those days back.

There was purity in my life before heroin, but I know that whatever false sense of sobriety I retain from writing this will be gone soon enough. I'll be willing to do whatever D. says I have to in order for us to score—that's just how it is. I still see some of my friends on the street sometimes, and I wonder how they're doing, and I know that if I were clean I'd allow myself to ask them in person. Knowing that I'm a fucking junkie makes that impossible. All I'd do is get excited, and then get embarrassed, and then get high. By the time I finally saw Ben or any of those kids again I'd ask them for money until they gave it to me or I was told to leave, and I'd probably steal anything that wasn't nailed down. And that's not even the worst part. The part I hate the most is that I could do all of that and as long as I was high, I'd be happy. That's all I really want, all any addict really wants.

So this is what heroin is like. People think it's some crazy high, like being drunk and stoned, this crazy storm of wastedness, but it's not. It's better than that. Heroin is the perfect high, one awesome moment that's there and then gone. Heroin is like that perfect second before you decide to dance on a table or beer-bong a forty-ounce, only it lasts for hours. Heroin is the best once your body gets over being sick, but it's never that good again. Not that D. and I don't try and find that moment. Not that I don't get on my knees or spread my legs for the chance to get that feeling all over again. And what I get from that spike is just good enough to keep me going.

I don't want you to feel bad for me. I don't even expect anyone else to ever read this. I guess I'm writing this down so that if I ever do get myself out of this hole I dug, I'll have something to remind me that even at my worst I was still a human, and that there are still good reasons for me to be alive. This isn't about recovery, not yet, but maybe it can be someday.

> *I dream of summertime.*
> *But when bright rays begin to flounder,*
> *the ice is on my mind.*
> *Now all I have is four cold walls,*
> *some whiskey, and a pen.*
> *A needle full of broken dreams,*
> *and nights that never end.*
> *It's cold outside,*
> *snow is raining down.*
> *But all I have is loneliness,*
> *and days that never end.*
> *I'd give everything for some comfort,*

the gift of a sleeping death.
The fear has left my body, love,
but I hate the parts he left.

Tonight I had sex with three different strangers so that D. could get right, but there wasn't even enough dope for me to do a skin-pop, much less really groove on a spike for a little bit. Normally that would destroy me, but right now I feel good. Even in hell there are sweet spots, apparently. I know I'll be on my back soon enough, though—that's how this game works. I feel so bad about being a whore that I want to get high, or I want to get high so bad that I don't care about being a whore. D. is yelling again and I can hear his boots on the stairs.

Kiss kiss,
Mandy

TWO

Betty Martinez had officially had enough of high school. It was her junior year, but she felt more grown-up than she ever had in her life, and the new grounding handed down by her mothers all because of some stupid boy was the last straw. Betty didn't even like Jake Norton that much. He was what she had considered one of the more interesting prospects available to her at Northview High School, but the thrill had worn off quickly, and the grounding over a few erroneous texts just added insult to injury. Now, as she pored over the Internet for research on a paper about the American women's suffrage movement—a topic that had once seemed so cool, but now seemed as edgy as cotton candy—Betty felt more tired than she ever had in her young life.

What Betty wanted to be doing was living in the music pouring through her headphones—in this case, an album by the obscure and long-dead band Discount. She wanted to just fade away into the noise. Betty was five feet four and fit from her years in gymnastics, along with Andrea's insistence that her daughter occasionally tag along for judo classes. She had purple hair that was ready for either a redye or a new color altogether, a ring in her nose and a stud in her lip, and plans for a small tattoo just below her left breast that would make going to the beach this summer a straight-up bitch if she ever got up the nerve to actually get inked.

Not that the moms were likely to notice, at least not right away. Andrea was always busy in her work as a children's psychologist, and Ophelia was just as locked down into her gallery and her own art. Betty would much rather have their approval first, but she knew getting her mothers on board with that first of many planned tattoos was about as likely as ever getting a straight answer on who her father was.

As busy and inflexible on certain points as her moms were, Betty knew they weren't half as bad as she liked to imagine. It would have been so easy to run away if Ophy and Andy had been anything besides wonderful, but they were wonderful, and it would have destroyed them if Betty had just disappeared into the wind like an ash escaping a fire.

Betty couldn't help but wish for some neo-Dickensian upbringing that would allow her to hear the lyrics of her favorite bands with real understanding, instead of a bystander's empathy. When Alison Mosshart sang to some unknown lover, "We wave sometimes to pretend that nothing is changing, but you've gone on and I've gone off to get lost and devastated," Betty sang along, wondering when she would meet someone worth being devastated over.

Forcing her attention back to the computer, Betty perused the links at the bottom of the Wikipedia page on suffrage and sighed deeply. The subject had seemed perfect for unsettling the seemingly sexist Mr. Evans, but he'd been supportive of it from the start, and Betty knew that her attempt to be subversive had missed the mark yet again. *Why is it so damn hard to be an outsider these days?*

It wasn't the first time that Betty had caught herself enjoying this spoiled, deluded line of thinking, and she felt a pang of guilt over it, like she always did. Still, was craving a little adventure so bad? God, the best she could muster was the half-joking text from

Jake that Ophelia had seen and that had set this whole ridiculous grounding machinery in motion.

"Send pix of bewbs pls."

Betty smiled at the memory of it, but it was bittersweet. She felt trapped, just like Alice Paul and Lucy Burns and all of their dowdily dressed, badass suffragette friends had been, but at least those women had done something with their lives. What had Betty done with hers? College was a lifetime away, so far off her radar it wasn't even funny, even though her mothers kept bringing it up.

Turning from her homework to the all-but-ignored guitar on its stand in the corner of her room, Betty vowed that she was finally going to play the stupid thing this year. Betty's heroes lived in a world of guitar, bass, and drums in cities run to the tune of a four-four beat, and she just knew that the one pure chance of escape available to her in the world would come in the form of a hastily recorded demo CD.

And yet, what was she doing about it?

Surely there could be some adventure in the two summers left before college, but there seemed to be an impossible amount of bullshit to shovel before she got to enjoy any of it, and Betty's fear was that somehow she was going to miss out on all of it. She had two wonderful mothers, a best friend named June Derricks that she could confide anything in, and her whole life before her, but right now she was a bored high schooler confined to her room, and nothing felt worse than that.

When Ophelia called up to her that it was time for dinner, Betty scowled, grabbed her phone, and left her well-furnished cell.

Dinner was grilled chicken, asparagus, and salads of mixed greens and fruit. The moms had been experimenting on the deck with the new grill after work, and though Betty had found their early work to be a mix of raw and burnt offerings, tonight the food looked like it might be good.

Andrea walked in just as Ophelia sat down, and Betty watched her mothers exchange a kiss before Andrea set her bag on the floor and sat at the table. As Ophelia ran to fetch another plate of food from the kitchen, Andrea focused on their daughter. "How was your day?" she inquired, her voice wearing just enough ice to let her daughter know that, while she cared, she was still more than a little pissed off.

Betty's mothers were as different in appearance and mood as two people in love could possibly be. Andrea was an ass-kicking children's psychologist with a history of work with the Grand Rapids Police Department. She wore her hair short and dyed the same raven color it had been when she was younger. She was addicted to judo, hated liars, and didn't trust most people. Andrea was hard from her job, but she could be sweet when she wanted to be, and she occasionally took off her thick skin.

Ophelia hailed from Greece and was fond of retelling in epic terms the story of the beginning of their love (a story that, to Betty, simply sounded like two people with similar interests had just decided to talk one day). Ophelia was much slighter than Andrea, her hair a natural gray, and her clothes and arms were almost always spattered with paint from one of her projects. Despite the seeming lack of attention to herself—or perhaps bolstered by it—Ophelia was impossibly, depressingly, unattainably beautiful. She was by far the sweeter of the two, always lending a shoulder to cry on or an ear to talk to, but Betty had been growing distrustful of what was starting to feel like the moms' good cop/bad cop routine.

"My day was boring as usual," said Betty. "My paper sucks."

"I doubt that," said Andrea as Ophelia set a plate before her, and then sat at the table at her own spot.

"What am I missing?" Ophelia asked.

"Betty was just telling me that she was bored. Now, why do you suppose that might be?"

Betty rolled her eyes as the two older women exchanged a glance and Ophelia replied, "I can hazard a guess. Betty, would you like to talk about any recently revoked privileges?"

"Not particularly," said Betty. "Unless you just want me to say again that I'm sorry, in which case I'd love to."

Ophelia sighed and shook her head, and Andrea said, "Not going to be that easy, I'm afraid." Here it came again. "You showed a serious lack of judgment, Betty, and the worst part is that we know that you know better. Neither of us is even sure what to do at this point, to be honest. This behavior just doesn't even make any sense." Sermon apparently concluded, Andrea plucked a piece of chicken from her plate and popped it into her mouth, then smiled at Ophelia. "This is great, by the way. Did you get any calls?"

"Thank you and not yet," said Ophelia, while Betty suppressed another eye roll. Her mothers' jobs could be so fucking important sometimes that it was almost nauseating.

As Betty poked at her food—the chicken was, par for the course, a little dry—Ophelia said, "I'm sure we'll get some contact soon, and even if we don't it's not the end of the world."

Andrea nodded in sympathy, and Betty stared at them like they were a pair of aliens. She loved her moms deeply, but this sort of drama over nothing was enough to make her crazy. Other than the romantic risk they'd taken twenty years earlier, had the two of them ever risked anything? After all, the concern about the gallery was meaningless. Both of them knew the gap in scheduling three months in the future would work itself out, and the worst that could happen would be if they had to give a bunch of self-important artists from a private school a chance to display their crappy paintings and sculptures at one of Grand Rapids' more prestigious galleries.

"I think the more important subject is Betty," said Ophelia in between bites of food. "Both of us have a lot going on with work, I know, but it appears as if our daughter might need more attention from us."

This time Betty really did roll her eyes, and when she looked back at her mothers they were staring her down. Andrea's eyes were pinched and angry, but poor Ophelia just looked hurt. Andrea was a battler, but beating up on Ophy just felt like some sick kind of matricide. Betty blushed at the sight of her.

"I'm not trying to be an asshole, seriously," she told them. "You guys are acting like I was really going to send that idiot a picture of my tits, and—"

"You sent him a picture of yourself in a bikini," said Andrea coolly. "There is nothing funny about that, Betty. Sexism and gender roles aren't going to go anywhere, at least not in our lifetimes, but there's no need to play into stereotypes. By sending Jake that picture, even if it wasn't exactly what he was hoping for, you're forgetting how you were raised."

"But—" sputtered Betty, but her response was waved off by the waving finger of Andrea.

"But nothing. You knew exactly what you were doing. We've discussed this, what? A thousand times? Pictures like that, texts, e-mails, they don't go away. Everything you put out there can be used against you, make you look like some piece of street trash when you're just a sweet little girl that got in over her head with a boy. You know better, Betty. That's the problem, not that you talk to Jake or write him mash notes, but that you know better and that you'd be so willing to act like a person you're not."

"I'm not hungry," said Betty, and then she stood and walked calmly to her room. Tears were running down her face as she hit the stairs, but making it from the dining room without crying in front of them was victory enough.

Betty wanted to yell at them, to shout that Jake had been the one who took the bikini picture in the first place, and that sending it to him had been a joke. It wasn't a joke now, though, at least not a funny one.

God. Jake Norton.

Jake had just been something to break up the monotony a little bit, just a minor stop in the quest to find The One. Betty knew who that was—some distant boy in some faraway town who had as many dreams as she did about disappearing into a life of glory on the road. He'd love her poems, call them lyrics, and play a wicked lead guitar. Betty smiled despite the tears. Yeah, and sleeve tattoos wouldn't hurt, either.

When Ophy brought her food up twenty minutes later, Betty was cheerful enough to hug her mother and take the plate without so much as a cross word.

THREE

The late-morning trip from the bus station to home only takes a few minutes on my bicycle, but my bike isn't here, it's locked up in the garage back at the house. Instead of walking I call Lou, my longtime cabbie friend, and like usual, he's at the train station in minutes.

"Home," I say, and Lou knows to drive me to the gas station by my house. If he's curious about where I've been for the last two months he doesn't say anything. Lou just drives, his eyes locked to the road like always.

I'm practically shaking when Lou parks, both from the pain in my side and my desire to be home, as well as the growing fear that something will have happened to the house while I was gone.

I pay Lou with money I took from Fillmore's office, knowing as I do so that I'm lower in cash than I've been in years, but also knowing that Lou needs to be paid in full every single time. For all I know Lou would be OK with getting paid in installments, but I'm not going to find out. Lou is a certainty right now, and I'm a lot lower on certainties than I am on cash.

"Pick me up in an hour?"

Lou nods from the front seat. Doesn't say a word, but I know he'll be back, and I know he wouldn't tell a soul about where he picks me up or drops me off.

The walk to the house goes quickly, though I do have a growing fear in my belly that the house will be inaccessible when I get there. The stuff inside is all that I have in the world and none of it was easy to come by.

My plain little house is still standing, at least. I wonder if my neighbors have noticed that no one has been coming or going for a couple of months. I live in the new suburbs—closed doors and windows, neighbors that don't know each other—but my absence has to have been noticed by someone. And when they did see me, would it finally be the tipping point to make someone call the law about the boy with no parents?

I rub the wound in my side and the pain rushes in, forcing the bad thoughts into the well in the pit of my stomach. Lately it's been even more crowded than usual in there.

I walk up the driveway as though it's the simplest thing in the world, but my mind is insisting that FBI boogeymen will come flying from the bushes, looking for answers about the blood I left in the snow. No one comes, though—not the FBI, not Gary, and not a neighbor wondering where I've been. I walk around the house to the backyard and hop the fence, take the spare key from the biometric lockbox I keep on the patio, and then unlock the back door to the attached garage.

I sigh. All of my stuff is still where I left it. Even my bike is sitting unmolested. There are a lot of things that I'm going to need to do in the next few months, both for myself and for other people, and for the first time I feel like I might be able to actually do them.

I could cry, but I don't. My last tears froze to my cheeks. *I'm home.*

The house smells like it did when I left—there's the acrid odor of marijuana still lingering like a skunk's cousin. Not that the odor bothers me, of course—it's just another cost of doing business. I still have a few bales in the basement, enough to make a quick sale, but that's the last thing I'm worried about right now. I want to curl up in bed, dive onto the Internet, or sit on the kitchen floor and hug my fridge, but I do none of these things. Instead, I walk to the bedroom and slide a long storage container out from under my bed.

My get-out-of-town box is exactly what it sounds like, the stuff that I would need to leave and never come back, and just like the stuff in the garage, it's undisturbed. I look over the contents quickly, and settle on a fiberglass knuckle-duster. Flexing my fingers in it feels good and makes me wish Spider was still alive so I could give it a test run and deliver the sort of death a man that evil deserves. Spider's dead, though—Spider, his friends, and Fillmore, all little more than ash by now. A good thing, for sure, though not, I know, some magical solution to the problems of all those kids in that awful camp. Even as I sit here on my bedroom floor, they're undoubtedly already being sorted out by the system. All I can do is try to shrug off that knowledge.

I distract myself from considering the meager stack of banded cash in the box by focusing on another interesting gadget, a little zip gun I made a few years earlier. The thing holds only a single .45 bullet, and is as likely to fail as it is to shoot, but it's the only firearm in my arsenal and seems sufficient for the task. I've always stayed away from guns, but that's another thing that's changed since my trip north. I want to surround myself with iron of all types, but I'm not going to, not yet. Guns can attract too much attention, and the absolute last thing I need is any more of that.

I close the box and slide it under the bed, and then clear out of the room. Comfort was calling to me, my bed looking inviting as hell, but my pockets are full of hate. Rest can come later. Right now, I have work to do.

Back in front of the gas station, I sit and wait for Lou while the civilians roll back and forth in front of me on their way to lunch. Then his cab rolls up and I get in, rattling off the address of the farm where Gary and I were growing dope. Lou grunts and we're off, my nervous energy playing games with my stomach.

As much as I've been relishing this moment, savoring the thought of putting my hands on Gary, I know the reality will be nothing to look back on fondly. I slide my fingers through the knuckle-duster in my pocket, flex them, and let the thing go.

Lou drops me off by the property without a word, and I hand him cash and tell him that I'll be in touch. He grunts again, a talkative day for my cabbie, and I get to walking.

The pole barn we grew in is visible, as is the little farmhouse next to it. I have a feeling Gary will be in the barn working, and the unnatural blue light coming through the window near the ceiling and the bass thumping through the walls confirm it for me. A shiver runs down my spine as I think about what led me here, about everything that happened at the camp. The image of Sam laid out on the snow is a tough thing to shake. It's good, though. I'm furious, madder than hell at this idiot and what he did for money. I can see Spider all over again, leading boys from the building while I sight down at him over the freezing stock of an M-14. My fingers were cold then, frozen to the trigger guard, but that didn't keep fire out of that barrel.

I take a deep breath, and the knuckle-duster and zip gun appear in my hands as if by magic, and then I'm sliding open the door to the barn and walking in.

Rap music blares from the chest-high speakers in the corner of the room, but other than the stupid, boastful lyrics and bone-vibrating bass, the place is exactly as I remembered it. Water runs from the system of drip hoses I hung over the rows of dope, and grow lights cast a blue glow onto the plants. The pot itself is still early in the grow cycle, the clones barely more than a foot tall, but they'll be taller than me soon enough.

There's no sign of Gary as I make my way slowly around the plants, my hands and their contents tucked in my jacket pockets, and I'm starting to wonder if perhaps he's in the house after all, when I smell a different odor. This pot's on fire. Somewhere in here Gary is burning dope and relaxing while he watches my labor rise from the soil.

I round the last row of plants and there's Gary, sitting in a folding chair with a joint pinched between a thumb and forefinger. His eyes widen as he realizes he's not alone, and then widen further when he realizes just who it is that's come to see him.

"Holy shit," says Gary. "You're back, man. That's great, supercool." He's up on his feet, stretching a panicked smile over his face. "Hey, Nickel. Spider couldn't be trusted, man, for real. He had me over a barrel, too. It's great you got past that crazy asshole!"

I can barely hear the words as I cross the room. Gary's busy staring a hole into a jacket lying a few feet away from him, and I know he's got a gun in there. Gary has never seen me train, never seen me fight, never really seen me as anything more than money, but he's about to learn all about me.

"Spider's dead, Gary," I say. "I shot him."

Gary's eyes dart to the jacket again, fight-or-flight battling with the haze of blue smoke fogging his thoughts.

"Spider's dead, and so are a lot of other people," I explain to him. "And you don't get to lie to me anymore. You already did enough of that."

"I'm not lying," says Gary, and I can only shake my head in disgust. He's backing away, getting closer to the coat, but the zip gun is out and my finger is on the trigger.

"Sure you're lying," I say. "You just told me this was all because of Spider. But if this was his idea, then why did he pay you?"

Gary doesn't answer me, just keeps inching closer to the coat. He's got nothing to say and we both know it. He made a deal with Spider to make me go away, and now I'm back.

Gary turns and dives to the floor for the jacket. I draw down on him as he frees a 1911 from the pocket—a classier gun than I would have expected—and I pull the trigger.

Nothing happens.

The zip gun falls from my fingers and I'm sprinting toward Gary, wishing I could try this all over and not be so cocky, use matches and gas and just forget about the money, but it's too late for that now.

It looks like slow motion as Gary raises the pistol and measures me up through the sights.

I leap to the left as he fires, landing atop a row of marijuana plants and rolling off them, onto the cement floor. Another shot rings out, shattering a plastic pot but missing me. I'm on my feet at the sound of the gun, moving fast down the row of plants and chancing a look back over my shoulder. I get a glimpse of him standing back there with his gun, watching me and probably thinking I'm heading for the door, so I duck low and head the opposite way. Hopping the row of short plants could have tripped me up and gotten me killed, but it doesn't. I land on my feet, sprinting as another shot echoes through the room.

"I swear to God I'll kill you if you don't leave!" screams Gary, but it couldn't hold less weight. He already did kill me, and here I am, back from the dead.

The problem is the gun. I'm a moving target, and Gary is clearly not the best shot, plus he's high right now. Not that it matters much. The closer I get the easier the shots will be, and I've been shot enough already for my liking.

Free of the plants now, I find myself near the back wall of the barn. Gary is doing me the favor of holding still, and I'm definitely closer to him, but the gun still stands between us like some immovable object. Gary fires again, the bullet missing me but striking the backside of the barn, letting a thin beam of light into the barn. None of that interests me however. I'm back on the path towards Gary. He's cursing and banging on his gun with his fist. There's something wrong with the thing, and it's time to cash in.

Gary is trying to rack the slide on the 1911, but one of the .45 hollow points he's loaded has gotten its brass stuck in the ejection port, and I close the distance between us just as the brass flies free. My world slows to a crawl as Gary raises the gun up, the hole at the end of it impossibly huge, and I launch to the right just as it goes off, the sound of it louder than anything in recent memory. This round doesn't get stuck, and Gary's readjusting his aim, but it doesn't matter—I'm too close.

A good punch is thrown not with your hand or even your arm, but with your whole body. Watch a boxer whip a haymaker sometime, or even better, go down to Rhino's gym and watch him. There's a reason he dominated the mixed martial arts world before the UFC put it in your living room, and it's not just because he grew up starving on the streets of Curitiba. Rhino throws a hook from the balls of his feet, through his pelvis, and then out his shoulder, putting his whole body together to deliver the pain. The results when Rhino does this now are electrifying, but watching his old tapes can be a squeamish experience. When Rhino hits you, soft parts bleed and hard parts bend, consciousness is unlikely, and he's just getting started. After all, there's a reason they call the man Rhino.

I can't punch like my teacher, but I can hit pretty hard, and unless Rhino was cheating, he wasn't wearing fiberglass knuckle-dusters under his gloves. My whole body vibrates, starting with my hand as the shot collides with Gary's face, and he drops the pistol and takes a hard seat on the floor. A mist of blood hovers over the fallen pistol, and then I'm on top of him, the first punch just the beginning. Gary screams while I rain down punches. All I can think of is Sam, and that just makes me hit him harder.

I do finally take a break, while he's still able and conscious enough to speak. In a minute or so, I know everything. The money's gone, spent on a new car and used to pay rent here and fix his mother's house up. He's coming to a bit, thinking he still has a future to speak of and telling me he's going to use this year's crop to get rich all over again and we can go halfsies, just like before Spider came and screwed us over. I want to tell him that isn't going to happen, that his plants look like crap and that the irrigation system I built is half-clogged with mold, but I don't. By then Gary's dead, and in another minute or so the barn and house are on fire, and I'm on the phone with Lou.

FOUR

Betty suffered through the first two periods of school—math and chemistry—and then made her way to the gym. Jake walked with her but the silence between them was palpable, even in the crowded and noisy halls. He knew she was mad, even if it wasn't really his fault, and he was making it abundantly clear that he had no idea what to do with anything on her face aside from smile.

"Is everything all right?" Jake asked annoyingly as they parted to head to their respective locker rooms.

"I'm fine."

"All right," said Jake as he left her in the hall. Betty didn't look back, but she knew there was likely one of those oh-so-predictable looks of male bewilderment on his face.

"You're such a bitch," called a voice as she entered the locker room, and Betty smiled at the sound. It was June. Betty gave her friend a wave and crossed the locker room to her.

June Derricks was an awkward girl, too tall, too weird, too loud, and possibly the clumsiest person Betty had ever met, but she loved her all the same. June's hair was the same color as Betty's, a quickly fading purple, but hair color was not the only thing the girls had in common.

June wore stainless steel in her septum and had paired studs in her lower lip, along with a tattoo of a heart on her left wrist. At the moment, she was stripping down from a short skirt and a hoodie covered in patches in order to dress in the ugliest clothes for gym that she'd been able to score thrift shopping before the start of the school year.

Betty dropped her bag on the bench next to June and began spinning the dials on her lock. June was mock-stretching on a bench, her bony physique in comic contrast to her baggy white shorts, the outfit tied together with neon-pink wristbands and a Spin Doctors shirt that had more holes than fabric.

"I'm serious, though," said June. "You are a bitch."

Rolling her eyes, Betty pulled her own clothes clear of the locker, then slid her bag off the bench so she could sit. "Fine, I'm a bitch. 'Fuck Martinez.' Like the song."

"You're not really a bitch, you're just callous," said June, who yanked a headband over her hair and then said, "Of course, the owners of those shattered hearts you've left behind might disagree with that."

"You're the worst," said Betty as she closed her locker. "You're my friend, and all you do is give me shit. Between the moms and this, I'm not really feeling the love lately. I should probably just run off with some carnies and smoke meth until my teeth fall out, and then when I come back you can throw me an intervention and I can tell you how you drove me away and I only had all of my carny children because you made me feel so bad about myself."

"And because you needed someone to run the Tilt-A-Whirl," said June. "Don't forget that part."

"Yes, and because I needed someone to run the Tilt-A-Whirl," said Betty. "Exactly right. Wait, hold up. Why are you so concerned about my love life? If I recall, there have been more than a few miscues for little old June Bug, too. Remember that guy you met on Facebook last year? Because if I remember right, you told him that you would—"

"You need to get that shit out of your mouth," said June. "I know all of your dirty little secrets, too, so if you want to get nasty, we can get nasty." June accentuated the words with a snap of her fingers and a quick but violent bobble of her head, and then both girls burst into laughter. "We need to hurry, though," said June as she sat to tie a filthy Reebok. "I do not need another gym tardy." She snuck a look over her shoulder. "And you know the Carp has her eyes on us."

"The hell with the Carp," said Betty, not quite brave enough to say the words at maximum volume, lest their gym teacher overhear the forbidden nickname.

June rolled her eyes.

"Seriously, though, Betty. You need to let Jake go. You're going to mess that boy up, and he's the regular kind. You'll leave some scars. If you really drag it out, he'll be one of those guys you see at Meijer's. You know the type, the ones following the wife around while she shops? Their eyes don't leave the floor, and it's all because some mean girl in school was playing 'collect them all' and fucked up a few innocents. True story."

"Jake is tougher than that, believe me," Betty said. "And he's just a thing right now. A fun thing, but that's it. I'm not trying to be mean; I'm just trying to enjoy myself." Betty frowned. "And I really don't think guys like that at the grocery store got that way from high school romance. I think that takes more of a slow beatdown from a domineering wife. Probably how Ophy and Andy would be if Ophelia didn't have such thick skin."

"Hey! Don't talk shit about your moms. They're the best. If I could, I'd move into your house right now. At least the moms don't hate each other. You've got easy street compared to my divorced idiots."

"Well, right now I'm grounded on easy street, and trust me, just because the moms get along doesn't mean they're always easy to get along with." Betty sighed. "They're still just parents, and right now they're pretty pissed off at me."

"All I'm saying is you need to stop dragging Jake along," said June. "I mean, I'm sure he's enjoying the fringe benefits of hanging out with a lady with your experience, but—"

"Fuck you," said Betty with a frown. "I'm not the one who lost my virginity at summer camp."

"Cold-blooded," said June as Betty tittered, and then the bell rang. "All right, we can debate this later, I guess," she said, and then they were running from the locker room with the flood of girls headed to the gym.

Down the hall Betty could see Jake and a few of his hockey-playing friends as they spilled into the gym from the boys' locker room.

He's cute, mused Betty, *but June is right.*

As cute or cut as Jake might be, he was so far from what she imagined in a boyfriend that it was hard to believe they'd lasted the few months they had. What the hell was she thinking? There was some edgy something about him, though he'd never been anything but funny, cute, and an utter gentleman with her. Maybe it was that dark streak that drew her to him. Jake rarely shied from a fight, on the ice or off it, and Betty had vivid memories of him beating a kid who'd asked for her number outside the mall last summer. The kid had been pushy, but Jake knew he was stronger, and he smiled when he hurt him. She hadn't been drawn to *that*, she knew that much. Betty could remember the kid's screams even more vividly than she could the images of the event that had been all but burned into her mind.

The girls mixed with the boys in the gym, and the class of sixty lined up in front of their PE teacher, Ms. Suzanne Carpowitz, a.k.a. the Carp. The Carp had earned her nickname from more than just a play on words: the unfortunately pear-shaped and utterly ageless gym instructor had an upturned nose and an absolutely enormous pair of lips. So far as anyone attending her classes knew, Ms. Carpowitz had been called the Carp behind her back since time out of memory, and there had been more than one occasion where another teacher had slipped up and referred to the aggressive woman by her less than complimentary name.

Fishlike or not, the Carp was a brutal taskmaster, and despite her unathletic appearance, she was as agile and strong as any of the varsity athletes. It was amazing. The Carp seemed to excel at whatever activity they happened to be doing, from tennis to wrestling.

With a wave of the Carp's hand and a growled "Warm up," the coed class began some light calisthenics. Two minutes later, the Carp blew her whistle and the class began to run between the painted lines of the track that rounded the perimeter of the gym.

Betty had never been much for running. She enjoyed cardio, at least as it pertained to the judo classes she took with her mother, but felt like there was something inherently stupid about just running in a circle. Still, she was dutifully running along in a group with June, not speaking, just pumping her legs and waiting for the Carp to blow her whistle, when she felt a tap on her shoulder.

Still running, she turned her head to see that June had dropped out of the pack and that Jake was now jogging next to her. He gave Betty a short wave, and she faked a smile.

"What's wrong?" Jake asked for maybe the two hundredth time. "Please don't just tell me you're fine again, I'm serious. Was it something I did?"

"I'm just grounded and irritable," said Betty as she spared a look to the Carp. The gym teacher had a hawk's eye and a hatred for talking in place of sweating.

All Betty could think as she looked at Jake was what a stupid mistake this whole thing was. The poor boy obviously felt something for her that was never going to be mutual, but she couldn't think of a single way to say that without sounding horrible. *You really are a bitch*, thought Betty, and the thought carried a weight that the words spoken by June had been missing.

"I get it," said Jake. "And I know that it's all at least half my fault, and I'm really sorry—"

"*Half* your fault?" she said. "You have got to be fucking kidding me, Jake! You sent me that stupid message, and you weren't joking. And so I did the only thing I could think to do and—"

A whistle cut her off, and then the Carp's voice boomed from across the gym. "Martinez, drop and give me ten!"

Betty groaned and walked to the side of the track, assumed the push-up position, and got to work. She could see Jake running away from her, his perfect calves carrying his muscled body across the floor. Perfect Jake was somehow coming off clean again, even though he was the one always asking to see bewbs and then talking while running.

Betty heaved against the floor, doing the push-ups as fast as she was able while her classmates circled the track, and for what felt like about the millionth time that week, she wanted to be anywhere except where she actually was.

FIVE

My temperature got up to 103 degrees in the week after I killed Gary, but I never even considered the hospital. Instead, I worked my way through my purloined drugs and tried to sleep as much as possible.

Bad memories came and went with the fever, some of Sam, a lot of Fillmore and Spider. Spider had been easy, in retrospect. I shot him and he fell. When I went after Fillmore, the camp had been put to the torch, and he was in his office trying to make some history disappear. When all was said and done, my hands were raw, he was dead, and there was a money roll in my back pocket. I thought I'd leave it all behind me, but the flames of that day haunted my fevered mind in wakeful dreams and nightmares that have faded in and out ever since.

The wound in my side had opened up during the fight with Gary, my hand was swollen up like a balloon, and all of my other nagging injuries were finally taking their toll. Coming out of that fever was like being reborn. I had yet to tell anyone besides Lou that I was back in town, but I didn't even worry about it while I was boiling at home alone. Either I'd see Jeff and Rhino again or I wouldn't. They know what I do, and I think they both know that one of these days I'm going to just disappear.

Even now that I'm on the mend, seeing my friends will need to wait, unfortunately. I need money, badly, and there are a legion of messages left for me on dummy Facebook accounts, e-mail addresses, texts, and calls on burner cell phones. I know before I even get started that most of these leads have undoubtedly dried up in my absence, but I start from the top anyway. Gary was supposed to be my salvation, but instead he'd damn near killed me, and now I needed to pick up the pieces.

It's two hours later, and the leads are even drier than I expected. The few people who've responded to my follow-ups have either given up on the problem or taken to other means to solve it. I'm craving the work that I normally hate—finding out if somebody's old lady is cheating, or if some employee isn't quite as injured as they say they are. Those are the boring jobs, but they're also the ones that pay, and that's exactly the kind I need.

Don't get me wrong, I'll never forget about what Dad wants me to do, and I sure won't ever turn down a kid that needs help. I just need a few things to get me back on my feet. Pot grows fast, but it won't be done tomorrow, so I need a solution that I won't need to watch grow.

And then, right when the outlook's blackest, I get a legit response. A woman named Claire tweets me and wants to get together to talk about some concerns she has for her daughter. She balks when I mention money, but I assure her that we'll be able to work something out, just as long as she understands that limited funds mean a limited amount of work. I'd love to be a charity for everyone out there that needs help, but this is not the time to be looking out for the rest of the world.

We cover the fine points, I explain how and where to meet me, and just like that I've got a meeting with a client. I'll admit, it's not exactly lighting my world on fire the way a spat between a lawyer and a doctor would, but hey, worst-case scenario, I make a few bucks and help the lady out.

SIX

Betty soldiered through the rest of school, ignoring Jake's texts as they came through with increasing frequency. She knew that her moms rarely looked into the phone stuff, thanks to the unlimited plans on their cell phones, but she would have been shocked if they didn't look this week to see if their whore daughter and that awful pimp, Jake Norton, hadn't been communicating.

It was enough to make her sick, and it was only the respite of getting behind the wheel of her ten-year-old Volkswagen Beetle that had any effect on her mood. She drove home while the Ramones sang their mindless and catchy punk through the speakers, and by the time she was home she was smiling despite herself.

Betty could hear the music before she opened the front door, and though she couldn't imagine what Ophelia could possibly be painting that would be best influenced by 1990s gangsta rap, she did feel that her mother's muse was a good one. Suppressing a grin, she walked inside and shut the door after her, grabbed a bottle of water from the fridge and trudged upstairs to work on her homework. In addition to the suffrage paper, she had math homework, an English test in two days, homework for her chem lab in three, and what felt like a mountain of other bullshit on her shoulders.

Betty sat at her desk and slid her computer from her school-bag, uncased it, and then waited for a few minutes as it fired up. When the laptop was ready, Betty tossed on a pair of cheap headphones, flicked the mouse to a playlist on iTunes, and then got to work on the suffrage paper.

As always, she started with Wikipedia. There wasn't a teacher in the world that would have allowed her to cite from a website so easily, and so often mistakenly, altered by random users, but the bibliography at the bottom of each page was a gold mine. Betty, like most students, hated the search for good sources, but here they were, all properly organized and ready for a couple mouse clicks to transport them to the bottom of her own paper.

When she was satisfied with the shored-up back end of her paper, even if the majority of the writing was yet to be done, Betty slid the headphones from her ears, stretched in her chair, and headed to the kitchen to see if there was anything worth eating.

After a brief inspection of the refrigerator, cupboard, and fruit basket, Betty settled on a handful of raspberries and half an apple one of the moms had left in the door of the fridge. Deciding that the fruit would hold her over until that evening's meal-and-fight, Betty trudged back up the steps, Ophelia's music providing a bass-driven rhythm that made it impossible not to feel like she was dancing along as she moved.

Halfway up the steps, though, there came a knock at the door. Most likely the UPS driver. Heaving an annoyed sigh, Betty walked back down and swung open the heavy door without checking the peephole or attaching the U-bolt—both major no-no's in Andrea's book—and found before her not the UPS man, but a grinning June.

"What are you doing here?" Betty asked. "I'm grounded, remember?"

June shook her head and said, "Doesn't matter. Does not matter." The way June's eyes were bugging out of her head had Betty wondering if her friend might not have decided to embark on a second and more successful attempt at their previous summer's goal of buying magic mushrooms, but then she saw the piece of paper June was waving in her right hand.

"What is that?"

June pushed past her into the house and on into the dining room. "I rushed over as soon as I saw this," she said, shaking the paper. "I stopped by Vertigo to see if they had the new Captain, We're Sinking—they did—and on my way out, I saw this." She held the paper aloft and shook it again for emphasis, but she was rattling it too hard for Betty to learn anything other than the fact that the paper appeared to be some sort of a flyer.

"What is that?" Betty asked again, but June didn't appear capable of staying still long enough to tell her what she was so excited about. She walked past the dining room table into the kitchen, the paper fluttering in her clenched fist, flung the fridge open, and grabbed a can of Diet Coke.

The snap of the soda opening reminded Betty of a television gunshot—especially with Ophelia's music in the background—but June took a long, leisurely pull off the can, yanked a seat from the dining room table, and plopped down onto it.

"Do you have any idea how much trouble I'm going to be in if Ophy comes out here and sees you?" Betty said as she sat next to her friend. "I'm like the most grounded person ever, and I'm pretty sure that even covers crazy best friends."

June shook her head with a smile and then smacked the flyer down on the table in front of Betty.

Betty made an O with her lips when she read it, and then looked to June, who was beaming. "Holy shit," said Betty.

The flyer June had taken from Vertigo Music advertised a show that was to take place at the Pyramid Scheme, a local bar and punk rock venue. Numerous bands were listed as playing, but the most prominent one on the list was a band that hadn't played a show that either of the girls had been aware of in a very long time. Old Croix Road had achieved no small amount of local press after winning a high school battle of the bands by a wide margin, but the kicker was that the oldest boy in the band was twelve at the time. That had been back in 1997, before either of the girls had been born, and neither had ever imagined there would be an opportunity to see them live.

Betty took the flyer off the table and gave it another look. In addition to Old Croix Road there were a number of other smaller regional acts—Alkaline Trio, the Lawrence Arms, Mustard Plug, North Lincoln, Mixtapes, Hamilton, Walls of Jericho, Small Brown Bike, Smatch, and the Bounty Hunters were all listed as confirmed—but as Betty set the flyer down on the table she could already feel the excitement fading from her.

There were more words at the top and bottom of the paper, but Betty was ignoring them. The only important information was that the concert was happening on May 15, one month to the day from then.

"No way am I going to be able to go," she lamented. "I'll still be grounded, most likely, but even if I wasn't, this is on a school night. Plus, even if your parents and the moms were cool, there's still the matter of getting tickets. The Pyramid Scheme is small, June, and there's no way a show like this won't sell out instantly."

June shrugged and pulled two pink-and-white striped tickets from her pocket.

"Maybe it will and maybe it won't, and maybe we'll have to sneak out and steal cars or rob a bank to go, but I've got fucking tickets!"

"No."

June laid the proof on the table in front of her.

"They went on sale today, Betty. Right when I got to the store. It's basically a secret show, a benefit for some guy." June pounded her hand on the table. "We have tickets, and we're going, both of us. I don't care if I'm grounded all of senior year, there's no way I'm missing this, not for anything!"

Ophelia and her rap music forgotten, both girls began to shriek and jump up and down in their seats. Betty could hear pounding on the stairs as Ophelia charged from her studio in the basement to discover the source of the disturbance, but she didn't care. *Somehow I'm going to this, even if June's right and we are grounded for all of senior year.* It would be a worthy sacrifice, and with luck, maybe even a bit of an adventure to boot.

Ophelia rushing through the door to the basement didn't ruin the moment, but it did temper the excitement. "Hello, June," she said. "Betty, would you mind telling me why you have a guest when you're grounded?"

"It's my fault, Mrs. Dranias," said June perfectly and primly, and Betty could tell by the look on Ophelia's face that she enjoyed the correct pronunciation of her oft-butchered name.

"Fine," said Ophelia. "You both can explain, then."

Betty and June shared a grin, and then got to talking.

When they were done, Ophelia was frowning, and though they'd made a compelling argument, Betty knew that they'd failed. Even worse, they'd shown their hand; sneaking out would be impossible. Not only would her mothers be on alert that night, but they would also know exactly where to find her if she did leave.

Telling Ophelia had been a mistake, but it had been an unavoidable one, and as painful as the situation was, Betty was glad that at least June could go.

Betty and June watched as Ophelia snatched up the flyer, frowning at it with her perfectly sculpted face. As usual, she wasn't wearing makeup, and not for the first time Betty wished that somehow she could have shared in some of that oh-so-fortunate DNA.

As her mother pored over the flyer, Betty came to realize that it wasn't the bands or the date that she was concentrating on, but something else, what appeared to be a name at the top of the flyer.

"What does that say?" Betty asked the room, and while Ophelia stayed silent, June said, "It's a benefit show for some guy named Duke Barnes. I guess he needs to be freed or something."

"June, you should go to this," said Ophelia, "but I'm afraid that Betty will not be attending."

"Please, Mom? I'll do anything," said Betty.

"Let it go, Betty," said Ophelia. "This isn't a fight to have, not right now."

SEVEN

I walk into the park feeling like I own the place. I may as well—no one else does. Riverside is as much of a home as the place where I lay my head. I feel alive there. Maybe it's the plants, or maybe it's knowing where the bodies were planted. Hell, maybe it's just Eyepatch. Riverside is his, too, ours in a way that only people who truly love a place can possess it. Four summers ago he was trading bullets while I ran with a scared and wounded little girl. I caught lead (that's how these things can work), but so did the bad guys.

I think about those days like they're some faded flag, my personal mark of glory. I've done good things since then, but nothing like that, and all too often my hands come back bloody. I can deal with that, as long as I know that's how it's supposed to be, but at night when I'm alone, it can be tough to think about. Seriously, roll it over on your tongue: *I've killed people.* You'd think it would be easy, like it is on TV, but it's not. Even killing bad people like Gary or Spider leaves a scar. Why do you think so many soldiers wind up jacked up? It's not all black and white or singing songs around the old oak tree when there are bodies in your wake.

The park is mostly empty. Kids are playing, and moms are on their phones ignoring them, the whole world aglow in the light of computers that can slip into a pocket. Hey, I'm not immune. I keep a phone, too, but I'm not married to it. I think we're supposed to use them like tools, but instead they function more like a leash. When was the last time you saw someone leave a cell phone home on purpose and not make a big deal out of it? I know what I see when I watch a person with their nose in a phone while they drive a car or walk down the road: I see someone I can take advantage of. Not a civilian, but a pigeon, and usually a fat one that's just waiting to be plucked.

Today I'm meeting the woman I met on Twitter a few days back. I still have some reservations, but beggars can't be choosers. All I want is a neck above water and a head below the radar. Fat chance of either one of those things happening, with the fire at the farm all over the news, and I'm just waiting to see cruisers pacing me on my bike.

I see her as I cross in front of the playground equipment. She sounded older on the phone, and she looks rough, but I couldn't care less. All I really care about is that she followed instructions, and unless there are two forty-year-old women walking Riverside Park wearing boots, a skirt, and a sweatshirt, it looks like she has.

"How are you?" I ask as I walk up behind her, and she jumps. I honestly don't make an effort to sneak up on people. It's just that civilians are so oblivious. They think they're safe no matter where they are, and then they wonder why bad things happen all the time. Watch your six, stay worried, and get ready to run. That's how you stay safe. Leave the pistol work for the cowboys and the dudes in blue.

"I'm fine, are you—"

"Yeah, we talked on the phone. You're Claire?" She nods, still looking a little shell-shocked over getting caught off guard, and I give her a little grin to help break the ice before we start the heavy lifting. "So what's the trouble? I know you don't want to talk to the law or we wouldn't be here, so spill."

"I don't want to talk to *anyone* about this," says Claire, looking like she's scared someone else is going to jump out at her on her blind side. It's my fault. I got her blood pressure up, but still: she needs to learn to trust me if she wants me to work a job. After all, if there were someone coming, I'd be the first person to tell her to hit the deck.

"I get that," I say. "I hear it all the time, in fact. But telling me is like telling a priest or a doctor. My lips are sealed, and unlike a man of God, I get results."

"I'm worried about my daughter."

"Why?"

"We . . . Our family has some skeletons in our closet, bad ones, and I'm terrified she's going to get a look at them."

I nod, smile, and then lock eyes with her. "I need more than that."

She took a deep breath, then said, "There was a girl killed a few years ago," the words coming out of her slower than cold toothpaste. "I don't want my daughter to know anything about her."

"What was her name?"

"Mandy."

"Mandy Reasoner?" I ask, already shaking my head, and Claire nods in agreement, her words all spent for the moment.

"Look, I'd love to help, Claire, but there's a problem. I don't know how Mandy Reasoner could have anything to do with your daughter, but no matter what, you're asking me to handle something that already got handled, something in the past, and that's not the way this world works. You don't have the money to make me shut up everyone who might know about that case. There's just no sense in trying to make the truth disappear."

"I know you can't make what happened go away. I just don't want her caught up in it." Her eyes are glistening, and that soft part in my chest that I keep next to what's left of my heart starts playing a little song.

"Lady, I can do a lot, but I can't put the paint back in the can. There's always going to be a stain." I shake my head. "I have to ask you, though. Why does it matter? What are you so worried she's going to find out about Mandy Reasoner?"

"They're trying to get the man that killed her released, and I want my daughter to be safe."

"From the man who killed Mandy?"

"From everybody."

None of it is making much sense, but we've at least drifted into an area where I can operate. "I can watch your daughter if you want," I tell her. "Make sure she avoids trouble for the most part, but it's going to be tricky. Duke might get released, and he might not, but even if he did, how would he even find her? And why would he even want to?"

"Can you keep her safe, or not?"

If people could just come out and tell me stuff, my job would be a lot easier. "I'm going to need to know what it is you think is going on, lady."

She closes her eyes for a few seconds, like I'm causing her physical pain, and then she opens them. "You've heard of her, so you must have heard about the people trying to set Duke free, right?"

"Yeah, I know about that."

"What if they're right? What if he really didn't do it?"

I'm beginning to wonder if it's even possible for this woman to make sense. "Well, what if he didn't? What's that got to do with your daughter?" But before she can answer, something else occurs to me. "Claire, you need to be straight with me," I say, leaning in close. "Do you know who killed Mandy?"

"No. I've always assumed the court got it right, but now there are so many people saying he could still be out there—"

I put up a hand, cutting her off. I need to just simplify this loopy job. "How many hours a day are we talking?"

"My daughter is still in school, so not many," says Claire. "Just enough to make sure she's keeping her nose clean and stays safe. Whatever you can do to steer her away from this whole business, that'd be great. But it's even more important to me that she stays safe."

I nod, try to look like I'm just considering taking the job, but I know the score even if she doesn't. I need this job, I need the money, and I need to keep myself busy. Being lonely hurts, and most of the people I care about are never coming back.

"I'll do it," I say, and she nods. She's already opening her mouth, but then I tell her the terms and she stops nodding, starts frowning, but agrees to pay me. I'm getting a tenth of what I would have been paid even just a couple of years ago—I never would have guessed the economy would have crippled even a crook like me, but here we are—but she's looking at me like I'm stealing from the church bowl. "I'll need her name."

"Her name is June Derricks, and Mandy is her aunt," says Claire and she hands over a picture of her daughter. All of a sudden, everything begins to make sense.

"You know there's no way you'll be able to keep her from knowing about this forever, right?"

"I just want her to be safe," says Claire, and I nod.

Secrets won't stay buried forever, no matter how deep you make the hole. But safe? That's something I can help with.

EIGHT

Betty spent her night buried behind a wall of studying and wondering. The paper was coming along swimmingly, but she couldn't help but wonder what June's mom would have to say about the show. Most likely just that June was allowed to go and little else.

Betty wanted to ask Andrea about a possible reprieve when she got home, but the look on her mother's face told her that Andrea was in no mood for hearing about a grounding violation, nor did she look like she wanted to discuss a punk rock show, even a really important one. Still, Betty did her best to maintain the goodwill that Ophelia had shown her, so she was talkative throughout the meal, ate her salad with gusto, and then cleared the table and did the dishes without being asked.

Drying her hands with a kitchen towel as she returned to the dining room, Betty had been expecting some small amount of gratitude for the completion of the unrequested chores, but found the moms entirely focused on each other. Clearly they'd been talking, *really* talking. Instead of sticking around to hear if they were discussing her or one of the bleak tales that Andrea carried home from work, Betty scurried off to the safety of her room.

Betty was buried deep in her homework when her phone rang around eight o'clock, the time of day where she tended to feel the most bruised by her school workload. Betty grabbed the iPhone and saw that it said "June Bug" across the caller ID.

"What's up?" Betty asked in the way of teenagers that don't really care what's up at all, but June's voice surprised her. Unless Betty was mistaken, her friend was crying. "Hey, are you all right?" she asked, but hated the words as they came out of her mouth. If June was all right, she wouldn't be crying, so why was she asking her best friend such a stupid question?

"My mom is fucking crazy," spat June. "I'm serious, Betty. Claire has officially flipped her shit."

"Calm down," said Betty, "and try and talk more quietly. If Claire hears you calling her crazy, she's going to go fucking nuts."

"No worries there," said June. "Mother is at the bar, guaranteed. I showed her that flyer when I came home. At first she looked like she was going to pass out, and then she tore it up before I could even say anything." June sniffled. "Thank God I didn't show her the tickets. I mean, I get that my mom hates punk rock or whatever, but she's always been cooler than this."

"Did you try and call your dad?"

"Fuck him," said June in response. "All he'd do is tell me that he was really busy, and that I should listen to my mother. My dad doesn't care about me, Betty, he just cares about whatever piece of ass he's chasing. That's just how he is, and being mad about it is like getting angry at a dog for running after a car." Another sniff. "It's possible I stole that part from Claire."

"That's OK," said Betty, smiling at the small joke. She was jealous that June could be so tough, with all the bullshit she had to deal with, and blushed at the memory of her recent wish for some sort of struggle to deal with. She had it easy compared to June, really easy, and she was pretty sure being unable to appreciate it was making her a terrible person.

"It's not OK," said June. "None of this is. I mean, no offense, Betty, but Ophelia saying no wasn't even a surprise. I'm not in trouble—as far as Claire knows, I've been a little angel lately—so I just don't get why this would make her freak out so badly. I mean, good lineup or not, it's still just a dumb little punk show."

"I wouldn't say it's a little show," said Betty, "but you're right. Your mom flipping is really weird. She's usually pretty cool about stuff like this. Like when she let you get your septum pierced. My moms would never go for that."

"You already have your nose pierced, septum isn't any different," said June. "Not like any of that even matters right now. Listen, Betty: I'm going to this show no matter what. Seriously. Senior year is less than six months away, I'll be eighteen in less than a year, and the Pyramid Scheme isn't even in a bad part of town. There's no reason that I can't go to this stupid show, except for the fact that my mom is a crazy bitch."

"Maybe Claire just had a bad day at work," Betty suggested. "Andrea looked like she got hit by a truck when she came home today. Sometimes with parents the timing is the problem, not the question."

"Seriously, Betty?" June asked, the sneer audible through the iPhone's speaker. "I'm not a complete idiot, remember? Mom was in a fine mood until she saw that flyer, and—"

"Wait. Remember what Ophy said? She was staring at that flyer like there was something wrong with it, but she wasn't looking at the bands or the venue. She was looking at the name on it, remember? It said Duke something-or-other. Maybe there's some weird shit with that guy that we just don't know about."

"Maybe," said June, "but it's probably just my mom wanting me to be as miserable as she is."

"I don't know. Ophy was superweird, remember? She knew something was up, guaranteed. If it had been Andrea, we'd already know—she's not nearly the secret keeper Ophelia is."

"I think we just need to let this go," said June. "I have to get back to my homework. No sense in getting grounded before I get in trouble for sneaking out."

"Yeah, I guess," said Betty. "Hey, I had a question: Do you really think my situation with Jake makes me a bitch?"

"Betty—"

"I'm serious. I know you were joking around in gym, but I'm not talking about that. I'm asking for real. Am I a bitch for dating him when I know it's going to turn out badly?"

"Pretty much," said June. "But listen, Jake is one of the cutest and dumbest boys in school. Someone was going to break his heart this year, and it may as well be Betty."

"I'm not sure that makes me feel any better," said Betty with a frown. "I'm not doing it to be mean, it's just—"

"Betty, the problem is that most of the girls at Northview would kill for Jake Norton just to look at them once the way that he stares at you. The boy is seriously in love, and you know it, and you knew exactly what was going to happen if you dated him. It's part of the Betty Martinez experience, if the past couple years have been any indication."

"Fuck you," said Betty with no malice in her voice.

"Fuck you back," said June. "I need to get to work on my homework, all right? We can talk more in school, maybe come up with a plan."

"All right. I hope your night gets better."

"It won't," said June, and then she was gone.

Betty laid her phone down on the desk in front of her, then stared down the blinking cursor on her open Word document. The flashing line was mocking her inability to go to shows, treat boys decently, or write about the women's suffrage movement. With a sigh, Betty popped her headphones back on, fired up the same playlist from earlier in the afternoon, and then clicked on the browser tab at the bottom of the window. After a moment of thought, Betty punched "duke barnes grand rapids" into the search box and then waited as the results loaded.

The results came flying in, and Betty clicked on the first of them, a website with the URL www.freedukebarnes.com. The click led her to a page with a black background and a picture of a hard-looking young man. The guy in the picture—presumably Duke—had spiked hair and a dog collar with a bondage ring hanging off the center of it. Seeing no other links on the page, Betty hovered her mouse arrow over the picture and double-clicked the image.

The screen flashed and then loaded a menu with four options: The Crime, The Trial, The Aftermath, and How You Can Help. Betty figured the start was as good a place as any, and clicked "The Crime." The screen flashed again, then loaded a text-heavy page with a few pictures of Duke along the side. The background was black with a red spatter effect, the grim imagery removing any doubt that what she was about to read wasn't going to end well. Betty shut the playlist off, removed her headphones, and began to read.

On January 27, 2000, Duke Barnes was at the end of a tough period in his life. He had largely dropped out of the alternative music community that he had invested a great deal of energy in, and he was struggling with addiction issues. His friends were worried about both Duke and his girlfriend, Mandy Reasoner, and their worst fears came to fruition on that wintry day. Duke and Mandy had both spent a significant amount of time under the radar of modern society, at first by intent, and later through their crippling addictions to street narcotics.

At 7:45 a.m. Duke was returning home to the squat he shared with Mandy and several other transients on the south side of Grand Rapids. He had spent the morning earning money through prostitution, and according to several witnesses, Mandy was also engaged in acts of solicitation. Upon arriving at the squat Duke saw a man running from the building, and fearing the worst, Duke entered to find Mandy lying on the floor in a pool of blood.

Despite Duke's best efforts to revive Mandy, her wounds were too grievous, and eventually Duke left her to call 911. Upon police arrival Duke was detained and then released, but was later brought back to the Grand Rapids Police Department in order to straighten out the exact window of his arrival to the home. At some point this line of questioning turned into an interrogation, and even though Duke did not have legal counsel present, he was questioned for over seventy-two hours. When the detectives in charge of the investigation were finished, they had a confession on the table and a suspect in custody.

This confession came despite the fact that Duke was given next to no food during the interrogation, was suffering badly from opioid withdrawal, and was still grieving Mandy. Duke was recorded on both video and audio for the duration of the interrogation, and the detectives in charge of this case broke several Michigan statutes regarding the length of time that a suspect may be questioned without counsel present. Despite these issues, Duke was formally charged, arraigned, and brought to trial later that year.

Seeing the tops of more pictures, Betty scrolled to the bottom of the page, and then gasped. There were three more pictures of Duke—one of him on stage holding a guitar, a shot of him smoking a cigarette and smiling under falling snow, and one of him holding his fists up in a mock fighting pose—but Betty ignored all of those because there was another picture, a moment captured in time of a skinny and scared-looking girl with bright orange hair.

Mandy Reasoner.

Mandy had a ring in her nose and was wearing a Queers T-shirt and black jeans. She had what looked like track marks on her arms and a bright bruise on her neck.

All of those things were insignificant to Betty, however, because the girl in the picture was a dead ringer for June.

Betty found it nearly impossible to take her eyes from the shot of Mandy, June's impossible doppelgänger. The similarities were so striking—the shape of their noses, the corners of their mouths, their hairlines. Betty back-clicked and then began to pore over the rest of the website, ignoring the words now, entirely focused on the pictures.

There were lots of shots of Duke and Mandy on the page about the trial. In some they were together, but most of the time they were separate and alone, and it was easy for Betty to imagine that whichever was missing from the frame was likely the one holding the camera. The last of these shots, an awful image taken by a police photographer of a half-naked Mandy covered in stab wounds, was bad enough to make Betty tear up, but the words at the end of the paragraph chilled her to the bone. "I hope he rots in hell" was the quote from the victim's sister—and the name next to it snapped the final piece of the puzzle into place.

Claire Derricks.

"Mandy was June's aunt," said Betty to no one at all, and then her hands dropped off the keyboard and mouse as though they could burn her.

June's aunt was killed.

The thought kept repeating until it began making some sort of impossible sense to her, and then she moved on to the next.

How could we not have known about this?

Andrea had worked a great deal with the police department over many years. Surely she had to have known all about this. Betty supposed there was no reason for Andrea to share these sordid details with her daughter, but the issue had to have come up between the moms once the dead girl's niece became Betty's best friend. Even so, Betty guessed it wasn't surprising that they'd never broached the subject with her, particularly since June herself didn't seem to know anything about it.

That was the amazing part, now that she thought about it: How had June never heard of it? Even if her mom and dad chose to keep it from her, wasn't it pretty incredible that no one in the community at large had brought it up with her? Maybe not, though. A random junkie girl's death had probably never been front-page news. Still, especially with the grown-up June walking around town as the murdered Mandy's all-but-identical twin, it was remarkable that it had never come up.

June had never said much about her family, which as far as Betty knew was practically nonexistent. Betty knew that June's parents were split up and that June didn't have any living grand-parents, but that was about it.

How can we be such good friends if I know so little about her?

Betty felt almost sick at this thought, and then remembered the murky waters of her own past—her missing father, her non-hyphenated last name, the moms themselves. Especially when it got complicated, maybe it was just easier to keep family stuff to yourself. It just *was*, after all, and not talking about it didn't mean they loved each other any less.

Done thinking for a while—it was wearing her out—Betty folded the laptop closed with a satisfying snap, grabbed the bottle of water from her desk, and ventured out of her room and back to the kitchen.

She found Ophelia and Andrea sitting at the table there. "Hi," she said.

"Why don't you have a seat," said Andrea.

Betty nodded, realizing as she sat that they'd been waiting for her. That they'd probably heard her phone ring and knew who'd likely called, and at least some of what they'd talked about, and where her curiosity would probably take her after she'd hung up.

"OK," said Betty. "I want to know everything."

NINE

"That's not going to be possible," said Andrea.

The moms were holding hands, Ophelia's over Andrea's on the tabletop. Betty wondered how long they'd been waiting for this moment. She'd been friends with June since the second grade, they'd gotten their first periods a month apart, and Betty's moms had known all along that June's aunt was dead and that June's parents wanted it all to just go away.

Now Betty found herself pissed off again. *Things like this don't stay buried forever*, she said to herself in her seat, fuming, her eyes flitting back and forth between her parents.

"Why not?" she asked, and even though she knew her tone was shitty she kept her eyes locked with Andrea's.

"Because we still don't know everything, Betty."

Exhaustion was evident in Andrea's voice, and normally Betty would have recognized that and realized that the conversation could wait a day or two, but not this time. Betty wanted to tear the information from their minds, and then get back online and read everything she could on the subject. She wanted to know all there was to know about Duke and Mandy. She wanted to know why Mandy was dead and why people thought Duke was innocent if he'd confessed to the crime. She wanted to know how June could have grown up in the shadow of all of this but was left with no information.

"I don't understand," said Betty. "Should I go look online some more, or can you tell me why in the hell no one knows about this?"

"Relax," said Ophelia. "You're getting very aggressive about this, but you don't need to. This wasn't a case of keeping something from you because we felt that we had to. There was just no reason to tell you about some poor girl that was killed over a decade ago."

"Why doesn't June know?" Betty demanded. "Why doesn't she catch shit for this from the mean girls and write sad papers about her cool dead aunt? Why was all of this a secret?"

"It's not a secret just because you're ignorant of it, Betty," said Andrea. "The information has always been out there. The fact of the matter is this: the man who killed June's aunt is a drug addict who has been locked up for half his life. His fingerprints were all over the crime scene—all over Mandy—he had a history of violent behavior, and he confessed to the crime. There was just no reason to talk about this. As for June's mother, well, not telling June was a decision she made when June was very young, and it's not up to us to decide if that was a good choice or not."

"What about me?" Betty whined, hating the sound of her voice. "Why couldn't you tell me?"

"You weren't but a year old when the poor girl was killed," said Ophelia, "and they've already convicted a man for what happened to her. Would you have even been interested in a story like that?"

"June would have," spat Betty, "but that's not even all of it. You saw the flyer for the show that she brought here. Why do so many people think this Duke guy is innocent?" She turned to Andrea. "I know that he confessed, Mom, but the website I found said that the police broke a lot of laws talking to him, and that—"

"How much bullshit have you read online?"

Andrea asked the question so coldly that it stopped Betty's stream of questions dead. It was all she could do to keep her eyes locked on her mom's heated gaze. For the first time, Betty wondered if more time researching this subject might have been a good idea before throwing ideas around the dining room table. "A lot, I guess," said Betty finally, and Andrea nodded.

"There are a lot of groups like this, Betty, and not all of them are trying to help an innocent man. Just because some guy looks cool and there's circumstantial evidence suggesting that he might be innocent doesn't really mean a whole lot. Cases of convicted people being exonerated get a lot of press, but believe me, they're few and far between. The fact of the matter is that it takes a number of gross mistakes for that sort of thing to happen, and—"

"This doesn't sound like that, Mom." Betty couldn't stop herself from interrupting. "Everything about this sounds really, well, interesting, at the very least. And not just because the girl who got killed was June's aunt. I only read a little bit about Duke, but it does seem possible that he's innocent."

"Betty." Andrea took a breath and sighed it out. "This guy was convicted by twelve of his peers and he's been in prison ever since. There's a reason for that, trust me on this. I see children every day that are at real risk of turning out just like that poor girl. Though hopefully they'll have a better end, there always seems to be someone around them like Duke. Men like that always find someone weak to be with them, someone they can lord over. And far too often, this is the result: a dead girl and a man sitting in prison and trying to figure out why he did what he did."

"You're really turning on that feminine charm, Mom," said Betty with a grin, and to her relief, Andrea smiled wryly back at her.

"That's one of my better traits," Andrea said, "and I thank you for calling attention to it. That said, how's that paper coming along?"

"All right, all right." Betty stood and then paused by the table. "Can I tell June about this?"

She watched her mothers exchange glances, and then Ophelia turned to her and said, "That's up to you, Betty. Just remember, this isn't going to be just 'interesting' or exciting for June. This is probably the biggest skeleton in her family's closet, and if you act like it's something to be played with, you're liable to get burned."

TEN

I was already pretty familiar with the Mandy Reasoner case before Claire mentioned it in the park, but I knew I needed a refresher to get up to speed, so that's exactly what I got to work on when I came home.

My office used to always be a mess, but these days I keep it pretty clean, at least by my standards. I'm sure it could still use a good deep cleaning, but I barely even know what that means, so I doubt I'm the right person for the job. That's OK, though—no one's been in the house besides me in years, and I like it that way. The house feels like my soul a lot of the time. It's one of the only things that's mine, and sharing it could just end up with me getting hurt, or worse. I've got experience to back that up: the last time a girl came inside, she broke my heart.

I got right on the hunt as soon as I sat down, even though I was pretty sure I knew what I was going to find. One of the best things about a trial that's received a lot of publicity is that there is a ton of information out there on it. One of the worst things is that most of that is bullshit. Take any crime tried in the public eye, and you're going to see a lot of wishful thinking touted as fact. I completely understand not wanting to think the worst of someone, and I fully believe there are a lot of innocent men sitting behind bars. I just don't think most of the innocent ones are lucky enough to snag a PR campaign.

It becomes apparent immediately that Duke Barnes has picked up even more support since the last time I looked into this mess. Not that I really care much either way. Duke is either guilty or one unlucky son of a bitch, but he's got public opinion on his side, so it's really just a matter of time before something happens for him. Granted, that something might not be what he's hoping for, but a second shot at a trial is still pretty good, especially when the body's as cold as this one is.

Speaking of the body, the pictures of Mandy blow my mind. When Claire handed me the photo of her daughter, I was struck by her resemblance to the dead girl. But now that I hold the picture up against the screen, I'm dumbfounded. Saying she's a dead ringer for this poor girl? Probably an understatement. They not only share the same alt look, it's like some cosmic trickster's at work. The girl *is* Mandy.

Which is all great, fascinating, even. Except what does it tell me? When Claire first handed over the photo, I was sure that resemblance had a lot to do with why she'd hired me to protect her daughter. But since then I haven't come a step closer to figuring any of it out.

Start with the facts: June is Mandy's clone, and at the very least, a blood relative. Could Mandy be her *mother*, and somehow June fell into Claire's care? Maybe, but highly unlikely. Surely that would've come out in the reporting of the case and in the trial.

No, June is Claire's girl. I feel that in my gut.

So . . . Claire is worried that maybe all of these rock stars and B-list celebrities that hopped onto the Free Duke bandwagon might actually spring the man who killed Mandy. And if Duke killed her once, he wouldn't be able to pass up the chance to kill her again, a decade and a half later? That's pretty damned far-fetched, even for a deep cable thriller. And even if that is Claire's thinking, why would she be so worried *now*, with Duke still safely fenced in?

I have no answer for that, so I move on.

Like she told me, now Claire's thinking maybe the Free Duke crowd is on to something. Maybe the man who killed Mandy is still free. All right, but if that's the case, that man's *been* free all of these years, probably walking the same streets as his victim's doppelgänger. So the same question comes up: Why is Claire so suddenly freaked out about the danger?

I'm getting this tiny headache in my temple, like someone's pressing a sharpened pencil into it. It's maddening how often my client's motivations turn out to be the deepest mystery in whatever job they've given me.

I just have to focus on doing what she's paying me to do, and doing it the best I can. She's paying me to A) do what I can to keep June ignorant of everything to do with Mandy and Duke and the whole mess, and B) keep her safe.

Part A is pretty much a lost cause. I've got a nagging suspicion the girl probably knows more than her mother suspects she does. At least according to Claire, June is out of the loop, but even if that's so, it's going to change eventually.

I open another window on my computer, hop on over to Facebook, and get to work. I keep up on all of this social media nonsense, because in my work it can be good business. Want some advice? Keep your kids off of this crap. Not only will they tell any thief within a few hundred miles when the house is going to be empty, but they usually set themselves up for identity theft as well. Of course, that's the tip of the iceberg. Much worse things can happen. Trust me.

I find June on Facebook after just a few minutes of clicking. It's always easier than it should be. I open a new window, log out of my work account, then start a new profile on Facebook. I populate it with a picture of a cute boy I find on an image search, then send out a few dozen friend requests. I've done this enough times that I usually get requests from myself in my inbox as all of these little webs come together. I always include my former profiles in this stuff. After all, my other identities are already friends with most of these kids, and it just makes things look that much more legit when they see how many mutual buddies we have.

Friends pour in like they always do, and June responds to my friend request like the rest of the sheep. I give her profile the once-over, see nothing out of the ordinary, and then move on to her friends, the real ones. No one has time to go through the whole list, but it's easy enough to see who the real buddies are, and that's what I do. Two boys and one girl later, I get a hit. A big one.

Her name is Betty Martinez, and excuse me for saying so, but she's pretty cute, and I feel like I've met her somewhere before. I try not to think about that stuff—it's easier that way—but I'm not going to hold everything in.

Still, cute or not, Betty has some pretty damning June-related evidence on her page, and I'm already thinking I need to call Claire. Stuck down among all of the comments and other crap is a picture for a flyer to an upcoming punk rock concert. The lineup is pretty good, almost good enough to make me briefly consider going out of the house for it, but that's not what's really interesting. Lo and behold, the concert is a benefit for Duke Barnes.

The Free Duke folks are back to work again, and judging by the string of comments under the flyer, this event will at least get Duke's defense some money. Probably not all they need—nothing bleeds a wallet like a team of lawyers working on an appeal—but maybe enough to get some of the boots off their throats.

I push back from the keyboard, giving the screen a frustrated look, but no dice: it's still got the same crap that I don't want to see on there. This is a loser's game, and I need to accept that my easy paycheck has just about gone up in smoke. June either knows or will know soon, so there goes half my scope of work with Claire. Part A is dust.

Which leaves me with Part B: keeping June safe from whoever might have the dead girl's double in his crosshairs.

There's only one way to move ahead on this half, and that's to look into the one man besides Duke Barnes I can think of who might have done it. It's a long shot, but I need to cross it off the list if I'm going to take Claire's cash in good conscience.

And if he does end up looking bad, Claire and her family are going to have a lot more on their plate than she already thinks they do.

ELEVEN

"This better be good," said June as they walked across the lawn to fourth period. "I'm serious. You sent me like five texts last night after I was asleep, and I woke up thinking something bad had happened." June grinned. "Not to mention, you know how impatient I am."

"How far are you on your paper for Mr. Evans?"

"Pretty far," said June. "I mean, I still have to find some sources, but most of the actual writing is done. I sort of think the paper sucks, though. I mean, what was I thinking? The class divides and death ratios on the *Titanic* isn't even that interesting a subject. It's really kind of obvious. Like, of course there were more poor people that died. Most of their rooms were below the waterline on the boat, and there were way more of them than there were rich people." She sighed. "I'll probably give it another look tonight, scrape together sources, and then turn it in early. Maybe that'll get me some points."

"I think we should ditch the papers that we have now and talk to Mr. Evans about setting up a project with special circumstances, maybe even letting us extend the deadline."

June stopped and stared at her. "You're crazy. In a new way, but still crazy. I've put a ton of time into that paper, I've got math coming out of my ass, and don't get me started on this Biology 2 bullshit."

"Look at this." June crowded her as she took her phone from her purse and pulled up the preloaded Duke website. When Betty had looked at it in the morning, she'd set it up for exactly this moment, with the picture of Mandy Reasoner centered on the screen.

"Is this some sort of weird joke, Betty?"

"Look again." The girls bent to the phone again. "That's not you. It's your aunt."

"I don't have an aunt," said June without looking at Betty. "You know that. This lady does look like me, though. It's kind of creepy."

"June, you had an aunt," said Betty. "This is her. Her name was Mandy Reasoner and she died when we were about a year old."

"That's not funny anymore, Betty." June glared at her. "Who is this really?"

"I'm serious, June. This is your aunt. She was murdered by the guy on that punk show flyer. That's why Ophelia got all weird and why your mom freaked out. This whole thing is a big secret for some reason, but the other crazy thing is that the guy who got arrested for this might not have done it. That's why all those big bands are playing. That's why Old Croix Road is playing. They think the guy who was convicted of killing your aunt is innocent."

"I need to sit for a second," said June, who promptly sat down. "Are you serious, Betty? You promise you're not fucking with me?"

"Scout's honor," said Betty, holding up two pinched-together fingers. "It wouldn't be a funny joke, and I'm not that mean. Just think about what I said about the project. I mean, I know this is a lot to take in, but who else has the chance to research something this crazy?"

"All right," said June as she stood and dusted herself off. "I feel sort of like I'm dreaming, but I think I'm in. I do want to know everything about this, but if my mom didn't want me to know about her, she must think she has a pretty good reason. I don't know how I'm going to keep my mouth shut around her, but I want in." June frowned. "What exactly are we going to tell Mr. Evans? Even worse, what if he tells my mom what we're up to?"

"I'll handle that," said Betty. "You just follow my lead." Betty and June snapped their heads at the faraway sound of a buzzer going off in the school, and then they took off running across the campus. Asking Mr. Evans for a change in subject as well as an extension was going to be tough enough without being late, too.

Betty waited until the end of class to make her way to Mr. Evans's desk, June doing what she had asked of her and following at her heels. Mr. Evans was discussing something with another student, a nice but nerdy boy named Robert Hellman, and when the two were done Mr. Evans smiled at them and said, "Ladies, how are we doing on this fine April afternoon?"

"Pretty good," said Betty. "We have some questions for you. June and I were wondering if we could change the topics for our research papers, and then work together on a new one. We'd need an extension, probably like three extra weeks, but I think we could actually do something cool, instead of just regurgitating ideas from books."

"Convince me," said Mr. Evans. "You girls are smart. Show me what you want me to see. I just hope this isn't a letdown."

"My aunt was murdered fifteen years ago," blurted June. *So much for following my lead*, Betty thought. But Mr. Evans had gone from bored-looking teacher to very interested friend in a matter of seconds, so she let June roll. "It's some family secret or something, I guess," she continued. "I never knew about it until today. Betty found out last night, and she just told me on the way here."

"Her aunt's name was Mandy Reasoner," said Betty. "She looked just like June, and she liked punk rock like we do."

"I'll need more than her iPod track list," said Mr. Evans, "but I'm about halfway there, so keep going."

"She was murdered by her boyfriend," said Betty, filling in some of the facts she hadn't had time to share with June. "He's locked up in Jackson right now, but there are a ton of people that don't think he did it. There's going to be a show in a month or so with a bunch of huge bands playing it—even Old Croix Road is playing, and they never play anymore. Anyway, the reason for the show is that they're trying to get the guy who was convicted of killing her aunt a new trial. He confessed to the police, but it sounds like he changed his story later, and they broke the law when they were questioning him. There's a bunch of other stuff, too.

"We want to tell Mandy's story—that's June's aunt—but we also want to look at as much evidence as we can to try and prove whether or not the guy who's in prison really killed her. My mom works at the police station sometimes, and I think with a little work we might even be able to talk to some of the cops that were working back then."

"Consider me convinced," said Mr. Evans. "This is very compelling stuff." Mr. Evans shuffled papers on his desk and then raised his head. "I'm going to grade this the way I would a college paper, ladies. Do a good job, don't add a bunch of padding, and keep me updated. If you're going to really work for this thing, we don't even need to set a due date, but I want to be in the loop." He turned to June. "Are you sure you're up for this, Ms. Derricks? There could be some ugly family history buried somewhere."

"I know," said June. "I just want to know more about my aunt, and this seems like a good way."

Mr. Evans nodded and smiled. "All right, then. Keep me up to date, and get out of my sight. I won't have you late to your next class on my account."

TWELVE

Not everyone is easy to find, but I locate Jack Derricks after just a few minutes on the Internet. Jack isn't a lock for the death of Mandy Reasoner—no one really seems to be except for the version of Duke Barnes that was convicted a dozen or so years ago—but there are a few interesting things that stick out about the man.

For starters, he was familiar with the victim. Next on the list is something Claire barely mentioned, that she has an ex-husband. But it was the way she spoke about the case that made me wonder why. Claire might not have been able to see that June's dad would look pretty good as a perp, but I sure can, and if Claire wants June safe, this angle needs to be looked into.

I find Jack Derricks pretty quickly through social media, but I did have to think outside of my usual go-tos. Jack is on several dating sites, and after a few minutes of looking, I've got an address and some recent pictures. I'm feeling less confident about my detective skills in regard to his possible guilt—Jack looks like more of a Hair Club for Men candidate than a killer—but I've been wrong before, and there's something about Jack Derricks that just gets my hackles up.

I make Jack's neighborhood in about fifteen minutes, then stow the bike and get to walking. I didn't bring anything too fun on this trip, just a little digital camera, a lockpick kit, and a pair of discreet binoculars. One of the advantages about not going to school or being on the clock at the same time as everyone else is that when most folks are working, I can see what they think they're hiding. Criminals make time to play when everyone else is busy. Jack should just count himself lucky that I have no intent on taking anything—assuming he's actually gone—unless it could be used as evidence. I still have my doubts, of course, but the man had proximity to the victim, and history proves there are plenty of killers that don't need anything else.

The house looks normal from a distance. No surprise there, they almost always do, but looks can be very deceiving. I glass the house from down the block, making sure no one is around to wonder what I'm up to, and then I stow the spyglasses and wrap my bike chain around my wheels and a stop sign. I don't use a lock—never have—but my reasoning is pretty sound. It's a big-ass chain and *looks* like it's locked, and if I need to get away, really need to leave in a hurry, I won't have to spend time messing around with undoing the lock. Bikes can be replaced. Still, it pains me a bit to walk away from it. For the first time in years, I don't have the money to replace it if it does get ganked.

The lots are big here, the houses small—a sure sign of a real estate development that didn't pan out quite as intended. Stopping in front of his house, I give a quick look to his windows and his neighbors', don't see anyone, and then snap a couple quick pictures.

As far as his house is concerned, Jack Derricks lives a pretty normal life. It's time to find out if the inside tells the same story.

I walk to the door like I have every right to and ring the bell. I can hear it in the house, but what I don't hear is a dog or footsteps, a very good sign. I stand there waiting and ring the bell again, though I know no one's going to answer it. It's dead in there. It's hard not to turn around to make sure that my six is clear. Easy fix for that: I take a burner out, cut to the crappy camera, and shoot a few pictures over my shoulder. To anyone else it looks like I'm texting, but even my throwaway phone can give me a pretty clean view of what's at my back.

The pictures let me know that everything is good behind me, and out from the backpack comes the lockpick kit. I've been messing with this thing for a few years now, and the truth of it is, most locks are easy to pick. It makes sense when you think about it. Most people just buy one from a hardware store or use the bolt that came with the house or apartment. What that means for a guy like me is that if I can pick one, I can pretty much pick them all. Some have more tumblers and take a little longer, but if I have time, I will get in. Jack's house proved to be no different. A few clicks and wiggles, and I was inside.

There was a house I was in a few years back that was hiding a little girl in its belly. I came in through the back and it was like I was walking into hell, but there was the strangest thing out front: no mess at all. The criminals in that place knew they were hiding in plain sight and needed to keep up appearances.

It only took a few seconds in Jack Derricks's home to realize he wasn't too worried about keeping the inside ready for a guest.

The house wasn't trashed, but it did look as though it had been paused midparty. There were beer cans and bottles piled on the coffee table, an ashtray overflowing with both cigarette butts and roaches, and a baggie holding a pretty familiar shade of green. I gave the room a quick once-over and decided even the most brazen psycho killer wouldn't hide an old souvenir in a room that obviously saw so much entertaining. Despite what the television might make you think, criminals aren't all stupid. In fact, some of them are incredibly intelligent.

Moving out of the front living area, I pass through a small kitchenette and down a short hall. There are a pair of bedrooms at the rear of the house, one neat enough and probably rarely used—at least judging by the dust on the light fixtures—and one that looks like a bar and a Laundromat had a filth contest and every-body won the grand prize. The smell hits me as I walk into Jack's room: an ugly reek of ass and black mold, with a few dried-up condoms on the nightstand to add to the ambience. I shudder, put my game face on, and get to work.

Despite the mess on the floor, bed, and nightstand, the dresser is full of neatly folded clothing. Mr. Tidy. I rifle through each drawer, being sure to check the underside of each of them as I do, all while keeping an eye on the Timex on my wrist. So far I've been in the house less than five minutes, discovering nothing, and I'm starting to hope there's not a crawl space or attic.

I give up on the dresser after hitting the bottom drawer, and come away with the revelation that Jack and I have a bit in com-mon. As it turns out, we both essentially wear uniforms. For me, that means punk shirts and hoodies, Converse All Stars, and jeans. Jack's is a little different: flannel shirts and Carhartt outer-wear, some camo for hunting, and then a bunch of white shirts, briefs, and socks. It's all boring, nothing tucked under any of the drawers—no bloody knife, smoking revolver, or baggied trophy of victim-hair anywhere—and I'm starting to think this is more snipe hunt than investigation.

There's no blood-stained coat to be found as I shuffle carefully through the closet, no punk records or heroin needles in the night-stand, and no diary packed with confessions. A little dejected at not solving the decade-plus-old murder, I walk out of the bedroom and give a look out the back door to the rear yard.

Jackpot.

THIRTEEN

The last two hours of class dragged on long enough that Betty was sure there was something wrong with the clocks. Finally it was 2:20 and the last bell of the day sounded, and Betty walked to her Beetle while she texted June.

She'd already decided she had to convince the moms somehow to let her break the grounding so that she and June could work on the project together, and she knew her only chance of doing that was if they agreed to do the work at her house. Betty knew what they were going to lay down as a precondition, though the thought of having to look Jake in the face and break it off made her throw up in her mouth a little. It would probably be for the best just to get it over with.

Betty made it to the car at the same time she was hitting "Send" on her phone. The message she sent to June told her about the plan and gave her a couple of different websites to check out for more information on Duke, Mandy, and the bizarre set of events surrounding the murder and the trial. "K" came through a few moments later, and Betty dropped the phone into a cup holder before throwing the car into reverse.

Betty was home ten minutes later, and she parked the car behind Ophelia's and then walked in the house. Ignoring the loud techno coming from the basement, Betty grabbed a water and headed upstairs and got to work on the part of the website labeled "The Trial."

The Duke Barnes trial started going sideways before it began. For starters, the court had a very hard time appointing an attorney for Duke. Not only was he furious and recanting his testimony to the police, but he'd beaten up two men in the county lockup he thought were jailhouse snitches. Worse still, he was suffering from extreme withdrawals from heroin. By the time he finally did have a lawyer, the man could do little but attempt to slow the trial, but to no avail. Six months after Mandy Reasoner was found dead, Duke's trial began.

Betty didn't even feel like she needed to research the matter to know that three days is an impossibly short span of time for a murder trial to take place, but in The People v. Duke Barnes, that was all that was necessary. Duke not only sounded guilty, he looked guilty. He was covered in tattoos, with the pinched and worn face of a junkie to boot. He was unpleasant, had to be threatened with being gagged, and was generally disagreeable with everyone he came into contact with. Duke's lawyer did the best he could under the circumstances, explaining that Duke had so many opiate metabolites in his system at the time he confessed that there was no way the confession should be legally binding, but the judge allowed it to stand. Duke was convicted and sentenced to twenty-five years to life in the Michigan penal system.

At the time of his conviction, it didn't sound as if Duke had a friend in the world, and for the next few years, nothing about that appeared to change. Interestingly, five years after his conviction and now stone-cold sober, Duke made his way back into the culture that he'd loved so much through a series of letters with the magazine *Maximum Rocknroll*, letters that eventually turned into a column that was still running. According to the website, the majority of the articles penned by Duke, a.k.a. Prison Punk, were about prisoner rights and how easy it can be for normal people to be railroaded by the legal system if they aren't careful. The columns were what set things in motion. Even though Duke tried to remain anonymous, someone finally figured out who he was and the snowball began to grow.

Eight years after his trial, the Free Duke Barnes campaign was in full swing, and while it lacked A-list celebrities, it had a fervent grassroots following. The efforts of the group seemed to be focused mostly on getting Duke a retrial, but as she read the words on the screen, Betty found herself even more interested in the other side of the coin. If Duke really didn't do it, then who did? If the person who had killed Mandy was still free, was he still in Grand Rapids? Had he killed again?

Betty took a long drink of water and leaned back in her chair, then gave a look to the clock. Impossibly, the five minutes or so that she'd been home had actually stretched to a little more than an hour. Standing to relieve the growing ache in her back, Betty decided to hop downstairs to see if Ophelia had made her way out of the basement yet.

The electronic music had been shut off, so Betty was unsurprised to see Ophelia standing in the kitchen with her nose in a cookbook. "This should not be so hard," said Ophelia without looking up. "It makes me think there's something wrong with me."

"Well don't look at me," Betty said. "I'm worse than either one of you. I think when I look for a husband, his ability to cook a decent meal is going to be pretty high on my list of necessary attributes."

"Can Jake cook?" Now Ophelia was looking at her.

"I have no idea, but probably not. Doesn't really matter, though. I think Jake and I are about done."

"I can't say that I'm very upset over that," said Ophelia. "I won't go off on an Andrea-style rant on the subject, but I will tell you that you can do better than a boy who sees only your body. You have a good head on your shoulders, Betty, and it would be a shame if you got pregnant or did something else to mess up your life. Do what I didn't: enjoy your childhood, and don't rush it."

"I know all that, Mom," said Betty. "Jake's a good guy, and I know it's hard for you to believe, but he really was joking. He knows I'm not the kind of person to sext him or send him pictures like that, and that's why my response was to send him a picture that he himself had taken. I mean, I get that it was a little risqué because I was in a two-piece, but it really was just a joke between us."

Ophelia gave a tiny, unconvinced shrug and sank back down into her cookbook.

"Look," Betty said, "I'm sorry. I know we've been over this and I'm not trying to start a fight."

"It's fine," said Ophelia. "So what were you headed down here for?"

"I wanted to ask you and Mom a question." Ophelia looked up again and nodded. "I have a paper due next week, the suffrage one that I told you about, but June and I decided to work on another bigger project instead. Mr. Evans said that he was fine with it. He even agreed to give us more time so that we could properly research everything, but I wasn't really thinking about my grounding when I said I could do it. Is there any way we could lift my grounding so that she can come over and we could work on the project together?"

"Well, I liked the idea of the paper on suffrage," said Ophelia. "I think it's a more relevant subject than people your age, hell, people my age, give it credit for. The fact that a hundred years ago half of this country wasn't allowed to vote is a fascinating thing." She sighed. "That said, I have a feeling I know what the subject of this new project is going to be, though I'm not sure I want to confirm it."

Betty nodded. "This is pretty much the most exciting thing that we've ever been close to, and we want to know everything about it, but especially the part about why people think the guy convicted of killing June's aunt is innocent." Betty knew she was choosing to leave out the other part, about trying to figure out who really had done it, but figured there was no percentage in doing so. Either her moms would rear up at the prospect of them putting themselves in danger, or roll their eyes at how childish it sounded. Instead, she closed with, "I think if we work hard on it we could end up with something really special, something that could even look good on a college application."

"Don't push too hard," said Ophelia. "I'm already pretty well convinced, and I don't want to feel like I'm dealing with a used car salesman. Let me talk to Andrea, but I think between the two of us we can come up with something." Ophelia's eyes narrowed. "You were serious about this Jake business, though, right?"

"I'll dump him right now if you want me to," said Betty. "I think it's a little cold to do it over the phone, but if it's going to happen either way, then the sooner the better."

Ophelia laughed, shook her head, and said, "No, you can do better than that. Don't be so rotten! Let him down easy. He would have done that for you, I bet."

"So you think I can tell June she can come over tomorrow?"

"I don't think that will be a problem," said Ophelia, "but let me deal with the discussion. You just be a quiet little lamb in your room until I give you the all clear, all right?"

"Baaa," said Betty.

FOURTEEN

I have a rule of thumb. If something sticks out, it's worth looking at. Hidden basements, attics with secret accessibility, or in Jack's case, a pair of toolsheds out back. One toolshed? I would have looked, sure. But two? I need to know.

I walk swiftly to the leftmost one, making sure to check Jack's fenced-in rear yard for anyone hiding out or peering in, and then get my kit back out. This lock is harder than the ones on the front of Jack's house. Still doable, but I'm eating time like a bowl of potato chips.

The first lock clicks open after a few minutes of frustration, and as the door swings open I'm hit with a chemical smell. Letting my eyes adjust to the darkness, I see something that I never would have expected to be here.

I'd been ready for Jack to be a monster, but either he's one that will be remembered for a long time, or I'm way off the mark. This first shed, perfectly waterproofed and climate controlled, contains an amazing woodworking setup.

I know what you're thinking: So what?

But seriously, Jack has everything, to the point that it's hard for me to imagine the man having time for another obsession in his life. There's barely even room to move for all the equipment.

Which begs the question of how he even uses the stuff within that little space.

Then I know the answer's next door.

I secure the first shed, walk to the second, and fiddle the lock open. Swinging the door wide, I know there's no reason to give it much more than a glance, but I can't help myself. Shed one was for storage, but shed two is where Jack puts in work.

Right now he's in the middle of stripping an old hope chest, but the walls are lined with pictures of other projects. The man knows his stuff. Why this fastidious dedication to his craft doesn't transfer to the rest of the house is beyond me, but Jack is off the list, at least for me. The only thing that stands out is an old press for loading bullets, but there's no ammo stacked on it, just a few cartons of powder underneath of it, along with a few boxes of empty shotgun shells. None of it matters, though, not even the equipment for reloading. Jack might have known the victim, might've been in the right place at the right time, but nothing else fits with my profile.

He had to have been discussed by the cops working this case. Still, it's hard to imagine even a really good detective being able to turn away for long from the smoking gun that was Duke Barnes, especially since Duke confessed. And now, all these years later, I certainly don't hear anything shouting otherwise at me. It looks like Duke Barnes has a few more days in jail ahead of him.

So why then, walking away from the house to my bike, do I feel like I missed something, like I should be trying harder to find some sign of Jack's possible secret life? Maybe it's because I can only name half a dozen humans on the planet I completely trust. Some people see things in shades of gray, and some in black and white. I see mainly black, and while I have my reasons for that, it doesn't mean it's an accurate view of the world.

So I keep walking, letting Jack's lonely home fade in the distance. Claire hired me to watch June, so now it's time to find her and see if there's anything that her mother doesn't know about.

FIFTEEN

Betty shared the good news with June as the two of them walked into school the next morning, but Betty could tell that the reality of the situation was sinking in for June. She wasn't talking much and seemed detached when she did speak. Betty frowned at the second of these oddly flat exchanges—something was bothering her friend—but they had to split up for class.

When fourth period finally rolled around, Betty felt as if she'd spent a week inside Northview High, instead of just a few hours. Seeing June waiting for her by the door made her smile, though. June was smiling, too, and they began walking without a word.

"I seriously considered asking my mom last night, Betty," said June after they'd walked awhile. "I wanted to tell you earlier, but I felt bad for even thinking about it. There's no way my mom would let me do this project if she knew what it was about, and I really want to learn more about Mandy."

"June, listen to me," Betty said. "If getting answers from your mom is what you want to do, then go for it. There's school, and then there's life."

June threw an arm around Betty at that, a gesture that almost saw the pair of them face-plant to the concrete before correcting their footing, and then unleashing a spray of laughter that sent birds flying from the budding trees.

"Jesus, you're going to kill somebody if you're not careful," said Betty, which only made June laugh even harder.

"I think I want to meet him," said June as the laughter faded. "Duke, I mean. Do you think your mom could set that up?"

"Probably." She'd had the idea herself, but she wasn't all that sure she really wanted to meet Duke Barnes face-to-face. The old photos made him look cold, almost as if he was willing whoever was holding the camera into a fight, or was perhaps sizing up the camera itself. Even in the earliest, prearrest photos Duke had a look about him, a hard look, and Betty doubted that a false imprisonment would have done much for his demeanor.

"It was just a thought," said June. "I don't really know how far any of this can go, anyway. We're at, like, the worst possible age for this sort of thing. We're smart enough to know what's going on, but no one is going to take us very seriously because we're still just a couple of kids."

"I guess we'll just have to see," said Betty. "We're still a long way from even being well educated on the case. I mean, there are tons of people that have spent a lot of time working on this, and they're no closer to getting any real answers than we are. The advantage that we have is it sounds like a lot of the research has already been done for us, but everyone is reaching the same conclusion. All we need to do is find a different finish line, and then we'll really have something."

"Easier said than done."

"I have some ideas," said Betty as they made the doors across the campus. Betty swung the heavy door open, and they returned to the bustle of a living and breathing high school. "I'll go over it once we get some privacy," she said. "Maybe Mr. Evans will let us work in the library." And then she and June were splitting the crowd so they could get to Mr. Evans's room on time.

———

As it turned out, Mr. Evans suggested the library idea before they could even bring it up. They left the quiet class behind them, the eyes of their classmates locked on their backs, the others wondering if those two had fucked up or were getting special treatment for some reason.

When Betty and June got to the library, they walked immediately to the row of desktop computers at the back of the room. Younger kids gave them a wide berth as they passed through the rows of books, the smell of the aged hardbacks as welcome as the blissful hour away from Mr. Evans's classroom. Finally they had privacy, and as Betty got to work on Google, June grabbed a chair to sit next to her.

The website loaded slower than it did at home, but soon enough it was up and the two of them were staring at stylized blood spatter, Duke Barnes, and the pretty and impossibly familiar face of Mandy Reasoner.

"God," June said. "Seeing her face is . . ."

"Unnerving?"

June nodded, still lost in contemplation of her tragic mirror image on the screen. Finally she broke away and turned to Betty. "So," she said, "spill."

"All right," said Betty. "I think we need to task ourselves with the things that aren't on the website." She tapped the monitor with her fingertips. "For example, whoever set this page up can tell you thirty different ways that Duke's trial was unfair. What they don't do is explain how Duke was really innocent, and not just a victim of a poorly run court. I don't see even one theory as to who the killer could really be."

"Do you?" June asked hopefully, and Betty shook her head.

"Not really. I mean, there's some pretty interesting stuff here, but nothing to really go off of. For example, the site basically accepts it as fact that Duke was working as a hooker that day, and Mandy was probably out doing the same thing."

"He looks like a fucking creep," said June, her voice raised well above a library whisper. "Seriously, just look at him. I mean, I usually think hard-looking guys like that are cute, but this guy . . . He might be innocent, but you can tell he still did bad things." She shuddered. "He's not cute, not even a little. He looks like he's been angry his whole life."

"So what is our goal going to be?" Betty asked. "Mr. Evans said college grading, and I don't even really know what that means, other than that he is going to be really hard on us. I feel like he gave us this challenge for a reason, but I can't really tell if he wants us to fail or succeed. It's not that I don't think we can do it, but if all we do is spit back what we found on a website, Mr. Evans is going to kick our asses, and he'll probably smile while he's doing it."

"Well, shit," June said. "What are we going to do?"

"We'll keep it simple to start with. We're going to spend the rest of the hour reading that website, and then we can move on from there. Also, I'm sure they're boring, but I bet we can get our hands on an actual court transcript.

"As for a goal for the whole project, that seems pretty simple, too. Our aim shouldn't be to try and prove that Duke is innocent, but to try and find out who else could have done it. If I'm right and Mandy was hooking, then we should look into anyone with an arrest for hiring a prostitute back then. I think that information's all public. And we also look into who was living with Duke and Mandy at the time."

"Damn, Detective Martinez," June said. Betty couldn't quite figure out if she sounded impressed or was mocking her. "OK, then. How do we find out who was living with them?"

Betty answered with a pair of mouse clicks and some scrolling before pointing her index finger at the screen.

"Look at what it says right here," said Betty, and June crowded back in. "This says that Duke and Mandy had roommates, that their house was basically a place for homeless people to stay illegally, and that lots of other people stayed there, too."

"So this is going to be impossible, basically," said June. "That's just great. My mom already hates me enough. A failing grade on this project should infuriate her in ways I didn't even know existed yet."

"Oh, get the knot out of your thong."

June scowled and socked her on the arm. "I'm serious, though, Betty. This all sounds pretty flimsy."

"We don't even know that yet," said Betty. "Like I said, we'll look over this page, read it all, top to bottom. And then, as far as I'm concerned, we have three things to figure out. We need to know who was with Mandy in the week or so before she died, we need to find out where they lived and if it's somewhere we can visit, and, unfortunately, we're going to need to learn a lot about Duke."

"God," June said, her eyes settling against their will on the man's sneering image on the screen.

"He's the only person who knew who was there that day," Betty said. "We need to read his articles from *Maximum Rocknroll*, we need to find out why the cops were so sure it was him and not anyone else, and if worse comes to worst, we really might need to find a way to talk to him, face-to-face."

"Christ," said June. But then she took a big breath and took over the mouse, scrolling down to the next screen of text. "I guess we better get to it."

I don't like Mondays. It's pretty much the worst cliché, but I really don't. Mondays were always the end of the party when I was still in school—or at least had friends in school—and I never really got over it. I never got over that blunt feeling that life really will catch up with you.

Example: take your average nine-to-fiver. Do they like their job? Nope. Are they satisfied with the money they make? Nope. Do they realize how lucky they are? Oh hell fucking no. I get it, though, at least now I do. Being some modern Kerouac-esque vagabond seems pretty romantic, at least it did to me, but when you realize that you never travel and that you'll do anything for heroin, it sort of takes some of the shine off. God, I feel like such shit right now, so fucking weak and useless.

I want to get high and listen to Jawbreaker, let Blake just soothe me into a coma. I want to shoot speed and listen to Motörhead, stop giving a fuck. More bands, too, all with drugs that match the music—cocaine and Avail, a buttload of beer and Hot Water Music, weed for any of them. Vodka for Crass, everything for the Dead Kennedys. That's how my brain has been for so long, it's hard to see it any other way. Heroin can be the best for relaxing, but it needs to be the right shot. The kind I can't find, the kind Duke can't find, that first blast of good clean pure shit. The kind I'll never have again. But I'll fucking chase it.

Jason came on to me last night, and I know what you're probably thinking, that Duke would kill him if he found out, but is that even the truth anymore? The stuff that Duke and I do to get a fix isn't what most people would consider good for a relationship. I mean, even if you discount what I do, having a boyfriend that goes to the rough trade district selling bareback sex can be a strain. If that sort of thing is OK, then why is it that I know that Duke would be furious about Jason sitting next to me on the couch last night? Nothing really happened, not really, at least not from what I remember, but the stuff that he told me was so sweet. It made me feel like maybe I was worth something, like maybe I could even turn all of this shit around if I got my act together.

I know I won't, though. I'm too scared of getting an HIV test, too scared of life without getting high, and way too scared of having to face my family ever again. For all I know they think I'm dead, and I may as well be at this point. Dead, gone, and forgotten, like a real-life zombie just sticking around for a fix. Have to go.

Better now. I saw Duke when he came to shoot up, and after he left again I finally talked to Jason. Nothing happened last night, so there's nothing to worry about. He said he was sorry I thought he was hitting on me. He was just messed up and being friendly. I don't remember what happened, but I think he's probably telling the truth. There was a time where I would have known for sure, and probably even freaked out about something like that, but all I can think of now is how good it felt to sit on the couch with his arm around me. If something else did happen then I don't remember it, so it doesn't matter.

I wish Duke and I were like that again, instead of just living like animals. I just want to have someone care about me. I want to feel as good as I used to on dope. I want to feel like more than just something for men to get off on. Jason made me feel like that and he says nothing happened, so I believe him.

This is the first time I've ever felt like I should just destroy this journal. Maybe in the morning, but right now I'm going to lay down for a little bit, it might help with how sick I've been feeling.

Kiss kiss,

Mandy

SIXTEEN

When Betty and June tromped inside the house, they grinned—Ophelia was back on a rap kick—and then headed upstairs to Betty's room. Once the door was shut behind them, they sat on the floor at the foot of Betty's bed, laptops laid out before them, and June pointed at her screen. "I found an archive with the last ten or so MRR articles written by Duke. I haven't read more than the first few sentences, but check this out."

Betty leaned in to see June's screen, and June began to read aloud from it. "'Another day, another lack of a dollar here in prison. Money can't buy happiness, but I would love to know why it's legal for the state to pay us only 74 cents a day. In all fairness, a skilled worker here can make almost five times that, and take home the lump sum of $3.87 a day, but that still isn't exactly minimum wage. Rehabilitation is supposed to come from within, but how can you rehab a man's spirit when all you do is remind him of how broken he is? I'd understand if prison was solely about punishment. Then they wouldn't have to pay us at all. But when there are men here for months or years, working 12-hour days punching out license plates for less than three quarters a day, and then they're expected somehow to reenter society? Something is broken.'"

"Wait," June said, scrolling down. "It goes on like that for pages. This is one seriously pissed-off dude."

"He's got a point," said Betty, "but I'd be shocked if there was anyone really listening to him up until this campaign to free him started. Now, who knows? There could be thousands of prisoners and civilians reading this sort of thing, and you know what they're all thinking: 'How could someone this smart commit a crime that was so senseless?' Hell, I'm thinking it and I hardly know anything about this stupid case."

"So he can talk and write OK," said June. "That's not that big a deal to me. He's complaining about rehab, but it seems like it worked fine on him." June rolled her eyes. "To me, he comes off like a total dick. Maybe he did it or maybe he didn't, but if he acted like that in court it's no wonder things didn't go his way."

June had turned tomato red while she was speaking, and Betty was desperate to see the subject changed. "All right then," she said. "So, nothing else interesting in here?"

"Nah," answered June. "I just read the same stuff you did. It makes me really angry. Yesterday I was pissed off that I was out of the loop, but now I'm just pissed off that she's dead. She was like us, and she would have been our friend, I just know it. Instead, some asshole killed her, and even if it was the guy convicted, no one knows why. It's not fair."

"No one said it was fair," Betty said quietly. "It's like the least fair thing ever. But what also isn't fair is if Duke is innocent."

June just shook her head and looked away.

Betty slid her laptop to the side and grabbed a notebook and pen from her bag. "Let's start with what we know." She tapped the tip of the pen on the lined, spiral-bound page. "Duke was convicted of doing it, so he's suspect number one, no matter who his friends are. Who else do we have?"

"The article on the Free Duke page said there were two roommates," offered June, and Betty nodded and wrote down "roommates" under the line that said "Duke."

"But it also said there were a lot of homeless people coming through, too," said June. "I know that isn't much help, but it's still something."

"No, that's good," said Betty. "I had another thought, too. Do you suppose there would be any way to find some of her customers from back then? I mean, they might not all have been awful, but the kind of person who would pay to have sex with someone who was that damaged . . . I don't think these were good people." Betty scratched "homeless roommates" into the third line on the page, and then added "customers" underneath it. "How old was she when she died?" Betty asked, and June took her computer and did a quick search.

"She was twenty-three," said June. "That's really young. Even younger than I thought."

"I was guessing around that age," said Betty quietly. "Any non-Duke theories?"

"It feels like sort of a stretch, but it could have been a teacher," answered June. "I don't mean, like, a teacher that sought her out. But maybe one that knew her from school, saw what she was doing and just couldn't get over it. So he pulled over and got her in the car, and then it just went bad. I suppose that could go for any of her customers. I was just trying to think of people we could connect her with."

"What other men would she have been in recent contact with?" Betty asked, and the question gave the girls pause.

"Probably my dad," said June solemnly. "I'm serious, Betty. I don't know if my folks were around her at all then, but if they were, my dad probably would have been apt to take a pass at his wife's little sister. That doesn't mean I think he did it or anything, and for all we know Mandy never saw either of them, but for right now he should probably go on the list."

"I don't know," said Betty. "I think I'd feel awful putting your dad on the list."

"Think like a cop and remember what Mr. Evans said about college grading," said June. "Put him on there, and hopefully we can cross his name out soon. It's not like it's uncommon for the victim to know who killed her. Why should this one be any different?"

"You are cold," said Betty, and the joke broke the tension, sending the girls into peals of laughter. "All right, all right," said Betty. "I think, first things first, we need to find out who these roommates are. It's safe to assume the cops haven't followed their lives since then, not with Duke's conviction, but I bet their names are listed somewhere."

"Yeah, like the police station," said June dejectedly, and then as if she had been reminded of some impossible secret, began beaming. "Wait, your mom's practically a cop, right? Maybe she can get us a couple names. If she did, all we'd have to do is look online into where those guys are, and then we could try and see what they've been up to for the past twenty years or so."

"I don't know," said Betty. "I think my mom would say no. And anyway, despite the fact that these guys were near the scene of the crime, they're also the people the cops would have looked at the hardest. Even if we could find them, I don't think we'd really be able to find out much information that isn't already out there. I mean, if one of these guys looked good for the crime or had like a history of being a rapist, the cops would have looked a lot harder at him than at Duke."

"For sure," said June, "but the cops wouldn't have thought to find out anything he did *after* she was killed. If one of the roommates did it, maybe Mandy was just the first, and everything they've done afterward they either haven't gotten caught for or it wasn't as bad as killing someone."

Betty stared at her. "God, you're right. That totally makes sense. Like, why would the cops go after them when they already had a conviction, a trial, and a guilty verdict? Why go through all that again if in their eyes they had the right guy all along?"

"Damn straight."

"All right, I'll ask," said Betty, though the truth was she didn't know what Andrea might say. She wasn't totally sure she even wanted to ask the question. Telling Andrea she needed to talk to the cops would mean the project was a little more serious than she'd sold it to the moms, which would either impress her mothers or make them wonder why in the hell their daughter was so obsessed with a crime that most people considered solved.

June must've caught the uneasiness in her voice. "You don't have to ask your mom," she said. "But Betty, this is my aunt we're talking about. Even though I didn't know she was alive until yesterday, I still want to help her. It's too late to save her life, but maybe we can make sure that whoever really did hurt her gets in trouble." She paused and then said, "Or maybe just stays in trouble."

"Hey, I'm sold," said Betty, raising her palms to June as if warding her off. "Now let's get back to work. There's still a ton of ground to cover before we even need to be worrying about talking to a cop. I can't imagine much that would be more embarrassing than having my mom set up time for us to talk to a detective or something and us realizing that we don't know even the most basic stuff about this case. That's going to mean finding stuff written by people who want Duke to stay locked up too, not just the stuff written by people who want him free because a few cool bands say that he should be."

SEVENTEEN

The rest of the study session was largely uneventful. June found a very informative site that covered the case with a less biased view, but even on that more news-oriented site it was clear that not everything had gone smoothly in the case of Duke Barnes. Maybe the deck wasn't stacked as much as the other site suggested, but there was enough odd stuff going on that it was hard to imagine everything on www.freedukebarnes.com was a falsehood.

The names of the roommates remained a mystery. Reading through other true crime stories to get a clearer picture of whether or not that was standard practice, Betty was left with the impression that none of the sites were telling the whole story and that talking to Andrea about her contacts at the police station wouldn't be all that bad an idea.

At dinnertime Betty said bye to June, then sat at the table where Andrea and Ophelia were waiting for her, their plates topped with a medley of grilled vegetables atop a white risotto. Betty stuck her fork in the rice and smelled it, smiling as the distinctive scent of parmesan cheese came wafting off of the arborio. "This smells ridiculous, and it looks even better," said Betty, and Ophelia smiled with pride at the compliment.

"I'm glad you agree," said Andrea with a grin, "but since we've been suffering and waiting almost two minutes to eat while your friend left, shall we get to it?"

"Absolutely." She hadn't thought about food for even a second while June was over, but now she felt like she could eat multiple plates of just about anything. She dug in with gusto, and after a few bites she said, "Research is going well. It's sort of a messed-up case."

"I remember reading about it," said Ophelia.

Andrea nodded. "Me too. I remember friends on the force talking about it as well."

"How old was she when was killed?" Ophelia asked.

"She was twenty-three," said Betty around a mouthful of food. "She'd be thirty-seven now if she hadn't been killed."

Ophelia shook her head. "So young."

Andrea nodded. "No one deserves a death like that, but her age makes it all the more tragic."

Both moms looked at her then, and Betty knew they were thinking about all the danger the world might hold for her. All she could do was smile back at them. They looked at each other then, one of their superconnected gazes, and then the three of them worked on their dinners.

Seeing her mothers like this made her long for someone she could care about like that, but none of the boys she'd ever met had come close to making her feel the way her mothers did about each other. Which then brought her mind around to poor Jake and the hammer she needed to drop on him. *He'll be OK, and we'll both be better for it, at least in the long run.*

Not for the first time, it was like her moms had a clear view into her brain. "Have you dumped that horny idiot yet?" Andrea asked, venom in her voice, a smile on her face. "Or are you playing us a little bit?"

"No, I haven't dumped him yet," she said, "but I'm not playing you guys, either. I just want to find the right time to do it. I know you guys think Jake is just some jock that's trying to take advantage of me, but I think it's actually going to mess him up a little bit after I tell him."

"I think Jake will be fine," said Ophelia, "but I wouldn't blame him if he did spend some time pining after you."

"So, I had a question," said Betty to Andrea, desperate to change the subject, even if this new topic could be fraught with its own perils. "I understand if what I'm asking simply isn't possible, or if you'd rather not get involved, but I was wondering if maybe you could set it up so I could interview someone at the police station?"

"You mean for your project?" Andrea asked.

"Yeah, exactly. June and I were hoping maybe you could use your contacts down there to get me an interview with someone who was on the force at the time. A detective would be ideal, but really anyone who was working back then who'd be able to give me some insight."

Andrea eyed her for a moment, working over a mouthful of risotto. "Assuming I can get you an interview like that," she said at last, "what do you mean to ask?"

"I don't know, exactly. Most likely just some questions about Duke and Mandy's roommates at the time of her death, and why they were ruled out in the crime. I'll probably come up with some other stuff, too, but if you're worried about me being insulting by asking about some of the bad stuff that people say the cops did, you don't need to worry. I want a good interview, not one where the person I'm talking to is irritated."

Andrea nodded at that. "No promises," she said, "but I'll make a call after dinner. Depending on scheduling, we might not hear anything for a day or two. Can it wait?"

"Yes, absolutely," said Betty, who stood and then rushed around the table to throw her arms around Andrea.

"I just said I'd make a call," said Andrea. "Don't get too excited."

Betty kissed her mother on the side of her head and then released her.

"If anyone's interested," Ophelia said, "I have some exciting stuff going on, too."

"Of course we are," said Betty, as she leaned over to kiss her other mother on the cheek. Ophelia smiled at Betty as she retook her seat, and then began to describe to them some breakthrough she'd had that afternoon with the new painting in the basement.

EIGHTEEN

I see Claire before she sees me, and I cover the distance between us quickly, giving her a short wave when she finally turns and notices me. I could have mugged her if I wanted to, but as interesting as her wallet might be, I'm a lot more interested in getting some information. I don't know how happy Claire is going to be that I looked into her ex instead of just checking up on June, but she needs to know everything at this point, and I want to see the look on her face when I mention Jack.

"You said you needed to talk?" Claire asks, but the words come out shaky, almost like she knows what I'm about to say, but doesn't want to hear it.

"I did," I say, and then pop a matchstick in my mouth. "I went by Jack's house the other day. Is there anything I should know about him?"

"Oh my God! Why would you go there? He's going to be furious if he finds out that—"

"There's nothing to find out," I say, and it's true. Jack isn't going to find out that I broke in, and even if he did, there's nothing for him to discover that would lead back to Claire.

"Jack has a temper." Her words come out measured and emotionless. "If he caught you there, he'd hurt you, maybe even worse."

Worrying about what didn't happen is a waste of time, so I press on. "How often does June spend time with him?"

"Every few weeks, but there's nothing I can do about that," says Claire. "He pays his child support, and so he has visitation rights."

"Not if you think he might hurt your daughter."

"I don't think that," says Claire, but the words don't assure me she's telling the truth. I wonder if she believes them. "Jack never had a temper like that, not with her. June's only usual gripe is that he ignores her when she's over there. No, he'd never get violent with his daughter."

I nod, not sure of what else to say. It still sounds to me like she's trying to convince herself of something, like there's some suspicion she doesn't want to say aloud for fear that might make it true. "Could Jack have hurt Mandy?"

"No," she says, the expression on her face screwed up and unfamiliar. "No, never."

I nod, but my head's racing.

I should believe Claire, but I don't. There's a wounded person inside of her, someone who wants to do what's right, but either doesn't know how or is too scared. "I just want June to be safe," she says again, like it's her mantra, or something she's chanting against demons while she shakes a rattle over a fire. I know there are no deeper revelations to be had today.

"All right," I say, letting a smile crease my face. "June's safety is what I want as well, so if you think of anything that could help me with that, be sure to let me know."

Claire returns my smile halfheartedly and then nods, but it's meaningless. She might tell me more dirty little secrets later, but at the moment, she's convinced that if she stays mum, the truth will stay buried forever.

———

The bike ride home from the park gives me a few moments to re-flect on things, and I have to admit, after talking to Claire my inter-est in the Reasoner case has been piqued all over again. The more I look at the evidence, the *real evidence,* the more I wonder how in the world the prosecutor was ever able to get a conviction. Don't get me wrong, Duke could be as guilty as Gacy, but that doesn't mean the conviction was clean. Of course, that's the real reason for all of the public interest. Duke and Mandy were already a good story, but add in a weak conviction? Gold.

Besides, the real meat of the job is to watch June, and if last night was typical, that should be a piece of cake. June is rarely alone, and she tends to stick to her house and school. If there's a boy-friend in the picture then he remains to be seen, and even though I only have one day to base her routine on, June isn't sneaking out at night. Claire wants her daughter safe, and so do I, but right now it seems like the best way to do that is going to be casually watching her and making sure her daily life stays on the straight and narrow.

Where I stand now, though, all of that's on the back burner. I need cash, and if this job with June is going to be as short-lived as I'm expecting, some drastic measures are going to be necessary. For years I had a connection to sell the pot I grow through a friend that went to a nearby high school, but that changed a little over a year ago. Now he keeps permanent residence in a hole in the ground, and I've been scrounging ever since. Don't get me wrong, it could be a lot worse. I could be the one in the hole, but it defi-nitely hasn't made life any easier.

Growing dope is easy, and dealing dope is easy. But finding someone you can trust to sell a quantity to—that's hard. And that's the only way it makes sense to do business, because it's much safer to sell a lot once for a low profit than it is to be the guy trying to make deals on every last scrap. It was hard enough to make an arrangement for that once, and it will be just as hard to do it again. Right now I'm in sort of a stasis on the matter. I try not to think about it, and the dope I grow just keeps piling up. The only good thing to come of it is that when I do finally make a big sale, it's going to pay off large, and there's nothing wrong with that.

I was supposed to go work out at Rhino's today, but the only person I made that deal with was myself and right now I'm not in the mood. I know it's lazy, and I know I need to keep in shape, but it's getting harder and harder to make myself walk in there. I trust Rhino like a father, and my friend Jeff is there all the time, too, but still I avoid the place. I think I'm just scared that they'll be able to see through me into the awful things I've done. Even scarier is the idea that I might finish a sparring session by spilling all of it, all of the mess. Life isn't meant to be easy, but when I look in the mirror I know what I'll see: hollow eyes wondering how we ever got to this point. The boy there is beyond wounded, and there's a trail of blood behind him a mile long. I'm glad I'm lucky enough to live like I do, but sometimes, I wonder what I would trade for the life of a normal teenager.

Instead of the gym, I just keep circling Riverside. Being here alone lets me breathe in the sights and sounds, and it reminds me of what it's like to be a hero instead of a demon. I've been both, but being a hero sure makes waking up more pleasurable, especially when you wake up alone. Some mornings, good memories and cereal are all you have to help you get by.

I'm half-tempted to just find June and talk to her, let her know she's digging in a hornet's nest and that her mom wants her out of it, but knowing kids, that might just make things worse. Of course, it wouldn't be purely altruistic. I like the idea of talking to June, or her friend Betty. I feel like I know both of them, in that creepy Internet voyeur sort of way. They have pictures and all of their likes posted all over their profiles, so I feel familiar with them already. I know that's a load of crap, and that all I'd do is freak them out if I did tell them I knew what was going on.

Doesn't matter, though. I'm not going to contact them. This job is going to fade away like they have been lately, and then I'm going to need to get back to moving some dope.

NINETEEN

Betty was slogging through another day of school when halfway through third period her phone buzzed. "It's a yes," said the text from Andrea. "Our house @ 4. Let me know if u cant make it."

Betty wanted to jump from her seat and run around the room, but instead she discreetly put the phone away in her pocket, making a mental note to text her mother back at the end of the class. Glancing at the clock as her teacher droned on about nonsense, Betty knew the text was only going to make time go even slower.

Minutes after the first text, Betty felt her pocket buzzing again, but this time when she took it from her pocket the message was from Jake. It was simple, short, and to the point: "We ned 2 talk."

The message filled Betty's stomach with a cold dread. Was *he* going to end it?

That should've been a happy prospect, right? She wanted things to be over with Jake, or at least she thought she did, but the idea of him wanting it to be over was sickening in a new way, and it made her feel awful that she could be so shallow. Betty had never been dumped, she'd always been the one holding aces at the end of every relationship she'd ever had, and the feeling that she was dump-able was gut churning.

Betty was just tucking the phone back into her pocket when the teacher, Mrs. Huevel, asked, "Betty, is there something you'd like to share with the class?"

"No, Mrs. Huevel," said Betty.

The scrunch-faced teacher smiled thinly. "Then put the phone away, dear."

Betty nodded but wasn't sure of exactly what to do, as the phone was already back in her pocket. She settled on rubbing the outside of her jeans, and the motion satisfied the prunelike teacher.

"Now, as I was saying," said Mrs. Huevel, and Betty once again drowned the older woman out, thoughts of boyfriends, detectives, and a dead girl from the past far too interesting for her to pay any mind at all to math.

When class was finally over, Betty grabbed her bag and walked out the door. The plan was to get to June, tell her about the meeting set for that night, and then text Jake and tell him that she'd be up for a phone call later on. After all, she was far too busy for a meaningless high school relationship right now, and if all Jake wanted was for it to be over, then that would work for her, too.

The thought died in her mind as a hand landed on her shoulder, and then a voice said, "We need to talk. Can I walk with you?"

Betty turned to see what her ears had insisted was Jake, but what part of her mind had argued was very likely an escaped and vengeful Duke. "Sure, we can talk if you want," said Betty, wondering why the Duke thought had ever come into her mind in the first place. Even if he were out of prison, there would be no reason for him to suspect that Betty and her friends were working on a project about the murder.

As Jake and Betty began to make their way through the crowded hallway, Jake said, "So I've been thinking—"

"Let's wait until we're outside." The words came out too blunt, too much of an order, and Betty could see Jake's face redden in her peripheral vision.

"All right," he said sheepishly, his eyes locked on the door ahead of him.

Betty kept her eyes locked straight forward, too. Before the text from Jake, all she'd wanted of the day was to escape school and get the interview that Andrea had set up, but now she would have been happy just to leave and imagine that none of this was happening. Dating Jake was supposed to be fun, just a little fling that never really went anywhere, but now Betty felt like she was destined to be thrown to the scrapheap that was the school's rumor mill, not to mention the emotional bruising that would come part and parcel with a breakup.

When they reached the doors, Jake pulled one open to allow Betty to walk outside, but without thinking she opened the door on the other side of the breezeway and then waited for Jake on the other side. June was out there waiting for her. In the stress of the Jake situation, Betty had forgotten all about their planned walk to the library. June shuffled out of the way as Jake followed Betty onto the sidewalk, and the three of them came to a halt and exchanged glances that covered the matter as well as words would have.

"Jake and I need to walk alone today," said Betty, as if the matter was really that simple, and June slipped back inside without a word.

"What's up with her?" Jake asked, and Betty wasn't sure what to say, so she answered him with a shrug. *June saw the look on my face*, thought Betty to herself, *and she wanted to leave before we started screaming at one another.* That they'd made it outside and the parking lot and lawn were devoid of people were the lone blessings of the situation.

Betty started across the sidewalk, then stepped over a curb and onto the asphalt, before crossing the road and hopping the next curb onto the lawn.

"You don't need to walk so fast," said Jake. "Besides, we both know I can outrun you."

"Especially if you get me in trouble and stuck doing push-ups," replied Betty, instantly regretting her bitchy tone.

Jake's face reflected the words' heat. "Betty, I'm really sorry about that," he said, "and about getting you in trouble at home, too. I do stupid things sometimes, like talk to you when we're supposed to be running, or that damn text, but I really do care for you."

Here it comes, the moment where he tells me that he likes me as a friend, or that he needs time for himself. Not sure why she was even upset, Betty just kept walking. *This is a good thing, it means you both get off easy. He doesn't get a broken heart, and you don't have to be the bad guy.*

But mainly, Betty was rocked by the fact that she'd never considered how she would feel in this situation. The reality of it was like seeing a semi bearing down on her. The idea of being the one dumped, and then seeing Jake with some cheerleader slut or whatever else had caught his eye made her feel like she could dust her shoes with her breakfast right there on the lawn.

She didn't, though. She just kept on walking, until Jake grabbed her arm. "Aren't you going to ask me what I want to talk to you about?"

"I figured you'd tell me when you were ready."

"Yeah, I guess so," said Jake. "This is actually tougher than I thought, though." Jake raised his face to the sky, sighed deeply, and then lowered his head to lock eyes with Betty. "I'm thinking about joining the navy." The words coming from his mouth were so unexpected that Betty wasn't capable of responding. She just stared at him with what felt like an impossibly dumb look on her face while he kept on talking. "I want to sign up so that as soon as I graduate I can go to boot and get it over with. My parents are totally supportive, and all I really need to do is talk to you about this."

"You want me to try and talk you out of it?"

"No," said Jake. "I want you to come with me. If we get married, then after boot you can come live with me on a base somewhere. I'll make more money if I'm married, and we'll both have insurance and stuff. I know we're young and this probably sounds crazy, but it would be the only way that you can come with me."

Betty opened her mouth to speak, to tell Jake that he was insane. She wanted to tell him that the two of them were nothing, just a little high school thing to keep from getting bored, and that his idea to join the navy and have a little family was probably the least attractive thing that she'd ever heard in her life. Betty wanted the wind in her hair and a guitar in her hands, she wanted to live before she was resigned to a house and a nine-to-five, she wanted to be the person that she'd always imagined, on stage and screaming about everything that had ever mattered to her.

"I don't know what to say," said Betty, one of the most purely true things ever to cross her lips.

"Don't say anything yet," said Jake. "I know it sounds awesome, but it's a big commitment, and we need to be totally sure before we do this. Why don't you give me a call tonight, if you're able to, and we can talk more?"

"I'll try," said Betty. "I'm still grounded, and that includes you, especially after what happened."

"Well, they're going to need to get over that," said Jake. "Either way, we're going to be together, so they just need to get used to it. We need to do this, Betty. This is going to be our life, and I'm not going to let anyone take that away from us."

Betty stared through him. Jake had always seemed dumb in a friendly sort of way, like a six-month-old dog, but this was a whole new depth of stupidity that she'd been completely unaware of. The Jake she knew, the jock that was dangerous enough to be interesting, was a far cry from this delusional little boy.

"I'll try," said Betty, and then the bell sounded from inside the school, an ear-splitting mercy.

TWENTY

Betty thought she'd be able to gloss over the details of her encounter with Jake and compile a list of what she should ask the cop later that afternoon, but June was far too intrigued for anything that reasonable. Once she was over the initial shock of Betty somehow being proposed to—a word that seemed more like a curse to Betty than it ever had before—June spelled out very clearly what she wanted.

"Every detail, Betty," said June. "Every single word, I want deets and I want them now. This is probably the biggest thing that has ever happened to us. I include my aunt in that—this is bigger."

"No, it's not," said Betty, the annoyance clear in her voice. All she wanted to do was work on the project, but June was going on like an idiot. *It's not even a big deal, it just means that dumping him is going to go even worse than I expected.* The thought was callous enough to redden her face. She was the one who had been terrified of being broken up with just ten minutes earlier, and she didn't even like Jake all that much. He was the one in love with her, and he was going to take it terribly. That was clearer now than it had been before.

"Yes it is," said June. "God, I cannot wait until this gets out. There aren't usually proposals until senior year. At least that's what my mom always said. Seriously, this is like the weirdest thing ever. How can you say it's not a big deal?"

"You swore you wouldn't tell anyone."

"I'm not going to," said June, and then she shook her head to indicate her unassailable loyalty, even in the face of such incredibly juicy gossip.

"I expect you to stick to that," Betty said, "no matter how exciting the idea of the whole school talking shit about me might be. God! I can't even believe we're talking about this right now. I have to meet some cop friend of my mom's tonight, and I'm going to look like a total asshole if I don't have good questions to ask him. We need to worry about that, not Jake Norton or his stupid fucking ideas."

"I'm not even sure I can think about anything else," said June. "I don't care how stupid that sounds, either. This is the craziest thing ever, and I just want to soak it in."

"All right, I get it," said Betty. "I still need help, though, I'm not going to have time after school to come up with good questions on my own, and we've already wasted twenty minutes of a fifty-five-minute class. We need to come up with something, and *now*."

June was nodding at her like she was totally getting her urgency, but when she spoke she said, "Will you keep Martinez, be a hyphen, or spend the rest of your days as Betty Norton?"

She asked the question with a smile in her eyes, but Betty couldn't take any more. She grabbed her bag from behind the chair and then stomped out of the library.

Betty could hear June calling after her in a hushed voice, along with a librarian shushing her, but she didn't care. She hated that she'd told June, she hated Jake for making a fool of her, and she hated that they were never going to figure out who had killed Mandy Reasoner.

Betty walked from the library straight to her car and started it without a second thought. When she reached the security post she blew right through it, almost hitting the guard's waiting arm. He wanted a pass that she didn't have, but Betty didn't care. She needed answers, but first she needed questions, and there wasn't going to be time for any of those during school. No longer clouded by thoughts of Jake, skipping school, or the guaranteed rage of the moms, Betty stomped the gas pedal and drove, no destination in mind.

TWENTY-ONE

Betty's mad dash from the high school ended at Riverside Park. She parked her car by a playground, then walked past a man wearing an eye patch and staring at the birds. He looked sort of scary to Betty, but also very comfortable in his surroundings, almost as if he belonged in the park. Betty settled on a bench across the playground from the man, and after giving him a sideways glance, slid a notebook from her bag. Betty flipped the notebook open, grabbed a pen from the bag, and then exhaled deeply before leaning back into the bench.

I probably could have handled that better, Betty admitted to herself. It was a rough truth, but it was true, and there was no way this was going to help with the grounding. Worst-case scenario, the school called Ophelia at home, Ophelia called Andrea, and Andrea called her cop friend to cancel the meeting. Even worse, now that she was separated from June, Betty found it hard to even find fault with her friend. If June had been proposed to in such an awkward and ridiculous way Betty would have been the first one on board to give her shit over it, but when it was her turn to take a little medicine, she'd run off like a spoiled little brat.

Forcing herself to accept the situation for what it was, Betty turned her attention back to the waiting notebook on her lap. The blank page was calling to her with the same siren song that a cursor in Word beckoned with, and Betty wanted nothing more than to fill the page with questions.

Gripping the pen in twitching fingers, Betty added notes to remind herself to ask about the timeline of events from a police perspective, rather than the one listed on the Free Duke site. Next, Betty added inquiries as to whether there had ever been other suspects, whether there had ever been any investigations after the trial, and whether Duke was suspected of any other murders.

Betty was so deep in thought that she didn't even notice that someone was approaching her until a male voice said, "Shouldn't you be in school?"

When Betty snapped her head up at the sound, she found a redheaded boy with a scar under his right eye standing before her. He was wearing a Hot Water Music shirt and grinning at her in a sideways sort of way with a matchstick hanging out of his mouth.

"Shouldn't you be?" Betty asked, annoyed at the intrusion, but also intrigued. The boy was familiar somehow, but even more oddly, he was cute in a mutt puppy kind of way.

"Nah," said the boy. "Not really feeling school lately." He cocked his head as if he were thinking and then said, "Rhino's, right?"

"Yeah, every now and again," said Betty. "My mom is a judo nut, and I train with her sometimes. You go there too?"

"Yep, I've been known to drop in and out on occasion," said the boy. "What are you working on?"

"A project for school," said Betty.

The boy looked from the notebook on her lap to the treetops. "Nature project?"

"Not hardly. About the most unnatural thing ever, actually." When he cocked his head at that, she found herself babbling away, filling him in. "No, it's this thing for school. There was this girl killed fifteen years ago, but a lot of people think the cops busted the wrong guy for it. My mom set up a meeting with a cop after school, and I'm supposed to be able to ask him a bunch of questions, but I'm still working out what I want to say. I was supposed to be doing this with my friend June but we got in a dumb fight and . . ." Betty let the last word trail off and then looked at the boy and said, "Why am I telling you all of this? I don't even know your name."

"My name's Nickel. What's yours?"

"Betty," she said, and then extended a hand. Nickel—if that really was his name—took it and gave it a quick shake. "It's nice to meet you," she said.

"It's nice to meet you as well. So what are you planning on asking your cop friend?" Nickel sat on the bench next to her, and then Betty quickly read him the words on the page. She still wasn't quite sure why she was doing it, other than that the boy was nice and cute in that weird sort of way.

When she was done, he looked at her and said, "Those are all pretty good. You've got a knack for this. You're missing a couple, though. Do you mind if I give you a couple of ideas?"

"Not at all," said Betty, deciding just to roll with it. She didn't know whether anything the kid had to say would be worth hearing, but he was the only one there to talk to besides the guy in the eye patch. The worst that could happen would be she just wouldn't use any of his suggested questions.

"Cool," said Nickel. "First off, some advice: Don't believe what the cop tells you, at least not one hundred percent. I'm not trying to say he's a liar. I just mean the stuff he believes about the case might not all be correct. There are three versions of a story like that: the cop's version, the criminal's version, and the truth. And the only person that knew the truth for sure is dead."

"All right," said Betty, not sure what else to say to the kid. He must have spent a lot of time thinking about this stuff, but what kid did that?

"As for questions, I'd make sure to keep your focus on the roommates as much as possible. From what I know about the case, that was one of the most contested—"

"Wait, you already knew about this?" Betty said, her voice incredulous, and her mind racing. "How is that possible? I just heard about all of this."

"I have an interest in this sort of thing," said Nickel. "Just in general, but especially because it happened locally. Anyway, aside from the roommate, I think you need to ask about the man in the green jacket, the one Duke Barnes claimed to see leaving the house when he was first arrested. He recanted later, and none of that testimony made it too far, but if your cop knows about the case then he knows about that."

"But how do you—"

"Like I said, it's just kind of a hobby, but I can be very thorough. Also, I think you need to ask why the police disregarded the existence of those roommates so quickly. Unless your cop was really close to the investigation, he's not going to know, but it's still worth trying. That was one of the things Duke's lawyers tried to get mentioned in court, but it was barred as evidence. There was at least one other person in that house at the time Mandy was killed. That's something Duke never wavered on, not even when he was first being interrogated and he was strung out on heroin and babbling out his confession. The only question is if the guy in the green coat was a roommate or some other guy."

"How can you possibly know all this stuff?" Betty asked the question with fear in her voice. Nickel looked to be the same age as her, but he spoke as though he'd been alive and watching the courtroom and interrogations as they happened.

"I just do," said Nickel with a shrug. "Like I mentioned, I find it interesting. I've considered looking into it further like you are, but I don't have a friend in the police department, and there always seems to be something else to do." Nickel paused and then said,

"One more thing. Ask about Mandy's diary. Duke mentioned it several times during his initial interrogation, but it never came up again. If it exists, it's likely the cops either buried it or never took possession of it in the first place. If the latter is the case, and Duke didn't destroy it himself, it's possible it's still out there."

"This is incredible," said Betty, scarcely able to believe the wealth of information this mysterious boy was sharing with her. *If he's lying he's damn good at it, and what reason could he possibly have to make all of that stuff up?*

"I have to go," said Nickel. "The person I was supposed to meet is going to be here soon." Nickel looked past her toward the parking lot, but when Betty turned to see what he was staring at, there was no one there.

"Here," said Nickel, a business card appearing in his hand as he stood. "It's just e-mail, but I'll get back to you if you send me something. Use it or don't, it's totally up to you." Betty took the card from him. It was white with black lettering and it said nickel1138@gmail.com.

"Thanks for your help," said Betty as she pushed the card into her pocket. "I don't really understand how you could know so much about this, but I really appreciate the help."

"I know," said Nickel. "Let me know if you need anything." Then he walked toward the parking lot without another word.

Betty watched him go with the sort of wonder on her face that's usually reserved for UFO sightings, and then Nickel disappeared into the parking lot. Betty shook her head, gave the man with the eye patch a look, and then stuffed her pen and notebook back in her bag. She doubted that her mother's cop friend would be able to give her all the answers she was looking for, but the help she'd gotten from a very odd stranger certainly seemed like it might be of some use. Betty stood, gave another look to where Nickel had disappeared to, and then began the walk back to her car.

TWENTY-TWO

Betty was braced for the fury to begin when she walked into the house, but all she heard was the thump of funk rock coming from the basement. She hurried upstairs and gave her phone a look. There were three text messages waiting for her: one from Jake that said he was thinking of her—a terrifying thought—and a pair from June, both of which said she was very sorry for what happened in the library.

Betty ignored the texts, too puzzled by the lack of enraged messages from the moms. She'd hoped against hope that the school hadn't called, but had resigned herself to the fact that of course they would have, probably before she was even out of the school building, much less the parking lot. *They'll probably call during dinner*, Betty thought, but she knew that they wouldn't. The second fifth period started, there should have been an immediate red flag at her absence and then a call to her parents, but somehow none of that had happened.

Suddenly her life was stuffed full of mysteries. The mystery of the missing call from school. The mystery of whatever the hell Jake Norton was smoking when he hatched the idea of them getting freaking *married*. And, of course, above all, the mystery of Mandy Reasoner's death, which she'd only scratched the surface of. And then there was the mysterious stranger she'd met in the park, with his wealth of information.

Betty spared a glance to the card on the desk and wondered how long she would be able to resist before sending him a message. Nickel was exactly the sort of guy that could make her swoon. He was smart, looked a little bit dangerous, and, judging by his T-shirt at least, liked good music. It was almost too good to be true. But Betty knew she'd never have the nerve to do much more than e-mail him. There was something dangerous about the boy that went far beyond his cryptic knowledge of Mandy's murder, something Betty couldn't quite put her finger on, and she didn't think that she'd be figuring it out anytime soon.

Trying to solve a puzzle for which she had so few pieces was impossible, so Betty grabbed her notebook and pen and left the card and thoughts of Nickel behind her as she headed back downstairs.

Ophelia's awful music was still blaring through the house, so Betty shut the door to the basement to at least muffle it a little and grabbed a water from the fridge. She had twenty minutes to kill before four o'clock and spent the time sitting at the table and staring at the questions on the sheet.

When the doorbell finally rang, it made Betty leap from her near-fugue state. She'd been thinking of Nickel and his bizarre appearance and information in the park, but it was the suggestions that she'd scribbled onto the page that had her attention now. He had told her things that she wasn't supposed to know, things that only someone with deep knowledge of the case could have known, and what was she going to do if the cop asked her where she had come by the information? Betty didn't know for sure, but she had a feeling that telling the officer a cute boy in the park had given it to her wasn't going to cut it.

When Betty opened the door, she found a pleasant-looking man wearing a gray suit waiting for her. He was taller than she was, about six feet, and barrel-chested. His hair and thick mustache were both salt and pepper—salt was winning the fight, especially in the mustache. Betty couldn't remember having ever seen the man before, but there was something oddly familiar about the half smile he gave her and the kindness in his eyes.

"You must be Betty," said the cop. "I'm Detective Dick Van Endel." He stuck his hand out and they shook. His hand was big but softer than she'd imagined it would be. Then again, why would a detective have calloused hands? "I understand you think I might be able to help you out with a school assignment."

"It's great you were able to make the time for me," said Betty. "I really appreciate it."

"My pleasure." He sounded like he meant it.

"Why don't you come in so we can talk? I don't know how long you have, but I have quite a few questions."

"All right," said Van Endel and followed Betty into the house and took the seat at the table she offered him. She sat down opposite him, the notebook a bridge between them. "Your mother has told me a great deal about you," said Van Endel. "It's been a good while since we worked a case together, but she and I have had a few adventures, and it's nice to finally get to meet you."

"Yeah, Andrea can be a little braggy," said Betty. "I hope it wasn't too annoying."

"Not at all," said Van Endel. "Any way we could get the music turned down?"

"Sure," said Betty, before pounding her foot into the floor. Van Endel grinned, and then a few seconds later the music became much quieter.

"Better?"

Still grinning, Van Endel nodded his head. "So," he said, "Andrea said you and some friends were working on a project for school. Something about the Mandy Reasoner case. I should be able to answer just about anything you want to know, so when you're ready just let me know."

"Did you work the case?"

"No, I missed that one," said Van Endel. "My partner at the time, a man named Phil Nelson, worked the case while I was on leave."

"Is there any way you could ask Phil if I have any questions that you can't answer?" Betty asked this slowly, stalling as the wheels turned in her mind, searching for a passable excuse that would help to explain away some of the insider information she was about to drop.

"Unfortunately that won't be possible," said Van Endel. "Phil passed away a couple years ago, and though I often find myself talking to him still, I've yet to get an answer."

"I'm sorry about your friend."

"It's all right, Betty," said Van Endel. "At my age it's pretty normal to have a few more friends underground than I would like. That said, Phil and I discussed that case over beers on more than one occasion, and I should be able to tell you anything you might want to know."

"OK," said Betty as she grabbed her notebook off of the table. "First off, what do you know about Duke Barnes's claim that he and Mandy may have had a roommate or two at the time of her death?"

"Hardball right away," said Van Endel with a chuckle. "I like that. Duke did claim to have a roommate—aside from Mandy—but other than some signs that other people slept there occasionally, there was no evidence they had any permanent roommates."

"Well, how could you tell?"

"Remember, they were staying at the house illegally, squatting there. And people living like that tend to be pigs. They hoard anything they can get their hands on. Leave plenty of signs. Plus, these weren't just poor people, remember. Duke, Mandy, and anyone they were associating with were hardcore drug users, who leave an especially recognizable brand of filth in their nests." Van Endel cleared his throat and then coughed into a fist before saying, "The entire house was like that, garbage everywhere, with one exception. There was only one livable room in that place, even for a really desperate junkie."

"Then why was Duke so insistent that he and Mandy had a roommate? I read that he never changed his stance on that, and that even today he still insists he had a roommate in that house."

"Well, there are two possibilities: either Duke is lying, or they had a roommate named Jason, like he claimed, and he or some stranger left just before Mandy was killed," said Van Endel calmly, but Betty couldn't help notice that the cop's brow was furrowed. *He didn't like that one too much.* Van Endel's face relaxed almost as soon as she'd noticed it, and then he said, "The problem is that we know Duke is and was a liar. He would have said or done anything back then to get out from under that crime, and the same thing holds true today. Regardless of what he might say about Jason, there is no evidence that definitively supports Duke's claim that there were other people living there."

"All right," said Betty. The answer wasn't all that satisfying, but it did go along with what she knew about the trial, and with what Nickel told her in the park. The cop's words also meant that the idea had been vetted by the detectives as they investigated the case, and that despite what the Free Duke site might say, there was a good reason why the roommate wasn't investigated further.

"I know you've got more than that," said Van Endel, the warm half smile back. "That sheet looked pretty full."

"I heard from talking to some people that run a Free Duke website that there was a man in a green jacket seen running from the house. Do you know anything about that?"

"Of course I do," said Van Endel with a smile. "Whoever you were talking to, they really know their stuff. We did investigate the man described by Duke, but the only man the neighbors saw in a jacket like that was Duke. You compound that with the fact that Duke was very high on heroin when he made his initial statement, and you have a very unreliable witness."

"Isn't it possible that no one but Duke saw the other man? That wouldn't mean he wasn't there just because there wasn't a witness around to watch him leave."

"True," admitted Van Endel. "The problem is that we never heard anything, even from Duke, about who that man might've been, or any other shred of evidence that could lead us to him. Contrast that with the evidence supporting Duke's involvement: he was covered in blood, high on drugs, and Mandy had been attacked very brutally—" Van Endel stopped himself, looking uncomfortable. "Betty, I'm not sure how bluntly I should speak with you. This is some pretty awful—"

"I'm fine, Detective. Really. I've already learned a lot of pretty graphic stuff about this case. I know what I've gotten myself into." Not that Betty was actually sure she did, but even to her ears, she sounded pretty sure of herself.

"OK, then," said Van Endel, apparently convinced. "Another damning bit of evidence was that Mandy's face had been covered by her shirt after the attack. Duke removed it before we got there, but the coroner put it all back together. An attack like that, the violence of it and especially the covering of the face, typically indicates that the murderer knew his victim and is ashamed of what he has done. Duke might not feel bad for what happened nowadays, but when he gave his confession he was very remorseful about how he'd let her live during that time, and he remembered very little of what had happened in the house that day."

"But Duke said later that he only confessed because he was held so long."

"Duke was held so long because of his toxicology," said Van Endel. "Those hacks on the Internet are right to think there are a few odd things about this case, but Duke being held wasn't one of them. He was hospitalized, not stuffed in some room at the back of the police station, and when Phil did speak with him it was for very limited periods of time and under the supervision of a doctor. Duke's confession was given under those circumstances as well, and it was strong enough evidence to stand up in court. Duke might not like that he all but convicted himself, but he was the one that confessed to that crime."

"OK," said Betty, giving a look to the notes. So far all the answers that Van Endel had given her seemed sound. The website had all the conspiracy theories and emotions, but Van Endel had facts, cold and hard ones at that, and Betty wondered how the creators of that site would feel if faced with such evidence. "What kind of timeline do you have on the event?"

"I can't recall exactly," said Van Endel. "Truth told, I think old Phil might even have trouble with that part after so many years. What I do know is that Duke went home, did what he did, and eventually called 911. There wasn't anything out of whack, at least not timewise, and from what I recall, everything happened pretty quickly. To play devil's advocate, if Duke were innocent then he walked into that home seconds after the attack."

"Wouldn't that support his story about walking in just after the man in the green jacket walked away?"

"If there was any other evidence that such a man existed, then absolutely. Unfortunately for Duke, there was no one else that saw him, and in his confession Duke didn't mention the man again. By the time the trial rolled around, there was no mention of green men at all." Van Endel caught himself with a chuckle. "Men in green *jackets*, I mean. Not that there was any mention of little green men, either."

They smiled at each other, but it felt weird to Betty to do even that when they were talking about stuff like this. "So, where was the house?" she asked.

Just like that, his smile was gone. "Why do you want to know?"

"We want to go take some pictures of it," said Betty, "assuming it's still standing, of course. Don't worry, I don't want to break in or anything. That's just plain creepy."

"Fair enough," said Van Endel. "Sorry for using my cop voice on you, it comes out pretty easily. I'll get the address tomorrow at work and send it over to your mother." He shifted in his chair. "But I will be pissed if it's still standing and you go inside. It was in pretty serious disrepair back then, and I can't imagine how it must look now."

"Just pictures, I promise," said Betty with a smile, and the cop smiled back at her. "I just have a couple more and then I'll be done. Is that all right?"

"It's fine," said Van Endel. "No rush. Barring anything particularly unfortunate happening, I've got the rest of the day off, and this beats anything else I might have had planned, even if you are sleuthing around a case I considered solved a long time ago. Still, better you than one of those nuts that think Duke Barnes really is without-a-shred-of-doubt innocent. I can understand doubt, but if you read some of the stuff we've had mailed to the station, you'd think Phil all but put a knife in Duke's hands."

"Well," said Betty, "I just don't want to be annoying." Van Endel waved a hand as if even the suggestion of such a thing was impossible, and so Betty asked him, "Did Phil ever mention if Mandy had kept a diary?"

"Is this another one of your Internet tips?" Van Endel asked the question with an even tone, but Betty saw a flash of something hard pass over his face. *Not much of a tell, but I bet if he plays poker he has some friends that know that look.*

"Yeah," said Betty. "I was told that Mandy had kept a diary, but that it never appeared anywhere after she died. Did Duke ever mention it?"

"He did, on numerous occasions, but if there really was one, it was never recovered," said Van Endel. "It drove Phil about nuts. They tore that house apart looking for it, but came away with nothing. That diary was either more BS from Duke, or it got swiped or tossed in the trash before Mandy was killed." Van Endel shrugged.

"I was really hoping that part might have been true," said Betty wistfully, and Van Endel nodded.

"That would have been a heck of a thing to look through. I'm sure it wouldn't have been a smoking gun pointed at Duke or anyone else, but it might have made some of this conspiracy crap go away."

"It could have given that conspiracy crap a boost, too, right?"

"That's true," said Van Endel. "I suppose in that regard there would have been a hell of an incentive for Phil to destroy it. Here's the problem though: Phil wasn't that kind of cop."

"What do you mean?"

"I mean he didn't have some vendetta against Duke or anyone else. There was no reason for him to have had one, and he just wouldn't have, in any case. Phil just wanted to catch the bad guy, not railroad some junkie." Van Endel drew in a breath, and by the time he let it out, his warm half smile was there. "You know those baby toys with the different-shaped holes, and the different-shaped pieces you're supposed to put in them?"

"Of course," said Betty.

"Being a cop and trying to fit a man for a crime is a lot like one of those," he explained. "There might be a time or two where a square peg gets shoved into a circular hole, like we're questioning the wrong guy, but part of being a good cop is realizing when that's happening.

"Duke Barnes is in jail because he fit that crime perfectly. If he was in the wrong place at the wrong time, then he sure did a good job of getting himself there." Van Endel paused and spun his head as the door to the basement opened and Ophelia walked through it.

"Detective Van Endel, what a pleasure to see you," said Ophelia, and then Betty watched as her mother hugged the cop, the sight of it bizarre in ways that she'd never experienced. *I get that Andrea knows him, but since when did she bring that part of her work home?*

TWENTY-THREE

The time after Van Endel left the house passed uneventfully. Betty's scribbled notes on the pad of paper felt like little threads of a far greater failure, and even looking at the Free Duke site felt a little silly now, childish even. If everything Van Endel had said was true, then there was no way Duke was going to be freed, no matter how many famous friends he might make. The site had described Duke as a hard man whose hard history had gotten him framed for a crime he didn't commit, but when Van Endel spoke of Duke, he didn't sound like he thought the prisoner was a dangerous man, just a pathetic one.

The only other useful thing to come out of the day had been the conversation with Nickel and his oddly helpful tips. Sure, the detective had cast doubt on all of them, but everything the boy in the park had mentioned at least had some bearing on reality. Betty believed the cop on all fronts, but unlike some of the things the detective had disproven outright, all the stuff Nickel had mentioned remained in the maybe-possible column.

The thought came to Betty with such finality that her mouth dropped open. She and June had tossed it out as a pie-in-the-sky possibility the other day, but the conversation with Van Endel had proven it to be a stone-cold necessity: she was going to need to convince the moms to let her go with June to Jackson to speak with Duke. He was the only one that would be able to answer their questions.

Not to mention, traveling across the state to speak to a man convicted of murder would be a serious boost to the project. Even if they ultimately failed in deciding Duke's innocence or guilt conclusively, she would still be able to say they had done everything they could in order to find out what had really happened to Mandy Reasoner.

Easy to say, but she knew there were going to be a lot of hoops to jump through. Betty had no idea how one could even go about setting up a meeting with a prisoner they didn't even know. And even if she did convince the moms to let her and Duke said he would meet her, there was still the matter of getting him to actually talk in front of Andrea, who would certainly insist upon coming along.

Even worse, if I ask her and she says no, then there's no way I'll be able to go. Maybe June will have some ideas.

This last thought set Betty's face to fire. She hadn't talked to June since the stupid fight at school. She hadn't even responded to her texts yet. She needed to make things right with June—this was *her* project, too. Hell, it had more to do with June than it did her. Mandy was her aunt, after all. And now Betty had so much to share with her. She needed to tell her about the meeting with Van Endel, about the house, and especially about the odd boy in the park.

Betty grabbed her phone from the desk and punched in a text to June that said, "Sorry 4 freaking out & being a bitch. Love you, and I need to tell you about today and ask you a couple of questions tomorrow. Still besties?"

Betty had only set the phone down on her desk maybe thirty seconds ago when it began to buzz.

"NO PROB! Sory I wuz so mean, totes just joking around but it went too far. Cant wait 2 c u 2 morrow so we can talk about it."

It was nice to have a person in her life she could fuck up with so totally and still call a friend.

The text conversation did remind her of Jake, though. Between everything else that had happened she'd nearly forgotten about her steady and his absolutely ridiculous request, and recalling it now made her feel nauseous. Being fodder for hallway mockery seemed far less a big deal to her now than it had earlier, but the idea of shattering a boy who obviously cared about her seriously made her feel like she might empty her stomach. Even worse was the fresh memory of walking through the hall and feeling like such hell because she was about to get dumped. Now it turned out he cared a lot more for her than she did for him, and she was going to have to turn around and put him through the same thing.

As Betty leaned back in her chair and let out a deep breath, Andrea called up the stairs that dinner was ready. Betty left the room determined to leave thoughts of Jake and Duke Barnes behind. There would be plenty of time for both of them soon enough, but right now she just wanted to be a teenager.

As she clomped down the stairs, Andrea shouted, "Hurry up, I want to hear about you and Dick."

Both Betty and Ophelia burst out in juvenile laughter at that, and as she walked into the room to see the moms giggling at one another, it struck Betty just how lucky she was to be a part of this little family.

TWENTY-FOUR

Our conversation the day before must have jarred something loose for the both of us. I spent the night reeducating myself on the Reasoner case, and now that we're together again at the park, it's obvious that Claire's been doing her own work. The first words out of her mouth are, "I want you to look into Jack."

"Excuse me?"

"My ex-husband. I want you to look into Jack as well."

"Yesterday, you said that—"

"I know what I said, you don't need to remind me. I changed my mind. If he had anything to do with that . . . thing, I need to know about it, for June's safety and my own sanity."

I nod, still trying to take it all in. Then things start to make more sense. The liquor on her breath and the unexpected change of heart are both fairly indicative that our conversation yesterday hit her far harder than I imagined.

"I'll need to do research more than just on him," I say. "I'll need to read about all the nuances of the Reasoner case all over again, but I need to remind you, I was in his house. There was nothing there."

"You think I'm crazy?"

"No, not at all." I'm trying to keep my tone neutral, but drunk divorcées that hire teenage investigators don't exactly strike me as the most balanced social demographic. "I do think, however, that I planted an idea in your head. I also think that if you really believed this idea, you and June would have skipped town for parts unknown a long time ago."

"I just want you to look into it," says Claire. "The other man is still locked up, and this is just an insurance plan."

"Is there anyone else it could have been? Anyone else that knew Mandy that the police looked into?"

"How should I know?" Claire asks, not even trying to hide her disgust. "The police never came around asking us any questions. They had their man, and that was good enough for me."

"So why do you want me to look into Jack now?"

"You've seen my daughter. Can you imagine what that would be like for him if he had done it, to see the girl he murdered whenever he looked at his own daughter?"

The rest of the conversation is just a lot of smiling and nodding on my end and ranting on hers. I want to tell her that I need to go, that people are almost certainly noticing our little meeting, but I'm forced to just let the storm die out on its own. By the time Claire is done yelling and back in her car, I've missed a couple of pages, both from the same number. Frowning, I grab my burner and dial the number, and the quick answer is telling. History has taught me that you know you have a drug dealer's attention when he answers on the first ring.

"Hello?"

"Hey, man, you paged me. Sorry about the wait."

"And who the hell is this?"

I sigh. I have a strict code, no names on the phone. But Paul doesn't care about codes, he only cares about proving to whoever's listening that he's in the power position. And it's been way too long since I've moved weed, so I'm ready to compromise.

"It's Nickel, man. I wanted to get together and talk about that thing."

"Yeah, I know that, *man*," says Paul, more bravado to back up the fact that the man has no backbone unless there's a heater in his pants and a friend or two to impress. I know the setup already: Paul in front of a room full of class clowns turned criminals, all having a joke at my expense. I can practically smell the reefer and hear Madden through the phone.

"So can we get together soon?" I ask, hating myself for having to put up with this nonsense. I can't believe I'm in this position. Not that it was my greed that put me here—it was all Gary's, and it's Gary's mistake I'm paying double for.

Of course, Gary did get a worse end of the deal than I did. Eventually.

"Are you still holding enough to make this worth my while?" Paul asks.

"Yeah, I am, and I'm willing to work on the price. The sooner I get off of this, the better."

There's silence on the other end of the phone, I'm guessing for either a video game break or a bong rip, and then Paul is back. "All right, that's good, that's good. I want to hook up soon, see if this smoke is as good as you say it is—"

"It's the same batch I gave you a bag of a few months ago," I blurt out. Any possibility that he doesn't think I'm desperate is gone now, and I wince, knowing I'm letting Dad down. I know what Dad would do with Paul and his friends, and it wouldn't be broker a deal. This is the corner I'm in, though.

"Yeah, I know that, Nickel," says Paul, all annoyed disdain. "I just want to get another bag, because as you said, it's been a few months. You want to move quantity, and I want to make sure I don't get stuck with a bunch of downtown brown, or a bunch of fire-damaged green."

"You know I wouldn't do that," I tell him, "and you know I don't know anything about that fire."

He just laughs at that, then gets serious again. "No, I don't know you wouldn't fuck with me, because we're not friends." That is sure as hell true. He's a connection, and not even a good one. That's the blessing and the curse of doing business in a city the size of Grand Rapids. It's hard to get caught up with some syndicate moving Peruvian bricks, but it's also hard to find a real operator and not a bullshitting weekend warrior. Paul is an unreliable wannabe gangster who smokes way too much of his own supply to ever be useful for much more than a few quick bucks, but he's all I have at the moment. "If we were friends," he goes on, "you'd be here right now, and we wouldn't be fighting over pennies."

"Paul, this isn't pennies." I know that he knows the rest, but feel like he needs a little reminder that we aren't squabbling over an eighth of an ounce. "I have over fifteen pounds, all processed and ready to go as soon as we can both get happy on a number. That's a lot of good green, and this is good green."

"I'll be the judge of that," he says, after a lengthy pause that's probably the result of him trying to remember if he's running offense or defense on the flat screen in front of him. "You can guarantee that, man: I will be the judge of just how much money this shit weed is worth. Where did you say you got it again?"

"I've got a knack for sniffing stuff out," I lie. "It just comes to me." Which is sort of true, though not with weed. I actually do have a talent for sniffing out monsters, and usually they do just come to me. That's where the scar under my eye came from, an angry man holding a .45 who hadn't realized he was about to go 120 miles straight to hell. As for pot—well, I just grow that. And I don't need Paul knowing where I stay or wanting to figure it out. Oh well, that's why they make burner cell phones, so that I can lose a number when I have to.

"Yeah, you better be able to sniff it out," says Paul. "If I find out this was stolen from some downtown dopeboy I'm going to be very pissed off. The absolute last thing I need is to do you a favor and have you sell me some shit that already has an owner. Get it?" I did, and told him as much, and then Paul said, "Give me a day or two. I'll call, you'll get back to me—immediately this time—and I'll get you a spot to meet me."

The line goes dead and I lay the phone down on my desk. Yes, I need the money, so yes, I need to work with Paul. But that doesn't mean I have to like it.

TWENTY-FIVE

"Was the cop cute?" June asked with a dopy-looking smile.

Betty frowned. "No—I mean, he wasn't ugly or anything, but he was old, probably as old as the moms, but men carry it differently."

"Old guys can be cute, too," said June, and that remark sent both of them into librarian shush-worthy titters, an affliction they managed to rein in before any actual punishment could be levied on them for daring to be amused in the temple of stacked books. "I am serious, though," said June as she wiped tears from under her eyes. "George Clooney is cute, Harrison Ford is cute, Tom Cruise is cute—"

"Those are movie stars. Of course they look good. Real-life old guys are gross. There's a big difference."

"I still don't get why you can't just ask the moms to drive with us to Jackson," said June. "I'd ask my parents, but there's no way they'd let me. I haven't talked to my dad in like a month, and if my mom even considered the idea that I knew about her sister she'd lose her shit, guaranteed."

"Shit," said Betty. "That's us stuck in the mud then. No way will the moms be up for it, and we're not eighteen so we need a guardian to go with us. Maybe it's just not meant to be. Besides, we don't know if Duke would talk to us even if we could get in to see him."

"He would, if we could get in," said June. "I'm sure of it. I mean, that's the whole point of what he's trying to do, drum up as many supporters as he can to help him get out. The problem is going to be getting into prison, but maybe we can figure something out."

"Well, I'm going to see if there's some sort of online form we need to fill out so we can see him. I'll just need to fudge our birthdays a bit."

"I suppose it can't be that hard," said June. "I mean, you hear about people breaking out of prison, why can't we break in?"

"Because I don't want to get shot?" Betty replied. "I can't think of a single adult that would even consider helping us out with this, June. Pointless though it is, I just need to bite the bullet and ask the moms. If we're already not going to be able to go, I may as well just ask. It's not like there are any other real options."

"Yeah, I guess so," admitted June. "This sucks, but it's weird, too. I never even knew I had an aunt, and now I'm bummed because I can't go meet the guy that probably killed her? What sort of fucked-up sense does that make?"

"It's not like you want to see him because you're some weirdo," said Betty. "We're trying to get a good grade in a really hard class, but more importantly, we're looking for answers. Do you have any idea how crazy it would be if we were the ones to figure this out?"

"It would be pretty cool to get some real justice for Mandy," said June. "I just don't think we can do that without talking to Duke."

"Then we'll figure something out," said Betty. "I don't know what, and I don't know how, but we'll figure it out." Betty didn't feel nearly as convinced as she was trying to sound, and she could tell her friend felt the same way. *Everything was going well until Van Endel made it sound like everyone already knows the truth. But if we can find some way to talk to Duke, then I can get us back on track.*

"Five minutes to the bell," said June. "That means we need to get back to Mr. Evans's class, and we never even talked about what we needed to do next."

"I'll do some research on the prison, and then I'll ask the moms," said Betty. "I guess we just cross our fingers and hope for the best."

The girls walked through the mostly empty corridors of Northview High School silently. Betty didn't know if they'd talked themselves out in the library, or if the subject matter had simply gotten too depressing to bear any further discussion. As they approached Mr. Evans's classroom, the bell signaling the end of the period rang out, and students began to fill the halls. Betty and June walked into the classroom as students flooded out of it, and Mr. Evans nodded as they came in.

"Ladies," said Mr. Evans. "How goes our research?"

"Good so far," said June, speaking the half truth for both of them, still preferable to telling their teacher that the path was beginning to look harder to traverse.

"Great," said Mr. Evans. "June, you may get on out of here, but Ms. Martinez, you and I need to have a quick word."

"OK," said Betty, trying to find confidence but unsure of why she was being singled out. She watched June leave and Mr. Evans close the door after her. He waited to speak until he'd walked back to his desk and sat across from where she stood, waiting for him.

"You cut my class yesterday."

"I'm sorry," said Betty. "It's a really long, stupid, and embarrassing story, and it won't happen again, I prom—"

"You're right," said Mr. Evans. "It won't. Forcing me to cover up your actions because you decide to just rush off isn't going to work again. June didn't tell me what the problem was, and I'm not sure I want to know, but I do hope that this was a one-time thing. Next time I'll call your parents myself, and to boot, I will give both of you a failing grade."

"I'm sorry, Mr. Evans. It won't happen again."

"I hope not. You have a good future ahead of you and there's no reason to let youthful stupidity screw it all up." Mr. Evans cocked his head and said, "Everything will be fine, Betty, just so long as you remember that high school is the start of your life, not the part that will define it. Does that make sense?"

"I guess so," said Betty. "Thanks, Mr. Evans."

"Thank me by not cutting any more class."

TWENTY-SIX

Betty found the visitor request forms online, talked briefly with her mothers during and then after dinner, but still found herself lacking in the courage department. If she had half a backbone, asking them to sign the form and then drive with her and June to Jackson should have been no big deal. Neither would calling Jake, or telling the moms that this grounding thing was going to need a fast death if she was going to retain her sanity.

Instead of doing any of those things, Betty ate, then fled upstairs and returned to the visitor request forms. There was no way it was going to work, not unless she got the moms to sign off on it, or they got fake IDs. The visitor request required both a birth date and a valid Michigan ID number. Betty had the ID, but she knew that her birth date wasn't going to hold water if she made herself a little older on the form. Getting a fake seemed about as likely as getting Andrea to sign the stupid form and then act as a jailhouse chaperone.

She kept a couple tabs open about Duke and Mandy so that she could at least lie to herself about working, but she just didn't have the stomach for it. Mr. Evans's words had been jarring, and Betty had felt sick ever since she'd spoken to her fourth period teacher, despite his kindness.

Betty doubted that Mr. Evans would really have failed both of them for her runaway routine the day before, but at the same time, he had told them he would be treating the assignment as if they were college students. As bad as it would have been to screw up everything for herself, Betty couldn't even imagine how fucked up the situation would have left June.

Mandy was June's aunt, after all—recently discovered family through pictures alone, but family just the same. Betty hadn't really spoken to June about how much the investigation must mean to her friend, but she figured it had to mean a great deal. They had a real chance not only to get a great grade, but also to either free or further condemn a guilty man, and even more importantly, they could be the ones to find justice for Mandy. That she looked so much like June was just the icing on the cake, and also the reminder that, with just a bit of bad luck, any one of them could be Mandy.

There were dead kids on the news all the time and school shootings and jealous boyfriends and abusive parents and texting and driving and a million other things, but they had a chance to fix something that had gone wrong when they were barely alive. They couldn't bring Mandy back, but ending the confusion over her murder would be the next best thing, and Betty knew she had almost blown it.

She needed to stand up and do what had to be done. And she knew where she needed to start.

Just tell the moms that you need to call Jake, dial his number, and be done with it.

Betty knew that would be the best thing for all involved, but still she kept her butt planted in her chair and left her phone lying on her desk.

Sick of herself, Betty turned her attention back to her desktop, checked her e-mail, clicked on www.punknews.org, bounced around on Reddit, and then her eyes fell on the card that Nickel had given her the day before in the park. She grabbed the card and flipped it over in her fingers a few times before clicking her mouse back to her e-mail tab and then clicking on "Compose." She wrote:

> Hi, I'm not really even sure why I'm writing this, but I'm the girl you met in the park yesterday. Not the one with the umbrella, the other one, with all the questions about Mandy Reasoner. I'm sure this is nothing you can help me with, but I never would have guessed you knew all that stuff either, so I thought I'd ask.
>
> I need to talk to Duke, and I need to do it soon, so letter writing is out. I know my parents wouldn't let me, but if I had a fake ID that said I was 18, they wouldn't have to know. It would need to be a really good one, like good enough to fool a guard, but I don't have a lot of money. I don't know if this is something you can help me with or not, but I thought it couldn't hurt to ask.
>
> It was super nice to meet you yesterday,
>
> Betty

Betty considered the e-mail for a few moments, then took a deep breath and clicked the "Send" button. She knew it was a long shot, but it was worth the risk. The worst that could happen is that Nickel would say no. Betty left the e-mail tab and went back to punknews. Nothing had been updated in the ten minutes or so she'd been there, but when she looked at her e-mail tab again she saw she had gotten a response. Betty smiled thinly, knowing it was far more likely to be junk mail than a response from Nickel, and then clicked on the button.

> Hey. I might be able to help with what you want, we can negotiate cost. Meet me where you saw me the other day when you get out of school. Come alone.
>
> N

There was something about the e-mail; even just how short and simple it was, was somehow exciting. Betty found herself already looking forward to meeting this mysterious boy again the following afternoon, though she was going to need to explain away her absence to Ophelia.

Not that a little fib to Ophy will be tough to pull off. Her head's been in the clouds lately with the new painting. Betty felt a touch of remorse at the thought. It was a little wrong to take advantage of Ophelia just because she was busy, but the whole grounding was pretty unfair. Betty didn't like herself for doing it, but she knew that when given the option of not meeting Nickel or bending the rules a little bit, bending was an easy pick.

I talked to Jason again, and this time he told the truth about what happened with us. What's been happening when he comes over. I think I've probably known all along. I'm not even sure that D. would be mad at him at this point, most likely he'd just be pissed at me, because lately Jason has a ton of money for smack, and that's all D. really cares about.

I hate knowing that about D. I hate that I stay, and I hate that I'm so weak.

Instead I just sit here and get high. I don't paint anymore, I don't go to shows—hell, I never even listen to music. I barely ever even write in this stupid thing. The only times that I even remember that I write a damn journal are when I'm so strung out that I actually start thinking like a human again. There is no reason why anyone should choose to live like this, but I'll bet you anything that I'm high again later today and that all of this is forgotten.

Things I will do when I am sober:

1. Go to a show and be clean and happy, no matter how much I hate the music, my hair, or my scars.
2. Call Ben and apologize. Let him know how sorry I am, and that the world needs another Old Croix Road record. I helped them record that first demo by hooking them up with a friend who had a four-track, and that was the best thing I've ever done, and now I can't even be around them. Not

*the way that I am now. Ben would try and help me, I know
he would, and in my current state I'd just lie and steal until
he never wanted anything to do with me ever again.*

*3. Do something positive to make other people know how
dangerous heroin is. This is a hard one, because I don't
want to be one of those nuts that kids laugh at, I want to be
their mom's cool old friend who's been there, done that, and
survived.*

*4. See the ocean. Both coasts, either coast, don't care. I want
to take my shoes off and get in the water. I don't care if it all
just swallows me up, I need to do this.*

5. Meet Claire's daughter. This one might never happen. ☹

*6. Be positive every single day, always think about using,
and still never do it.*

7. Write poetry that I'm proud of again. Pick up a guitar.

*8. Remember that I am a good person, and know that I have
worth.*

*9. Smile at Duke, and be so happy that we made it through
all of this together. There won't be many stories we can tell
our grandkids, but who cares.*

10. Live.

11. Live.

*Fucking Jason. Or, I suppose: I've been fucking Jason. I was
scared that it had happened once when I was too high to know what
was really going on, but now I know the truth. Jason who I didn't
want to move in with us, Jason the felon, Jason the drunk, Jason
the enabler. I thought it was a weak moment, but he said months,
MONTHS. How the fuck is that possible? I honestly feel sick when I
think about it.*

*I've been with worse men than Jason. Men that hit me or do
things that I tell them are off the menu. Men that fuck me and don't
pay me, men that lie about wearing a rubber, men that take and*

take and take, but somehow this is worse. I can't decide what would destroy me the most, if D. found out, or if D. knew all along.

I need help, I need some savior to just walk in the door and tell me to pick myself the fuck up, but I know that's not going to happen. D. doesn't even need me anymore, not since he broke down and started selling himself as well. He made money as a pimp, but he makes more as a rough-trade bottom. He hates me for that, I know he hates me for not being able to earn enough, like I could at first. Maybe that explains Jason, maybe D. gets off on seeing me used like that when I'm at my weakest. If that's the case, then it's the saddest revenge I've ever heard of.

I need help, but I'm too fucking weak to ask for any myself. I need my sister to come get me, I need Ben to come get me, I need any of those people that told me that they cared to come care right now. Right now my brain is begging me for that release, and my body is screaming for dope, and I know I'm going to tuck this away and get high.

I'm sorry to leave you like this, but I'm making a promise. Next time I pick up this journal, things are going to be better. I have no reason to lie to you, that would be like lying to myself, but next time things will be better. Maybe D. and I will be in rehab, or maybe just me. It's not like D. is who he was anymore, or like he and I have what we did. Of course, I'm not what I was anymore, either, but I think I could be. There are boots on the stairs.

Kiss kiss,
Mandy

TWENTY-SEVEN

Betty sat waiting on the bench for Nickel to show up. Not telling June what she was doing had been the hardest decision she could ever recall making, but it had been necessary, and not just because she didn't want to feel stupid if things didn't go well. She was still dating Jake, and she was meeting some other boy after school, a cute boy, and she didn't want to see the look on June's face when she told her she had to meet him alone.

Thoughts of Jake made her feel sick. He'd been giving her space, but she knew that wasn't going to last. He wanted an answer, and she had a bad feeling that anything other than the *right* answer was going to be catastrophic. *Why is he so wrapped up in me?* Betty knew the answer, though: because she'd made it happen that way. She had been the one singing the song he wanted to hear, filling his head with the things he wanted to believe, and certainly doing some of the things with him they both wanted to feel.

"How are you?"

The unexpected voice made her jump, and when Betty looked up she saw that Nickel had managed to sneak up on her a second time. "I'm doing good. You?"

"I'm OK," said Nickel. "Been better, but I've been worse, too." Nickel sat next to her on the bench, not too close, but close enough that Betty could smell him, a scent of fabric softener applied thickly, and something else that was indiscernible but familiar. "So you want to go meet Duke Barnes and you need a fake ID, huh?"

"Are you going to tell me you think my idea's stupid and I'll get caught?"

"You might get caught, no doubt about that," said Nickel, "but I don't think it's a stupid idea at all. Prison will be an eye-opener for you, I'm sure."

"Have you been?"

"Not prison, no," he said. "But close enough to it that I know I don't have any reason to rush to one."

"I never thought I'd have a reason to, either."

"I bet most inmates don't until they get there," said Nickel. "I bet that goes for visitors, too. When you think about it, prison as a theory is even worse than the reality can be. If your behavior is so out of whack with how the rest of society wants to live that you have to exist in a cage, well, that's pretty jacked up."

"I never thought about it like that," said Betty. It was true, though; the way he described it made it far worse than anything she could have imagined. *Is that really how it feels, like you're some dog that has to be penned up so it doesn't bite?*

"I have," said Nickel. "I was in foster care for a little while, and then later on, briefly in juvie up north. Everything worked out, but man, if that was bad, then prison has to be a special kind of hell."

"What were you in juvie for?" Betty asked, regretting the question as the words spilled from her mouth. That was the sort of thing you just weren't supposed to ask someone. It was like commenting rudely about religion in front of strangers. "I'm sorry," she said, her cheeks betraying her embarrassment. "That was rude; you don't have to answer me."

"Nah, it's good," said Nickel. "Besides, the truth is pretty boring. I thought I could trust someone I couldn't, and as a result I got locked up for a hot minute. It could be worse. At least I'm not there anymore."

"Were your folks pissed?"

"Not at all," said Nickel. "I think my dad was probably a little proud."

Betty didn't know how to react to that. How could his dad be proud his son got locked up?

"None of that matters, though," said Nickel. "Do you just need an ID for you?"

"My friend June wants one, too. Like I said, though, we don't have a ton of money, so maybe we'll just get one of them. Do you know how much it will cost?"

"It won't cost you a penny. I'll be doing most of the work."

"That sounds really great," said Betty. "I just don't want you to get the wrong idea about anything. I mean, I totally appreciate that you're offering to help with this, but I'm not looking for a relationship right now, OK?"

"Me either. I've got way too much going on for something like that." Nickel looked at Betty and for the first time she really saw into his eyes. There was something fragile in there, something far from the surface that had been broken more than once. Despite what she'd just said, in that instant Betty wanted to grab him and wrap her arms around his body, and then the moment was over as if it had never existed at all.

"Anyway," said Nickel, "the only problem is going to be finding a place to take your pictures for the IDs. I've got a good camera and the right color blue for the background, but I don't have a good spot to take them right now."

"Can we do it here?"

"Not if there's any wind," said Nickel. "Plus shooting with a background outside is going to look supershady. There aren't a lot of observant people around here, except for Eyepatch, but it would still be a risk we don't need." Nickel shook his head. "I'll come up with something, and I already have the template, so all we really need to do is get the pictures. The rest of it will be supereasy."

"You have a template for Michigan ID cards?"

"Yep," said Nickel. "You never know, it can come in pretty handy. Like I said, though, no good without some pics, but I'll e-mail you when I settle on somewhere."

"That's seriously so cool of you. If you change your mind and you want some money, just let me know, OK?"

"Completely unnecessary," said Nickel with a wave of his hand. "Like I mentioned, I'll be doing the work. I will ask you for a favor, though."

"What's that?"

"Assuming you don't get arrested, I want to know what Duke has to say. I think it could be pretty damn interesting to hear what he'd really be willing to talk about when confronted with a few questions face-to-face. I'll try and get a few loose ends wrapped up just in case there's any exploring to do when you get back."

"Of course I'll tell you what he says. But what do you mean by exploring?"

"We might have to go check some stuff out, depending on what he says, and if that happens, I want in."

Betty nodded. She wasn't sure why, not exactly, but something about Nickel being around for whatever might happen made the prospect a lot less daunting.

"Absolutely," she said, and when she smiled at Nickel, he smiled back.

TWENTY-EIGHT

"Running a little behind, are we?" Ophelia asked drily as Betty walked in, and Betty could only nod.

"Yeah, sorry about that. I was talking to June about our project in the parking lot and then I realized I was late. I was going to call, but I'm not supposed to when I'm driving, and I figured you would have been busy painting anyways."

"Well, I was busy working," said Ophelia with a frown, "but if you think I wouldn't notice that my child was late coming home from school, then you're crazy. Just remember, you are still grounded, and being tardy isn't helping that any."

Betty found it impossible not to feel bad for her. Andrea had always been the disciplinarian; Ophy the one most likely to wipe away tears and offer a hug. It was Betty's fault she was in this position, and Betty could tell they were enjoying the gentle dressing down in equal amounts.

"I know, I know," said Betty. "Speaking of that, though, how much longer do you think I have?"

"Have you broken up with that boy?"

"Not yet. It's harder than I thought."

"If you still have feelings for him, then maybe you shouldn't break up," said Ophelia.

"It's not like that," said Betty. *Should I just tell her what he asked me? She'd understand, you know that.* But she couldn't bring herself to do it. It was just another secret of childhood, one more strand of connective tissue broken, and the snap of the deceit sent a cold chill through her body.

"It's not like what?" Ophelia asked. "If you don't care for the boy, then why do you string him along?"

"I can hear Greece in your voice," said Betty with a smirk, and Ophelia shook her head.

"You know that only happens when I'm mad or have too much to drink."

"So should I go check the basement for empty bottles of wine?"

"I wish," said Ophelia. "This painting is tearing me in two. But none of that answers my question: Why won't you just end it with this loser?"

"He's not a loser, Mom, he—"

"Anyone who asks a girl your age to compromise herself in such a way is a loser in my book. Do you know how many times Andrea has had to talk to girls your age and younger because they destroyed their lives by doing something like that? She had a patient last year that killed herself because she sent pictures of herself to a boy and he put them on the Internet. Even her best friends called her a slut, shaming her because of a mistake she made so young, and now she's dead."

"Ah, spring in Athens."

"You see how upset this makes me?" Ophelia asked with a chuckle. "I get so mad that my voice forgets it's been in the States for thirty years. You still don't answer my question."

"Fine," acquiesced Betty, "I'll try to explain."

"Good, I can't wait."

"Jake's not a loser," said Betty, and Ophelia rolled her eyes. "I'd laugh if they got stuck like that. I'm serious, though. Jake can be stupid, and he's a total jock, but he's not a loser. He's a good kid who sent me something as a joke—that part I'm sure of—and I responded in kind."

"It's hard to believe."

"I know," said Betty.

"You want this grounding to end, yes?"

"Yes, of course," said Betty, "but I also don't think you guys forcing me to break up with my boyfriend is a fair way to get out of being in trouble."

"Hmmm," said Ophelia, "that may be true. What if the grounding ended, with the provision that you slow things down with Jake? I don't mean don't speak to him at school, just don't do things outside of school with him, and let the relationship cool off a little bit."

"Wouldn't that basically be the same thing as breaking up with him?"

"I'm sure it sounds that way," said Ophelia, "but remember, *you* said you wanted to break off things with him. This would give you some freedom, and the chance to think about what you really want."

"All right."

"Not too hasty," said Ophelia. "I need to talk to Andrea about this, and if you recall, she was the one that wanted your car keys and everything else over this." Ophelia frowned. "I know there's some part of this you're not telling me. You've never been one to drag things out when you were bored of a relationship. Why is this time so different?"

"I don't know, it just is," said Betty. "Will you talk to her tonight?"

"I will," said Ophelia, "but I want a favor out of you." Betty's eyebrows rose, as if to say, *Ask away*. "If she says no, you be respectful."

TWENTY-NINE

Betty sat alone in her bedroom. Ophelia had given her a perfect opportunity to fill her in on what was going on with Jake, but Betty had blown it. And she was still messing things up by not racing downstairs and just blurting it all out. She wasn't going to do it, though. It was sickening to think about her mothers discussing the matter, and Betty hated that they were deciding her fate without her even telling them the whole truth about the new developments with Jake.

Sick of even thinking about Jake Norton's stupid proposal, much less forcing herself to actually deal with the reality of the situation, Betty checked her e-mail. She was glad she did, as among the mostly bullshit contents of her inbox were three very interesting pieces of mail. She clicked on the first of them, a message sent to her mother from Detective Van Endel, and then forwarded to her.

Betty frowned—her mother had obviously removed part of it before sending it—and then decided it was probably just something about work. The e-mail said:

In any case, here's the address for you. 4527 Lincoln Ave.
I already told Betty not to go inside that house, but when

you give her this make it clear that I was serious about that. The area isn't the best, but if they go during the day they should be fine, as long as all they're doing is taking pictures from the car. There have always been transients living there, and there's no good reason to think there aren't any staying there now. Not to mention the place is probably falling apart.

Betty closed the mail with a grin. The get wasn't quite as exciting as talking to Duke would be if they pulled that off, but it was something more than just research on the Internet.

It would be the best if we could go inside that house, thought Betty, but she knew Van Endel was right. The idea of walking into the house where Mandy was killed was freaky enough. Happening upon a bunch of drunk-or-worse homeless people in an abandoned building did not sound like the best situation for two high school girls to be getting involved with.

Betty clicked on the second e-mail, this one from the Michigan Department of Corrections. It was all business, explaining that both of them would be permitted to visit with Duke Barnes. There was a bunch of legal mumbo jumbo below the important bits, but Betty ignored it. They would already be breaking at least one law by visiting Duke with fake IDs, and she didn't want to know if they were going to be breaking any others that might be buried in the fine print.

Finally, Betty double-clicked on the one she'd saved for last, a message from Nickel. It was short and to the point, just like everything with the mysterious ginger boy:

Problem solved. Meet me tomorrow with your friend, same time and place, and we can go to my house. My dad has to work so we'll have a few minutes to take care of everything without having to explain to him what we're doing.

N

Betty closed that last mail for a second, then rethought things and deleted it. Coming home late twice from school in the middle of a grounding would be bad enough. Being late because she was in a boy's house without a parent could easily threaten the freedom she planned to enjoy over the summer.

After hopping off the mail tab Betty began a bored perusal of the Internet, before finding herself back at the Free Duke page. She looked at it for what felt like only a few minutes, but when Ophelia called her down to dinner, she'd been at it for over two hours, most of it looking at pictures of Duke and Mandy and wondering about men in green jackets, disappearing roommates, and a missing diary.

Blinking twice at the shock of dinnertime, Betty snapped the computer shut and headed downstairs.

THIRTY

It's been a long time since anyone else has been in the house, years, but in just a few hours Betty and her friend will be here. It makes no sense, but for some reason I find the idea of letting a couple teenage girls into my house to be a lot scarier than brokering a several-thousand-dollar drug deal. That's stupid, I know, but I can't help it.

I *should* be damned scared about the drug deal. Paul is going to be calling me in a few days, and I'm going to need to get him about fifteen pounds of weed and haven't even figured out how I'm going to transport it. My old cabbie, Lou, is up for just about anything, but a job with weight like this is out of the question.

That's the problem I should be focused on—how to haul pot, make a sale, and then get out alive and with the money—but instead I'm spending my afternoon picking up the house, mowing the yard, and even sweeping and mopping the floors. All the while, there's a rotten feeling in my gut telling me that Betty and June aren't even going to show, and that all this stress and work is nothing but a waste of time. Yeah, I admit the house needed the work, but it didn't need to happen today.

Thinking about Betty and June coming to visit makes me think of the last time I had a visitor, when Arrow came over. The similarities are striking. I was involved in a job because of a girl, but got roped into something else because of another girl. While it's true I haven't fallen for Betty the way I did for Arrow, I'm a lot older now, and Arrow is so far in the rearview mirror she almost seems make-believe. Not that I'm likely to ever forget what made her unique, or what she did for me. She hired me to find her missing sister, Shelby, and I did it, but without Arrow both Shelby and I would be dead. Arrow was pulling the strings from behind the curtain the entire time, and then, *poof!* she was gone.

Arrow would be eighteen now. I'm sure she has a boyfriend and college plans, and everything in her life is going well, but I like to imagine she thinks of me sometimes the way I think of her. She and I were a menace together, and with her help I hurt some very bad people. That job was the one that gave me the confidence to take on some things I should have known were too ambitious, and if Arrow had been there to help me, maybe I could have saved myself a lot of pain.

Arrow was in my heart, though. She was with me inside when I sent those bastards up a roller coaster at 120 miles an hour without the wheels that keep it on the track, and I felt her behind my eyes when I was killing that piece of shit Spider at that damn camp. Spider was one of the worst men I've ever met, and I don't say that lightly. I've known some choice individuals. None of them enjoyed torturing kids any more than Spider did. Watching him fall and then bleed out in the snow after I led a rebellion was one of the vilest things I've ever seen, but it was also beautiful. Of course, the aftereffects of that scene weren't beautiful at all. Arrow could have talked me down from that. I was at my best with her, the purest version of what Dad wanted me to be, but since she left, the bad guys have gotten worse, and so have I.

The house is clean enough, I suppose, but I don't really have a good measuring stick to know if that's even true. I don't own a TV, and the only furniture is a ratty couch, my bed, a kitchen table and chairs, and the desk in my office. Plus, the house smells like a skunk from the dope in the basement. At least there is something I can do about that problem; I installed a pair of exhaust fans in the basement years ago, and they let out into an herb garden in the backyard. I hit the switches, then open the windows on the front of the house, a harder proposition than it should be, because I've never opened the damn things. When that's done I want to go to my computer, but I don't. Instead, I go to the couch, sit, and stare into the apartment.

I think it's probably in good enough shape. Now I'm not sure I am, though. Betty and June aren't coming over for a make-out session or anything, I get that, but I'm still nervous about letting someone in. This is my world, these are my secrets, and if I had just kept my big mouth shut I wouldn't be in this mess in the first place. Of course, not keeping my big mouth shut is how I met Arrow.

I check my pager again to see if I've missed anything, but I haven't. Checking for word from Paul has become a nervous twitch. I could check a thousand times in a day and still wake up every few hours to give it another look. I don't think you realize just how desperate you can become until your back really is against the wall, when you really need to put up or shut up. If this deal doesn't work, I'm going to be completely broke, but I'm spending my time printing fakes for a couple of teenagers.

Par for the course, I guess. June's mother is paying me to keep her safe, but instead of honoring my contract with her, I'm making her daughter a fake so she can visit a prison. Maybe I do have a thing for Betty, because otherwise this just doesn't add up.

THIRTY-ONE

"So who is this mystery boy?" June asked, and then both of them set to giggling. "Also, have you been to his house before? This home-alone stuff is pretty earth-shattering."

"Cram it," said Betty. "I told you I barely know the kid, but he's going to help us anyway. I think we should consider ourselves lucky." Betty gave June a stern look but failed in the attempt and both of them were laughing again, despite the glaring librarian and sign begging them to be quiet.

"Hey, do you think we should get Mystery Boy to make them so we're twenty-one?"

"I seriously wonder about you sometimes," said Betty. "First of all, the guy's name is Nickel. It's weird, but it's not like it's that hard to remember. Secondly, we're getting IDs that say that we're eighteen or nineteen. It won't do us any good to be able to maybe buy beer at shitty liquor stores if we get arrested for giving fakes to a prison guard whose only job is looking at licenses and cataloguing them."

"I guess so," said June, pouting. "So we get our fake IDs from Nickel, but then what?"

"I e-mail the prison with our visitor request forms to let Duke know what day we want to come," said Betty. "All he has to do is approve us, and then we're in, assuming our IDs work. Probably better not to think too much about that part."

"What else?" June asked, and Betty considered that.

"We could go check out the house, but I promised that cop we wouldn't go inside no matter what," said Betty. "I guess I'm sort of banking on this ID thing working out. If it doesn't we can go take some pictures of the house and then start writing the paper, I suppose. It's not like there's going to be a whole lot more to discover if Duke doesn't give us some sort of a lead."

"If he'll even talk to us," said June, sourly. "I still have mixed feelings about meeting the guy."

"Totally understandable," said Betty. "If you decide not to go I completely get it, but I'm going—at least, if Nickel comes through, I am. Mr. Evans made it clear that there was going to be a lot riding on this, and I don't think he was exaggerating."

"I don't think he was, either, but you can't think that he expects us to solve an ancient crime the cops still believe they figured out a decade and a half ago, right?"

"I don't know what to think," said Betty. "Not until I talk to Duke, and maybe I still won't know after that."

"Seriously, Betty, we don't need to do all of this just to get a passing grade," said June. "Even a paper written with what we've already done would be good enough, I bet, especially if we got those pictures."

"Like I said, if you want to stay home, that's fine, but I'm going to see Duke if I can swing it at all. We might not need to do it just for a grade, but I need to take this as far as I can. Not just because she's your aunt, and not because of some stupid concert. We need to go because we might be the only people left who actually care about finding out who killed Mandy."

"That concert is like the least stupid concert ever," said June. "Seriously."

"OK, fine. It's a great concert, but that's not my point. All of the adults knew about this, every single one of them, but somehow we never knew until we were at an age where we could have a chance to add our names to the story."

"So it's fate, then."

Betty just shrugged, then narrowed her eyes at her friend. June didn't seem to be trying to be funny, though. She just looked thoughtful, like she was trying on for size the idea that they could be fated to find justice for her dead aunt.

"Betty," June said after a minute, "you're already in trouble. Are you really sure you want to risk this?"

"Like I said, it's worth it to me. If you don't want to do it, or just can't bring yourself to, well, I understand. But there's no way I'm not going to go talk to Duke if I get half the chance."

THIRTY-TWO

Betty had seen Jake around the halls of the school on a daily basis since he'd made his offer to her, but they'd spoken only sparingly. She was hoping he'd decided the idea was stupid and felt bad for even bringing it up, but knew it was far more likely that he was simply waiting for her to decide it was a marvelous plan, and then tell him to go run off and play at being a soldier so she could be a housewife on base.

Her silence on the subject must have worn some cracks in his enamel, however, because as Betty walked to her car after school she felt her phone buzz three times in her jeans. All three texts were from Jake, and all bore the same grim words from a week prior, "We need 2 talk." Praying that Jake wouldn't be waiting at her car, she marched double-time across the parking lot.

Twenty minutes later Betty was free of the school's lot and headed south to Riverside to meet June at the park. The weather was fair for the season and Betty had her windows halfway down as she drove and sang along to the new RVIVR album. It occurred to her that ever since her discovery of the case, she'd hardly spent a moment during which she wasn't thinking about Duke and Mandy. How exactly had her dreams of the future been so completely forgotten in the wake of this investigation?

Maybe June was right. After all, if June could avoid this obsession, then maybe Betty really was taking everything too far. Mandy was June's aunt, not hers, but June's interest in the project seemed tempered. Betty felt sure that her imprisonment at home was a large reason for her obsession with the case. June still had a life, but Betty was trying to escape hers, and between Jake and the grounding, a little escapism was probably exactly what she needed.

Arriving at the park, she parked her car next to June's. The two girls got out of their vehicles at the same time and a minute later were crossing the grass together.

"I thought you said he'd be near the playground," whined June. "All I see is that pirate-looking guy over there."

"He'll be here. I'm sure of it." She shrugged. "He always seems like he's sneaking up on me, but I think he just likes to be sure of who he's going to run into."

"Sounds like he watches too many movies to me. I don't care if he wants to play secret agent, but I'm not drinking the Kool-Aid or asking for a decoder ring."

"Shut it," said Betty. "He's going to do us a huge favor, so knock it off."

"That's if he shows up." June shot nervous looks around them. "Right now this place is a ghost town. There's hardly even any birds!"

"Take a breath, June Bug. He'll be here."

She walked to the bench and then sat on the middle of it, with June plopping down next to her.

They had barely settled in when Betty heard Nickel's voice from behind them saying, "Hello."

"Holy shit," yelled June as she spun to her feet. "He really did come out of nowhere!"

"Sorry. It's sort of a habit." The redheaded boy extended a hand to June. "I'm Nickel."

June took the hand, shook it once, and dropped it. "You're Nickel, I'm June, and I want you to make it so I can buy cigarettes."

"Yeah, and I got your decoder ring, too."

June flushed crimson and Betty laughed. "Hi, Nickel," she said.

Nickel offered his hand to her as well and they shook quickly. "All right," he said. "I'll ride with Betty, and you follow, OK?"

"That sounds fine to me," said Betty, and then the three of them went marching back to the lot.

Betty walked next to Nickel, and could feel that June had shrugged off her embarrassment over him overhearing her secret agent crack and was now grinning hugely at Betty's back. If Nickel noticed, it wasn't showing on his face, but Betty felt ridiculous, like a middle schooler with a crush.

When they got to the parking lot, Betty unlocked the car doors with the key fob and then walked around to the driver's side. When she got in she saw that Nickel was still waiting outside the car, so she turned on the engine and rolled down the window before calling to him, "Are you getting in?"

Nickel nodded. A troubled look on his face, he opened the door and took his place in the passenger seat. "No fast driving, all right?"

"No problem," Betty said, giving him a sideways glance. She could hear him swallow thickly as she pulled the car out of the Riverside lot. He'd seemed really tough before, but now he was acting as meek as a fawn. Wondering if he was going to get sick all over the car, Betty hit the gas gently and got moving.

"I have no idea where I'm going," she said.

Nickel responded without turning. "Just stay straight, and I'll let you know when to turn. It's not far."

THIRTY-THREE

They arrived ten minutes later, but Betty wasn't sure exactly what they had arrived at. She and June parked on the street in front of a gas station, and Nickel popped out so quickly Betty didn't know if this was really it or if the short ride had just been too much for him. She shut off the ignition and once again she and June exited their vehicles in unison.

"What are we doing here?" June asked.

Nickel smiled. "We walk from here. Don't worry, it's not far."

Betty expected June to ask why they couldn't just drive the rest of the way, but she kept mum, and Betty enjoyed the silence. Nickel didn't look pale or weak anymore, didn't even look as he had earlier in the park. Whatever had been bothering him about the ride in the car was gone now, and he looked as confident as he had on the day she met him. *Confident and cute*, confirmed a particularly ill-timed part of her brain, and Betty fruitlessly fought against the flush she could feel rising in her cheeks.

They walked as they had in the park, with Nickel and Betty in the lead and June following. The neighborhood was a little run-down, but was more boring than trashy. Betty wasn't sure how she felt about the vibe. For one thing, nothing stirred—no pedestrians, no moving vehicles. Not even a stray cat. It was almost as if the houses had been built for use as a background on a movie set. Betty felt sure that if she walked behind them, she'd see they were nothing but fronts and sides.

"Nice and quiet," said Nickel, the statement coming as if he'd been in her head, and Betty just smiled.

"It sure is."

Nickel stopped at a house that was as plain as all the rest. It had one story and looked as though it could use some paint, along with a general update, if it were going to be on the market soon.

"Home sweet home," said Nickel. Betty felt sure she could hear some nervousness in his voice. As he walked up the driveway with the two of them in tow, he opened the garage door with a clicker on his key chain.

The garage was sparse. No car, and no sign of one—no oil stains or tread marks. A ratty-looking mountain bike sat on one side of the garage floor, and there was a massive black toolbox next to the door to the house, along with a padlocked metal cabinet. There was a clean workspace between the cabinet and toolbox with a weird-looking machine on it, along with various tools hanging on a pegboard above it. At the opposite end of the strange machine, a massive vise had been bolted to the bench, and several plastic fixtures sat next to it.

"Does your dad reload?" June asked, the sound of her voice startling in the garage's silence. When Nickel just blinked at her, she said, "I saw the press over there and figured he must because my dad does and he has—"

"Yes," said Nickel. "Dad reloads for his hunting guns."

June nodded and then Nickel hit the clicker to shut the garage before opening the door to the house and waving them on ahead of him. Feeling like a doomed actress in a PSA warning against entering the homes and vehicles of strangers, Betty walked into the house ahead of June, and then heard Nickel shut the door after them.

When he flipped on the lights, the house appeared to be normal enough, just as the outside and garage had. Yet all of it felt a little wrong, somehow. Hollow. The kitchen and dining room were spotless, and the living room was one of the most sparsely decorated living spaces that she'd ever seen. There was a couch but no TV. No carpet, no rug. No coffee table. Nothing on the walls. Curtains sealed the windows tight.

Betty let Nickel pass her, and he disappeared into a room down a hallway, and then reappeared a few moments later juggling a roll of paper and two metal stands. "Would you guys give me a hand, please?"

Betty ran to grab the stands before they fell and handed one of them off to June.

"Thanks," he said and walked ahead of them to the living room. "There should be plenty of light in here." He turned on a pair of floor lamps. "The real trick is to make it as unnatural as possible. They sure as hell don't use natural light when they shoot a Michigan ID."

Nickel laid the roll of blue paper on the floor, then took the stand Betty had given to June and snapped it open. It looked like a long-necked tripod, and when it was in place in front of the couch, Nickel took the other one from Betty and unfolded that one as well. With both up, Nickel took the paper roll—it had a metal spindle running through the middle of it—and placed the ends of it so they attached to the tripods. After yanking at the paper so that it rolled down to cover a few feet of air and a few inches of floor, he said, "I'll grab my camera. Who's first?"

"I'll go," said June. "It took me a minute, but now that I see what you're doing, I'm all in." She smiled at Nickel. "If you can really pull this off, I am going to be seriously impressed."

"Of course I can," said Nickel with an odd look on his face, and then he disappeared back into the room that he'd taken the paper and stands from.

"He is seriously weird, but seriously cute," said June in a whisper. "Betty, if you decide you don't want this one, I'm going to make it happen. For real."

"You're such a ho," said Betty, and the two of them burst into laughter just as Nickel emerged from the room with a camera around his neck.

"What did I miss?" he asked, and that just made the pair of them laugh harder.

"We're just being stupid," Betty said. "I think the thrill of being in a boy's house without his parents at home might be getting to us."

Nickel smiled with an odd look on his face, and began fiddling with the camera. Betty didn't know much about photography equipment, but the camera was obviously a serious piece of kit. It had the heavy look that high-end electronics almost always do, even when they're as light as a feather. Nickel raised the camera to the paper he'd put up and clicked the button a pair of times before checking the results on the little screen on the back of the camera. Apparently satisfied, he nodded at June. "You still want to go first?"

"Yeah, I'll go," said June. "Sooner the better, right?"

"One more thing. Do you guys think you're going to dye your hair before you go see Duke?"

"Ah shit, no," said June, "but we really need to, huh? I keep forgetting that it's all washed out."

"You both look really nice," he insisted, his face reddening as he realized what he said.

"Thanks," said Betty. "Get to it, June."

June crossed the room, taking off her hoodie as she went and laying it on the sofa behind the background stand before taking her place in front of the paper. She gave the camera and Nickel a smile, and then waited for the picture.

"Remember, you're at the DMV," said Nickel behind the lens, and June forced the grin from her face. "Better," he said, and then he pulled the trigger three times, rapid-fire flashes bursting from the camera. "I think we're good," he said.

When June walked over to see, Nickel leaned the camera over so she could get a peek. "I think they look good."

"They look better than good," said June as Betty crowded in to see. "Seriously, if they look that good on plastic then we're going to be in with no problems at all."

"I'm telling you guys, ginning these up's not as hard as you'd think," said Nickel as Betty walked to the background. She smiled at first—she couldn't help it—but then switched to a bored expression before Nickel could chastise her. He did the rapid-fire thing with the camera, and then waved Betty over to see her pictures.

"Not exactly flattering," Betty said, "but they sure look authentic."

"Seriously, with the template I have, the ID part is easy."

"What's the hard part, then?" June took the camera from him and grinned at the array of images. "You just paste these to a template, print, and we're golden?"

"Well, I guess the hard part was meeting Betty to begin with," said Nickel, taking the camera back and busying himself with it. "Walking up to a girl you've never met before can always be a little nerve-wracking."

June smiled and jabbed an elbow in Betty's side at the remark, and Betty elbowed her back.

"Yeah, like I'm so intimidating," Betty said. "You didn't seem so nervous. And you've been ridiculously helpful, and you're supernice."

His face pretty much on fire, he turned away. "Let me grab my laptop and we'll get to actually making these. You guys can go sit at the kitchen table, and I'll be right back, OK?"

Nickel didn't wait for a response, just turned tail and walked back into the room he'd gone to before.

At the table, Betty gave June a thin smile, trying to communicate that things were going as smoothly as they possibly could, and in response, June whispered, "He just keeps getting cuter. Normally the awkward thing does nothing for me, but this boy is adorkable. I just want to grab him."

"Well don't."

June rolled her eyes. "You're just trying to hog him. If you're going to keep stringing Jake along, I can't see why I can't at least try and throw myself at this one. Worst that could happen, he says no, but I think—"

"Think what?" Nickel asked as he returned to the room, camera still hanging from his neck and a laptop under his arm.

"You don't want to know," said Betty. "Trust me."

"All right." Smiling, Nickel grabbed the free chair between Betty and June and flipped the computer open on the table. He plugged the camera into the computer with a USB cord and, with Betty and June leaning in on either side to see the screen, got to work. If he was bothered by being crowded by girls, he didn't show it.

Betty and June watched as he pulled up a program that looked a great deal like Photoshop, but had a blank form on it that looked just like a Michigan ID.

"Betty first," said Nickel, and then he began rattling off questions as he filled in the form. "Full name?"

"Elizabeth Anne Martinez."

"Address real, or fake?"

"Does it matter?"

"Not if you get in enough trouble."

"Fake."

"Date of birth?" Nickel asked, and then added, "I want to use the real month and date, so if somebody tries to trip you up by asking your sign or something, you can just spit it right out."

"Oh, that makes sense," said Betty. "So, March fifth, 1998."

"Well, for the intents and purposes of this fake, we'll go ahead and list you as 1996. Sound good?"

"Oh. Yeah. Duh."

Nickel grinned and filled in the rest of the information before opening a separate window of the program and cropping her picture down to the right size for the ID template, and then copying and pasting it onto the template itself.

"All done," he said. "Are you ready, June?"

THIRTY-FOUR

The computer was back in whatever clown car of a room Nickel had gotten it from, and in its place were two still-warm fake ID cards. The difference between these and every other fake that the girls had ever seen was incredible. The IDs Nickel had made for them were printed on what seemed to be the same type of machine the Michigan secretary of state used, and on what appeared to be the exact same stock the state used.

Betty found herself transfixed by the hologram of the bridge and all the other little details designed to make exactly this sort of thing impossible, and when she looked up she could see June doing the same thing.

"I'm not sure how to thank you," said Betty. "These are incredible. Like, incredible, incredible."

"They are pretty cool," Nickel admitted with a grin. "The trick is to have the right plastic, but since I was able to order blanks from the factory that produces them, I was able to do better than just the plastic. These will hold up to pretty much anything until a cop swipes them, and even they'll need to really look at the picture on the screen in their cruiser to know that your ID doesn't match the picture in the database. I figure it's fifty-fifty at that point as to whether or not they hold you or just complain about the computer messing up, so just remember what I told you: be indignant but do it at the right time."

"I can manage that," said June, and when the girls started to laugh, Betty saw that Nickel was laughing along with them. "Seriously, though," said June, "this is amazing. We really appreciate it. I know we probably aren't going to figure all of this out, at least as far as my aunt is concerned, but we will wind up with an A if Duke actually talks with us."

"He will," said Nickel. "He'll take one look at you and he won't be able to shut his mouth. Hell, he might think you're Mandy's ghost and not just a relative. I know I was shocked when I saw you, but Duke lived with Mandy, and I've only seen pictures online. You know, that reminds me, I did have a question for you guys."

"Ask away," said Betty.

"As of right now, with all the research you've done, who do you think killed her? I don't mean you necessarily need to have someone else in mind, but do you still see Duke as a possible, or maybe even guilty as charged?"

"I don't know," said Betty. "I mean, we've been doing our best to find other suspects, but our evidence probably wouldn't even be good enough to be called circumstantial."

"Well, maybe talking to Duke can help with that. For instance, maybe he can tell you why he reported seeing a man in a green jacket, but the only person the neighbors saw wearing green that day was Duke himself."

"So what were the cops thinking?" asked Betty. "That that was somehow part of his confession? Him telling them he'd done it?"

"Who knows what the cops thought," said Nickel. "Likely they just figured it was some heroin addict's delusional rambling and round-filed it. Not that that stopped them from buying his full confession pretty shortly after that, though."

"From what I've read about the case, even people who didn't just write him off as totally drug-addled assumed Duke was grasping at straws with the green jacket stuff. You know, yelling about a one-armed man, that sort of thing. I assume the cops took the confession and the neighbor's testimony into account, and just assumed Duke was accidentally projecting himself onto this never-seen-again mystery man."

"But why would Duke do that?" June asked. "It doesn't make any sense."

"Does it need to?" Nickel answered. "The point is that we have a description of what the killer may have looked like, as long as we don't ignore Duke's initial statements to the police."

"So assuming Duke was telling the truth, then that makes Duke the only known witness to the real killer?" Betty asked, and Nickel nodded.

"Exactly. It's not perfect, and it doesn't prove anything on its own, but it is something else to look into. Just because the cops thought Duke was a stupid, lying criminal doesn't mean we have to."

"He's still an asshole," muttered June.

"Maybe so," said Nickel, "but what if he also happens to be innocent? Asshole or not, the goal is to find the person who actually did it. The cops that worked this case weren't stupid, but that doesn't mean they didn't go for the obvious answer instead of exploring all the evidence."

"Especially when some of that evidence was only offered up by the man who confessed a few hours later," said Betty.

"Exactly."

THIRTY-FIVE

Betty had hugged Nickel before they left, both of them had, but she had felt something when she'd let go of him, and it was a black thing that made her feel even worse for not texting Jake back yet. She didn't want to think she wanted to be with Nickel, though there was something there, and she knew the longer she strung Jake along, the worse the breakup was going to be. Still, she had yet to text him, she had no idea what to say, and if they really did go see Duke over the weekend, Jake was going to have to wait for answers until next week. Even worse was that Jake had been waiting dutifully by his phone for her to pay him the simple respect of responding to him, but she'd been at another boy's house the entire time.

When the girls stopped by their cars in front of the gas station, June smiled at Betty and said, "You sure know how to make friends. I don't know what that boy's been up to, and I'm not sure I want to, but that was really cool."

"Yeah," said Betty. "Nickel barely even knows us, even me, but he still spent hours putting our IDs together. We're going to need to do something nice for him."

"I'm sure you have something in mind," said June. "If not, then I'm willing to do my part to show just how apprecia—"

"Enough," said Betty with a grin. June could be so annoying, but at least she was always annoying in the ways that were so *her*. "I'll thank Nickel by doing exactly what he asked: as soon as we're back from talking to Duke, I'm going to let him know what Duke had to say. After that, I'm going to keep him up to date with everything we're doing, especially locally, and he said he might want to tag along at some point."

"Yeah, that'll be a problem," said June. "Who would want a supercool guy that's incredibly smart tagging along?"

"That's what I was thinking," said Betty. "Nickel won't do anything but help us with the rest of the investigation."

"And he might be able to interpret what Duke says better than we can. I mean, he knows all these little secret details about Mandy's murder that most people never knew at all, and for all we know Duke could tell us something that Nickel can make sense out of, even if it means nothing to us."

"I'm glad he's going to help," said Betty, "but I'm even happier you liked him so much."

"Yeah, he's supercool," said June, a frown crossing her face. "I thought his house was weird, though. There were no pictures in there, no art or knickknacks at all, and there was no TV. I can excuse the lack of pictures and other crap if it's just Nickel and his dad living there, but no TV? C'mon, two guys living together are going to have a TV."

"What do you think he was trying to hide?"

"I don't know," said June, "but when we first went there, I was nervous his dad would come home and get us all in trouble, but by the time we left I'd forgotten I was ever even worried about it at all. I forgot I was nervous because Nickel wasn't nervous about it. He wasn't worried about it *at all*. He had two girls in the house—there's not a boy I've ever met that wouldn't be nervous under those circumstances. He wasn't nervous, though, he was fiddling away with his computer and flirting a little bit and doing exactly what he told us he could, which if you think about is weird all on its own."

"How do you mean?"

"You think there's any boy at our high school that could do even half of what Nickel just did?" June asked. "They're all bragging losers by comparison. Hell, comparing them seems unfair. Nickel did everything he said he could, and he wasn't even proud of himself for doing it." June shot a look at her phone. "Look, I need to go. I have to get home and eat, and I have to do some math homework, too."

"Crap, me too," said Betty, her thoughts not just on schoolwork, but also on the limp-wristed text she was going to send Jake when she got home.

On the road, Betty's mind careened among fake IDs, Duke Barnes, Jake Norton, and a boy who seemed to neither have nor need a last name. Her heart felt as though it were caught between three worlds: Duke and Mandy called to her from the past, Jake from what should have been a normal year in the life of an American teenager, and Nickel from a world of shadow and mystery that seemed to link the other two with mysterious possibilities.

I got beat up. Not the first time, of course, but it had been a while and it was pretty bad. Not cool. D. tried to find the guy who did it, the guy who beat me and then hurt me even worse, but he couldn't. I knew he wouldn't be able to. I couldn't even describe him. Guys who get off like that and get away with it are almost always just normal-looking, forgettable guys. Not that I'll forget what he did to me. I can still see his fists raining down, his boot rearing back and driving toward me. It's going to be weeks until my face is in good enough condition for me to go back to hooking, unless I run a blue-light special or something.

Being hurt means I don't leave the house anymore. All I do is sit around and get high and look at my pictures and wish I could just disappear. Not die, that's too easy. I mean just not exist at all. It would be better for everyone involved, especially my sister and my parents, if I'd just never existed at all. The only people I can even think of that have actually benefitted from my existence are the guys from Old Croix Road. That was the old me, though, the dead me that's too sad for even me to think about. That me has been rotting for a long time now.

I knew Ben through his father, and then when his dad died, he and his brother, Joe, started coming around the record shop I was working at more and more often. They were always buying rock albums that were a little too cool for their age—Joe was barely even ten. Ben kept going on about being in a band, and I finally convinced my friend Mike to record them. I mean, I thought it would be cute, maybe a little funny. Duke and I picked them up, and that night four twelve-year-old boys recorded one of the best demo tapes I've ever heard. They got huge after that, but that isn't why I never see them anymore. I don't see them because of me, because of what I am. Ben isn't even eighteen yet, and I'm still too scared to call him because of what he'd think of me.

The only blessing from being hurt is that Jason isn't after me for sex. Apparently being as shallow as he is isn't always a bad thing. Even better than that is that D. hasn't really been hanging out with Jason anymore, or at least not as much as he used to.

The one good thing to come out of getting beaten and raped—and isn't it pathetic to find a silver lining in that?—is that I'm pretty sure I had a miscarriage. The baby couldn't have been D.'s, that's the really bad part, but since it had to be from Jason or a client, it seems like a blessing. I don't have a lot of dignity right now, but asking D. to sell his ass so I could get an abortion would be so low it's hard to even contemplate.

I can hear Jason and at least two other people downstairs, strange and loud voices, but without D. here I'm not going to say anything. I'm just going to hide in my little room, avoiding mirrors and trying to imagine the person I used to be and will be again someday. This is just part of my life, I'm sure of it, and someday I'm going to know how to escape it. Still, all I want right now is to get high. It helps with the pain, and there's nothing wrong with that.

Kiss kiss,
Mandy

THIRTY-SIX

Betty drove while June fiddled with the GPS and the iPod hooked to the stereo. It was Saturday afternoon and they were headed to Jackson to meet Duke Barnes.

Betty could tell June was nervous. Not that she blamed her; she was nervous herself, and not just over meeting Duke. Betty and Jake were embroiled in a string of communication, her own short missives inspiring some truly awe-inspiring strings of paragraphs about their new life at some base somewhere, and how all she needed to do was tell him she was ready to take the next step. Ophelia had been right: the best time to dump Jake had come and gone, and now it was just going to be a cruel joke no matter how Betty went about it.

It was hard not to focus all her energy on Jake, but with the wheels bringing them ever closer to Duke and a real-life conversation with one of the people who was actually there when Mandy died—if not the man who killed her—it felt sort of ridiculous to worry about her boyfriend troubles. They were going to give fake IDs to a prison guard, get vetted by a system built specifically to avoid something like what they were doing, and if all went well they would be rewarded by having a conversation with a convicted felon. There was some insane joy to be found in that—the euphoria of doomed women, as June had suggested while giggling an hour or so earlier—so why was the upcoming encounter with Jake all Betty could think of?

"You may as well just talk about it," said June as they passed a sign telling them Jackson was seventy-two miles away. When Betty gave her a confused look, June locked eyes with her and said, "Bullshit. Just tell me. I won't even give you any crap, I promise."

Even with that guarantee on the table, Betty didn't want to talk about any of the stuff going on in her head. Not only were her thoughts and worries private, they also seemed incredibly weak, especially considering that June was being driven to meet the man thought to have killed her aunt. But June kept staring at her.

"So much has changed in the last week and a half that nothing feels right," said Betty after a few moments to collect her thoughts. "First it was that show, and then your aunt, Jake's proposal, and well, Nickel. I feel like I'm watching a movie about myself, like there's nothing I can do to control the outcome of anything, except for what we're doing today. Isn't that crazy? The only thing I feel in control of is the one thing I'm doing that should be impossible."

"It's not impossible," said June. "Everything is going to be fine at the prison, except maybe Duke. You just need to let the rest of it go. What we're doing today and everything else that comes afterward is all that matters. The rest of it is just petty teenage bullshit."

"You sound like my mother."

"I'm sorry. I think I might have sounded like my mother, too. Do you think you'll ever have kids? I don't see how anyone could ever want to burden themselves with something like that."

"That's too out-there for me right now," said Betty. "I've got a delusional boyfriend who wants to get married and join the navy, we're going to go try and have a civilized conversation with a guy who may have murdered one of your family members, and last but not least, there's Nickel."

"In this order," said June. "Meet Duke, dump Jake, see what happens with Nickel. We're fucking sixteen, Betty. The only important thing we need to do with a boy is not get pregnant. Everything else is just passing the time." June smiled broadly at Betty. "OK, now I sound like you. That should have been a Betty Martinez original right there, and I just tried to steal it before you could even say it."

"Very funny," said Betty, "but unfortunately, I think you're right. It sounded more annoying coming out of your mouth, though."

"I was thinking the same thing, only in reverse."

"Ugh," grunted Betty. "Now I'm even annoying to myself."

"Just let it go. We still don't know exactly what we want to ask Duke, so let's worry more about that and less about the trivial stuff."

"If you were having boy trouble I wouldn't call it trivial."

"If I was having boy trouble you'd be holding a parade," said June. "Let's just be ready for this. I'm superscared to meet Duke in person, even with guards there, and I think it's only going to get worse the closer we get."

"June, all you need to do is sit there and look at Duke, and I'll ask the questions. He's going to be so freaked out that someone from Mandy's family is there, someone who happens to be her spitting image, that I don't think there's going to be a lot of venom left in him."

"I hope you're right."

───────

Though neither Betty nor June wanted to discuss it further, they were both terrified as Betty pulled off the highway to finish the trip to Jackson State Penitentiary. The iPod was off now, and both girls had tucked their legitimate licenses into the glove box, replaced in their wallets by the fake ones Nickel had given them. Betty pulled past the prison's main entrance and then turned next to a sign that said "Visitors." As she spun the wheel she said, "From here on in, no more talking about it." June nodded. They were in someone else's world now, and the razor wire–topped fences and the still-distant cement and brick buildings were all the proof of that they needed.

Betty pulled up to a gate in the middle of the road, and then waited as it opened up. There was a sign next to the road that said "5 Miles an Hour, Strictly Enforced" and then one next to it that said "All Guards in This Area Are Armed." June looked like she wanted to say something, but snapped her mouth closed without a word as Betty pulled up to a checkpoint station between the fences and rolled down a window. Betty set a notebook on her lap with Duke's info on it, and when the friendly-looking man in the small building asked who they had come to see, Betty replied, "Duke Barnes."

The man at the checkpoint nodded, neither interested nor impressed with their choice of inmate, and then asked them for their IDs. Feeling trepidation like nothing she had experienced in her life, Betty took June's wavering fake, stacked it atop her own and handed them to the man. He took the licenses, copied information from them, and handed them back through the open window. Betty handed June her ID and then stuffed her own in her wallet. It was hard to control her breathing, but so far things were going as well as they could.

"You know your license?" the guard asked.

Betty blinked in response, her heart feeling like it was about to blast out of her chest. "What about it? You need to see it again?"

The man blinked at her now, then smiled. "Oh. No. I mean, do you know your car's license number?"

"Oh!" A manic laugh escaped her. "Um. Do I?"

Now the man laughed. "Well, I don't know. How about this: just pull up so I can write down your plate number, and I'll give you a wave when I'm all set."

"Great!" *God, calm down.* She needed to keep it together. Everything was going OK. "I'll go on, then."

"Sounds like a plan," the man said with a grin.

You're not doing anything weird in this guy's eyes, she assured herself. *Most people must be nervous when they come here.*

She took the car out of park and pulled forward. Neither she nor June spoke, and when she saw the guard wave in the sideview mirror, she put her foot on the gas and drove through an iron gate that provided the lone break in a razor wire–topped concrete wall.

"Holy shit," said June.

"Yeah," said Betty. "I need to calm the hell down. That was actually a good sign. I mean, with the licenses. So we just keep smiling and being polite. We'll be inside soon."

June said nothing in response. Betty watched her friend and the road in alternating gulps—the prison road was straight and dull, but June looked as though she were looking into the face of God.

Jackson State Penitentiary was not a tall building, but the plain concrete structure rising from the dirt carried the weight of those living inside its walls. Just knowing that it housed thousands of the state's most-hardened cons would have made even a Chuck E. Cheese's seem intimidating. Guards could be seen at rooftop positions, and at the center of the largest part of the prison was a large tower that would have looked like part of a capitol building had it been placed elsewhere.

Signs in front of the building indicated they had made it to the right spot for prisoner visitation, so Betty parked and she and June got out and stretched. The air was warmer than it had been at home, but there was still a bit of the bite of Michigan winter in it. Betty and June looked at the concrete building waiting for them, then looked at each other over the roof of the car. Both of them swallowed drily, then began walking to the massive front door of the building.

On their way they passed two state cops leaning on the edge of one of their cruisers, and Betty had to force herself to stop staring at them. The cops looked bored and in no particular rush to go anywhere or do anything, but to Betty they appeared as great white sharks do to a skin diver, menacing and awful in a way that only a predatory animal can. The cops took no notice of the girls as they made their way to the door, and then Betty was tugging at the handle and they were inside.

A stout woman wearing a name tag that said "Helen" was working a desk to the left of the door, and just beyond her was a metal detector staffed by a pair of guards. The guard monitoring the people coming through the line looked alert, but the other, older one charged with telling people where to put their keys and wallets as they walked through the metal detector appeared bored, and perhaps even a bit hungover. Betty had a sickening flash of all three of these people snapping to attention when the girls tried to pass through security, the cops outside yanked from their break and forced to haul the pair of them off to holding cells somewhere.

"You two visiting someone today?"

God, they'd just been standing there in the doorway. "Yes," said June, and Betty knew instinctively that June was the one holding it together now. "We're here to see Duke Barnes."

June slipped her ID from her purse and slid it across the counter, and then Betty was next to her and doing the same thing, feeling all the while like she was on marionette strings. The woman took their licenses wordlessly, and then slid them both forms to be filled out with their names, addresses, and ages, along with a number of boxes to check and questions like, "Do you currently have any State or Federal Warrants?" Betty couldn't imagine that anything good would happen to a person that checked yes on that particular box.

She and June finished the questionnaires at the same time.

"Don't worry about filling in the prisoner number," said Helen. "Lucky for you, Mr. Barnes usually sees at least a couple of guests a week, so I know his by heart." Helen took their forms one after the other, scribbled a series of numbers and letters on them, stapled them to copies of their driver's licenses, and then stuffed the two sheets into a massive folio labeled with the date. "Now you're all set, ladies. Assuming there's nothing you want to bring back to your car. They'll call a sheriff for a knife with a blade longer than an inch or anything worse, and just about anything else will go in the trash. If you brought phones, now would be a good time to toss them back in the car."

"No, we're all set," said June. "We've been reading over the conduct rules on the website, but thank you for telling us."

"Well, all right then," said Helen. "You go have yourself a nice time, or at least as nice a time as a couple of young ladies can have in a place like this." Helen slid their IDs across the counter, the girls replaced them in their wallets, and then they were walking to the metal detector.

THIRTY-SEVEN

The pager buzzes and I grab it, then flip it over and look at the number. *Paul.* I take the burner purchased for this occasion out of my pocket and dial the number. I'm working quickly, so that I'll be on the phone before I even have a chance to get nervous, and Paul answers so quickly that it actually works.

"Hey, Nickel," says Paul. I know he's trying to get a rise out of me by using my name, but I'm not going to let it work. We're going to have an in-person soon, maybe even tonight, and I need to be in a good place with him.

"Hey," I reply, all business. Get the show on the road.

"So here's what I'm thinking," says Paul. "You stop by the house with a bag, me and my boys toke on some smoke for the next day or two, and then maybe we work something out. Sound good?"

"Sure, I just need an address," I say, but the truth is something else entirely. Paul and I have already been down this road—he's had my stuff and he knows it's good. Which gives me a sinking feeling in my gut, like maybe he's just looking to score for a party, nothing more, but all I can do is hope that he can really come through on this.

Paul rattles off an address and I grab a notepad and pen to write it all down. When he's done, he says, "So you can bring that by soon? I'm going to have some people over that will be able to help us both make some money, assuming this is the same green you brought by last time."

"It will be, no problem," I say, and I mean it. I might not be willing to negotiate on price or broker a bigger deal than he wants, but there's no question that the product is the same. The same bale I took bud from the last time is where this bag is coming from. I mean, I don't smoke this stuff, so if no one's buying, it just accumulates.

"Good, I'm glad to hear it," says Paul. "I'd hate to be let down." He pauses, and then says, "One more thing, Nickel. How much did you bring by the last time you let me taste this shit?"

"An eighth."

"Yeah, that's what I thought," says Paul. "We're going to need more this time. An ounce, actually. Like I said, these guys I've got coming over here are serious, serious dudes, and they're going to want to taste the goods, you know?" An ounce of my pot is worth a few hundred bucks, and Paul is expecting me to give him a weekend of bliss for nothing, likely so he can show off and then never contact me again. It's just like him using my name on the phone. He's only doing it because he can, and I'm not exactly making a good case for why he shouldn't.

"I can bring an ounce by later today," I say, hating the sound of my voice, and hating myself for giving in even more. I'm acting weak, not like myself, but everything in me wants this sale to go through. Even the parts of me that hate dealing with a guy like Paul at all are insisting that I just shut up and bring him some dope.

"All right, Nickel, we'll see you in a little bit then," says Paul, and then the phone clicks dead. I know what he wants, dope in a heartbeat, and even though I resent myself for doing it, I plan to get it to him as fast as possible.

I stuff the burner in my pocket and walk downstairs to the basement, letting myself through the twin doors that lead to the pot. Even with the blowers on, the room smells like a few skunks are having a turf war, but that's a good thing. I've had more than one person call my pot the best they've ever had, and I've seen the results in person. I might not smoke the stuff—I need my clarity—but I do take a certain amount of pride in providing a good product.

For the longest time, my dealer Gary and I had a great working relationship, but his greed put me in the spot I'm in right now. I'm still not really sure why he wanted to kill the golden goose. I mean, if he'd been thinking, he would have realized he was not born with a green thumb. Yeah, he could make more money without our split, but that was all dependent on him having grass to sell. When I came back from the dead looking for him, the warehouse space we'd been using was on the decline, and Gary looked like he was on the decline himself.

Thinking about Gary doing what he did makes me feel sick, so instead of dwelling on it, I cross the room to a few packaged bales of dope. Next to them lies a bag with about a half pound of some very clean-looking bud. The quality is the same as what's packaged in the bales; these kinds of pieces typically fall aside during the cleaning phase. Think of them like butcher's cuts from a cow, the kind you never see unless you know a guy in a bloody white apron.

I weigh the dope with my eyes, then drop a very pretty-looking bag onto a digital scale. I'm shy about an eighth of an ounce, so I toss a few more buds into the Ziploc, and this time the numbers dance and wind up just above an ounce. *Perfect.* I seal the bag, and then hit the lights and go upstairs, closing the doors behind me. Even through the bag the pot stinks, and since the last thing that I want to do is have a conversation with a cop about why I'm hauling a skunk corpse around town, I head to my laundry room.

One thing that you need to have if you're going to be transporting dope in quantity is a masking agent. I'm not sure who invented dryer sheets, but somebody owes them a couple of beers. Dryer

sheets smell so much like laundry that the mind goes there immediately, even if it should be obvious that no one at Lollapalooza is
going to be taking a break between sets to get their darks done. I
toss a couple sheets into a backpack, drop the dope on top of them,
and then throw in three more sheets for good measure. Satisfied
with the smell, I throw the backpack over my shoulder, head for
the garage, and jump on my bike. I close the garage with the clicker
and then ride to the gas station under the drooping sun, the same
place where I had the girls leave their cars.

I leave my bike leaned up against a pole, and then do my trick
with the lock and chain. Once the bike is secure, I pull another
burner from my pocket and call Lou. I doubt he'd care even if he
knew about the ounce in my bag, but I know that despite the fact he
drove me to Rhino's gym with a bullet in my arm once, he wouldn't
drive me crosstown with a few pounds of dope in a duffel bag.

That will be a situation to deal with when I get to it, though.
For now all that matters is getting to Paul's house and making
everybody happy. Once I get an offer of cash on the table, then
everything else can happen. For now, I just sit on the curb and
wait for Lou. Like it always does, thinking about Lou brings back
memories of Arrow.

Pretty girls get a pass in this world, but they also wear a target.
I'd love to have that advantage, but I like the anonymity even more.
That was the best part about Arrow. She could run the distraction
while I came from behind with the garrote. Thinking about Arrow
makes me think of Betty, and then I'm wondering how she's doing
at the prison. I've been so busy with the dope that I almost forgot,
but once I remember it's all I can think about, Betty and June and
Duke Barnes. I hope Betty can get something out of him, and not
just for the case. I want today to go well for both of us, and I want
her to call me. I want to talk to her again, and I'd love to say I don't
know why, but I do. I want this to go well, and I want to help her,
and with that in mind I stand as Lou pulls into the gas station.

I get in, throw a pair of twenties over the seat and mumble an address. Lou grunts, hits the gas, and we go. Betty will have to wait, because she's at the prison and I have to deal with a deeply unbalanced egomaniac. In that regard, I guess Betty and I are doing the same thing, but at least Duke will have bracelets on.

THIRTY-EIGHT

Everything had gone perfectly so far, and now the girls sat in the room with the rest of the visitors, waiting for Duke's name to be called. None of the people here to see friends and loved ones looked all that happy to be where they were. Babies and small children cried out from frustration and boredom, wives and girlfriends sat around looking sad in clothes that were either ill fitting or fit for prostitution, and a pair of older people looked scared and miserable. Everyone in the room jumped as the doors on the sides of the room opened, and when either the wrong name was called or one of them returned from visitation, all the heads would droop back down to return to the seemingly endless wait.

Betty heard "Barnes" called and felt as though the words were pulling her from a deep sleep, but then she felt June yanking at her arm and the two of them stood. All around them the room was already returning to disinterest as they approached the bored-looking guard by the door on the left.

When they got to them he said, "IDs, please." After a quick verification to make sure they hadn't switched with someone else in the waiting room, the girls found themselves following the guard to Duke.

Betty felt like she could throw up as the guard closed the door after them, but it faded to a kind of low-grade, sustained panic. Circular tables filled the room, about half of them seating men in orange jumpsuits and cheap plastic shoes and their visiting family members and friends. No one except for Betty, June, and the guard was standing, nor were they touching one another. Instead of leading them to a round table of their own, the guard ushered them to the far side of the room and one of a line of small tables bisected by glass partitions. Their side of the table had a pair of phone handsets; past the scratched glass, another handset waited for Duke.

"Go ahead and take a seat," the guard said. "Mr. Barnes will be out in a few minutes. Do not stand while Mr. Barnes is at the table, do not touch the glass, and only communicate through the handsets. He knows these rules as well, so if he acts confused about them, he is trying to play you. You can be arrested for a violation of any one of these rules, so do not break them."

"All right," said Betty.

"If either of you want something from the vending machine, you can call me or one of the other guards over to your table by raising your hand, just like in grade school. We will come to your table as fast as we can, and then one of you can walk to the vending machine with me. Are there any questions?" Betty and June shook their heads, and the guard locked eyes with them one after the other, before leaving them to their seats and the void on the other side of the glass.

"I can't believe we're doing this," said June in a choked voice. "I can't believe we're going to meet him. I'm not sure if I feel excited or sick."

"You'll be fine," said Betty, though not at all sure she was going to be fine. "Trust me. There's guards all over the place, and he's going to want to talk to us, not come over the glass and hurt us. This is going to be good, I know it."

June nodded but didn't say anything, because the door in front of them was opening and two guards and Duke Barnes were walking through it.

Duke was thinner than he'd looked in the recent pictures on the website, but still not as thin as he'd looked in the pictures from before he went to prison. His arms were sleeved in mottled greenish and gray prison tattoo work, and similar designs were climbing out of his cuffs and collar. Duke had huge knuckles—from fighting, Betty assumed—and though he was rail thin, he also looked taut, as though what was left of him was all muscle. His clothes were the same orange as the rest of the inmates', but his were ill fitting, draped over him as though it had been impossible for the prison to find the proper size for him to wear.

Betty and June watched the man as though he were a movie star or punk rock hero that had been zapped into place in front of them. Duke was no one to lust after in schoolroom fantasies, but he had been all they had been thinking of for weeks. Seeing him in person felt both perverse and impossible, Batman brought from the pages of a comic book and presented to them in human form.

As the guards set Duke before them behind the glass, Betty could tell he was trying to pretend disinterest in the audience. It occurred to her for the first time that Duke might have a legion of female followers, girls that believed in the words on the website and not the story about a girl who'd been beaten into submission and then stabbed to death by a man more animal than human. Whether Duke was guilty or not, Mandy was still dead, and there should have been respect for that. Instead, Duke was the champion of a popular movement that should have been interested in proving his innocence by finding the man who had really committed the crime, rather than solely focused on freeing the one who might not have.

When Duke looked from Betty to June, his face changed. It was gone in an instant but both Betty and June had seen it, and

Betty knew what had caused it. Duke was seeing Mandy, a Mandy before dope, an impossible Mandy even if she'd survived her Duke days. June was Mandy as she'd been before, before she was left to bleed out on the dirty floor of an abandoned house.

Duke cleared his throat, and the guards walked off without a care in the world. Betty found herself wondering how long it would take them to come back if Duke decided to launch himself over that partition, after all. She figured it would be too long by half. Duke was pale and yellow, but his tattooed forearms sheathed iron sinews.

The three stared at each other for what felt like forever, Duke's eyes switching back and forth between them, and then Duke picked up his phone and, eyes drilled into June, said, "Is this some fucking joke?"

"No," said Betty into her handset.

His gaze flicked to her.

"No," she said again, amazed that her voice was steady. "This is Mandy's niece. She didn't know about you or Mandy until just a few weeks ago. Her parents never told her about either of you."

"Not a bad call," said Duke, his voice raw gravel as it came through the phone. "What are your names?"

"Betty."

"June."

"All right," said Duke. "Now tell me why in the hell you're here."

"We want to know about you and Mandy," said June.

"We want to know everything," said Betty.

"You two have heard of the Internet, right?"

"We want to know what you told the police about the man in the green jacket, we want to know about your roommate, and we want to know about her diary," said Betty. Her voice had risen as she spoke, but looking around the room she could tell the words had been lost in a fog of noise. People at every table were talking loudly—men complaining about the lack of money for the commissary, women complaining about money for rent, and not a happy child within earshot.

"All right," said Duke. "Well, you know some things that most people don't, good for you."

"Tell us about the man in the green jacket."

"You know this only goes a half hour, right?" he asked, seething with bitterness. Duke was used to being the idol, and now he was back in the hospital, a confession demanded from him. It was clear he was used to people that believed in him coming to visit from the land beyond the wall, and now he had two would-be adversaries holding court across the table from him.

"A half hour is plenty of time to tell us the truth," said June.

Duke held his hands up in front of himself. "Look, I need you to be quiet," he said to June. "Let your friend talk. You look and sound way too much like Mandy, and it makes it hard to concentrate."

"Because of what you did?" June snapped back.

Duke nodded. "Why else would I feel bad about it?"

THIRTY-NINE

I have Lou drop me off about a half mile from Paul's house with instructions to meet me in the same spot in an hour. The sun is threatening to go away for good soon, so I get moving. I can use the exercise, and I really don't want him to know how I've arrived. The next time might be on a bike, or pulling a Radio Flyer decked out with a few bales and a sign that says "Not Weed" for security reasons. I know I'll need better than that, but Lou is out, the bales are too big to just throw on a bike, and there is no way I want Paul knowing where I live. I could ask Betty to help me drive it in her car, but I don't want to ask, and I can't even imagine what would happen if we got pulled over. I'll need to think out of the box, but that's all right. I do OK at that.

When I get to Paul's house I pause at the base of the driveway. There are a few cars in it that scream, "Drug dealer inside!" but I do my best not to think about it. I need to go inside, so there's no point in getting nervous about it, especially when I'm already wound up like a top.

I weave my way around the cars, and the closer I get to the house, the louder the music gets. It wasn't audible from the curb, but it's clear now that there is a very loud stereo inside. Par for the course. The house is a dump, the neighborhood sucks, and there's a few hundred thousand bucks' worth of cars in the driveway. It's a sure bet the house is furnished like a rapper's mansion.

Three knocks on the door gets me nowhere, so I do it again, and this time I'm met with a very polite "Hold the fuck on!"

I do, even though following instructions has never been my strong suit, and a few minutes later a young gangbanger opens the door and looks me up and down. "What the hell do you want?"

Now there are a few ways to handle this sort of impoliteness, but I think it's important to note that the young man I was speaking to was wearing a semi-auto stuffed into his pants. I'm a firm believer in politeness, but also in seeing the inside of my house again.

"I'm here to talk to Paul," I say. Giving the backpack strings a tug, I add, "I have the stuff he wanted."

"Oh shit, you should have said that. Come on in," says the kid, grinning.

He's my age, maybe a little older, and he's running the door for a drug dealer with a gun in his waist. I might share with him my estimate of his life expectancy—somebody sure as hell should—but I err instead on the side of caution and follow him inside.

The smell in the house is sort of like the music: mildly pervasive outside, in-your-face once you step in. Smoke, both tobacco and marijuana, has formed a nearly impenetrable cloud. I watch as the young banger locks the door behind us, then follow him down a short hallway past a filthy kitchen where a half-naked woman is sleeping on the floor and on into a packed family room.

All things considered, "family room" may not be the best way to describe it.

Paul and his friends are spread out on a sprawling couch and the floor. Beer bottles, glasses, and improvised ashtrays provide an idea of what the afternoon has entailed, and the sight of an Xbox One and a flat-screen TV showing Madden confirm any suspicions that I might have had.

The room ignores me, everyone focused on the TV. These guys are worse than civilians: they're sitting in a house that's a thief's wet dream, and they can't even be bothered to turn around at the appearance of a new body in the room.

Paul is sitting on one end of the couch. He's holding a mixed drink and a girl that doesn't look like she's legally able to get a driver's license. She's smiling, but the sight of it puts a rotten feeling in my stomach. Knowing you have to lie down with snakes is one thing; being happy about it is another.

Paul still hasn't seen me, his focus on the TV and nothing else.

"Yo, Paul, your delivery boy is here," says the kid who brought me in.

Paul turns, spilling some of his drink and forcing the girl off his lap. "That was fast," he said. "I like that, people don't always jump when you ask them to, but you look like the kind of motherfucker that would ask me how high and on which leg."

I nod. Whatever he wants to think is fine with me. I'm rusty, I know that, but I could rip this prick's head off without breaking a sweat, even while his friends filled me with lead. *But that's not how we play.* The voice is an ice pick in my brain, Dad telling me not to be so shortsighted.

"Where's the shit?"

"In my bag. Can I get it?"

"Do your thing," says Paul. "If you try and pull a piece or do something stupid, I have a feeling you know what's going to happen."

I do, no lack of clarity there. Football is paused, and all eyes are on me. Since I figure these idiots have all the trigger discipline of a freshman on prom night, I play it as cool as possible. Unzip the bag, one hand in, nothing but a sack of green comes out.

If I'd been expecting a *wow* moment when the dope cleared the nylon, I'd have been sadly let down. There's no reaction at all, other than the kid who let me in taking the bag from my hand and bringing it to Paul.

Paul takes it from him, opens the bag, takes a sniff, and then hands it to the girl who'd been on his lap. "Go roll blunts, bitch," he says, and like a dutiful dog, the girl takes the bag into the kitchen. I hate him so much at this moment that it's hard to look relaxed, and it's all I can do not to say something, anything to make him react and give me an excuse to hurt him.

Instead, the moment fades and Paul says, "You can get going. Rio will show you out. I'll be in touch, Nickel, but I really hope you didn't waste my time." The other guys in the room are nodding, trying to look tough while they sit high, drunk, and distracted by digital men playing a game none of them had the talent to even attempt in real life.

"You'll like it, man," I say. "Just let me know what you want me to do."

Paul nods, but he's already watching the TV again, the distraction immediate. Rio taps me on the arm and I reshoulder my backpack and follow his lead. I don't want to be there any more than they want me interrupting their little party.

I'm walking in front of Rio to the door when I see something I don't like at all.

On the bottom of the steps heading upstairs there's a coloring book. I can see the scribbled-in pages from where I stand, and just a few steps up sits a little boy clad in only a pair of briefs. He's clearly malnourished, eyes sunken into his head, and biceps thinner than his wrists should be.

I'm a coward, act like I don't see him, and go outside.

I could hear Dad screaming at me as I passed the boy, could hear Sam's last breath rattling in his throat out in the snow at the camp. There was nothing I could do, not with Rio at my back, and not with a room full of thugs a hallway away. The only question I have now is whether I'm going to follow through as planned and hope Paul actually pays, or do what's right. Thinking back to the woman passed out on the kitchen floor clouds my thought process further, as it seems a fair conclusion that the sleeping—or worse— woman was his mother.

I leave the house, deciding that I'll walk a few blocks before calling Lou. Pointless precaution, of course, as even Rio has better stuff to do than watch me walk down the road alone. Still, I walk, and I'm halfway to the end of the block when I see the sign, and despite what happened in the house, I'm grinning. I might decide not to do the deal with Paul, or I might swallow my pride and go for the money, but at least one problem is solved. The asking price at the garage sale is only thirty bucks, and with a few mods, my dope transportation issues have been solved.

FORTY

"So you admit you killed her?" Betty asked, and Duke nodded.

"Absolutely, just not in the way you're thinking," said Duke. "You've got an idea in your head that I put that knife in her, but I didn't. I loved that girl. Hell, I still love her. That's why it makes me feel sick when she talks." Duke was looking at June, wincing as if seeing her physically pained him. "The sound of your voice makes me feel even sicker than I already am. It makes me feel like I'm already in hell."

"But you killed her?"

"By putting her in that house, and in that situation, yes, I killed her," he admitted. "I was the junkie, she just loved the punk scene, and she was looking for what she thought was going to be a relationship with a really cool guy." Duke smiled sadly at them. "I wasn't all that cool. I wanted to be, but what the hell does that even mean? I was a mess, although I might be worse now."

The man is an emotional wreck, and he looks like something is eating him alive. But no, Betty thought. *He's just trying to play on my sympathies.* She wanted nothing to do with that. His life was sad, but that would have been true whether he'd killed Mandy or not, and there was no good reason to listen to him bitch about the things he'd ruined.

"You saw a man in a green jacket that night?" she asked.

Duke heaved a sigh at that, already ditching his woe-is-me approach for bored annoyance at having to talk about his case with these schoolgirls. He did finally answer, though. "Yes."

"Well, why didn't you stick to that story? You saw a person leaving, and then your girlfriend was dead inside the house. If that was me, I'd be screaming about what I saw, but you dropped it and confessed."

"I was stoned out of my mind, and I was sick after seeing her like that," said Duke, heating up. "I saw a man—that part's true— but I dropped the story because they refused to hear it, *refused* to, and I was coming out of my skin with withdrawals. So, yeah, I stopped saying the pointless words. What did I care? I wanted to die. Dying would've been a mercy."

Once again, Betty was shocked that no one was staring at what was beginning to be a tense conversation. Duke was glaring at her through the glass, then the air seemed to go out of him.

"Listen," he said. "What it came down to for them was getting me convicted. They never tried to catch anyone else. Maybe if that neighbor had seen the guy in the green jacket—would've seen both of us, I mean, him and me, two green jackets, instead of just the one, which could've just been me—maybe then things would have been different, but that's not what he saw." When the two of them just stared at him, he shook his head. "Look, this is pointless. You're gonna believe what you're gonna believe."

"We didn't come here because we're sure of what happened," Betty said. "We want to hear it from you."

"All right, I'm telling you. I was high on shit when I got to the house, but I'd also just scored, and I was about to get a lot higher. That was how it always worked. Mandy and I would go sell ourselves and then score dope and go back to that fucking house. That was the toilet our lives had become. It probably sounds pretty unbelievable, but I was happy to go back there with heroin to share with her. I'd had a good day and I'd bought good tar because of it. I can still remember how I felt, I can remember the weather, and there wasn't a single part of me that was pissed off enough to hurt her."

"What does that have to do with anything?"

"It has to do with the fact that even though I was a shitty person and a junkie, I still cared about her." Duke seethed. "If I'd been mad enough to want to smack her around a little bit, I would have remembered that, too. It might even have been enough to make me convince myself I had done it. I was a little cloudy from dope, I can admit that, but I know where my head was, and I wasn't thinking about hurting her."

"Tell us about your roommate," said June. She hadn't spoken since Duke had asked her to stop talking, and his head spun as if someone had fired a revolver next to his ear. The expression on his face wasn't anger, but great surprise and pain.

"I'm serious," he said. "Let the other one talk. Please just keep your mouth shut."

June dropped her eyes to the table, and Betty felt sick thinking Duke's disgust might be the only real proof they would ever get. *He won't look at her because she makes him see that day all over again,* thought Betty. *But is it guilt poisoning him, or regret?*

"We had a lot of people in and out of the house," said Duke. "The last roommate we had was a guy named Jason, but he moved out three days before Mandy was killed. The police thought I made that all up, too, but I didn't. Jason left and then Mandy died. If he'd been home, then she'd probably be alive, or at least we'd have a better idea of who killed her."

"Why did he leave?"

"He and I got in a fight."

"Money?"

"No," said Duke with a sardonic curl on his lips. "We weren't real roommates, remember? Ask a cop. No one paid rent, and besides, Jason had plenty of money from selling pot."

"Was the argument over Mandy?" Betty asked the question slowly, distracted by the incredible fact that it sounded like Duke honestly thought a man who had moved out just three days before Mandy's death shouldn't be on the list of suspects.

"No," said Duke. "It's worse than that. Jason was holding some stuff over my head, and finally I'd just had enough. He wouldn't have killed Mandy. That wasn't the type of person he was, but he and I did have a beef."

"What were you fighting about?"

"I was selling myself on the streets, and sometimes when Mandy was gone or passed out I'd sell myself to Jason," he growled. "I don't know why I can admit to peddling my ass on the street like it's no big deal, but when I talk about what I was doing for him it makes me sick. But that's just how I feel. Jason finally pushed too far and it was time for him to go. He picked the not-getting-his-ass-kicked version of getting the fuck out of the house, and that was the last I ever saw of him."

"Did Jason have a last name?"

"Lattrell," said Duke, "not that it will do you much good. Jason is gone, thrown to the wind like a handful of ashes. I bet you could find a few Jason Lattrells if you really looked, but I doubt you'll find the right one. He wasn't a junkie, but he was a fucking mess just the same. You're not going to find him cleaned up and working some kind of plugged-in life."

"You might be wrong," said Betty. "Finding people's gotten a lot easier. I bet I'd find a lot of Jason Lattrells out there, and I could easily get a hold of them one after the other. Jason could be a hell of a character witness if we could find him and you ever got a retrial."

"That sounds great," said Duke, "but like I said, it's not going to happen. For all I know, Jason wasn't even really his name. This is a guy that sold dime bags to high school kids, you know? He was a scumbag with a murky past and an even murkier future. You can do all the searches that you want, be my guest, but even if you call a hundred Jason Lattrells, you're not going to find the right one. My lawyers couldn't find Jason to testify, and I think they actually managed to get that part of their job right. They looked."

"All right," said Betty. "One last thing."

"Better hurry up," said Duke. "Half an hour, remember? You can be damn sure we're pushing into that."

Betty looked around. The tables surrounding them were still full of people, but the faces were different. "We have time," she said, unsure if they really did. She didn't have her phone, didn't have a watch, and had no idea how long they'd been speaking with Duke. "Did Mandy have a diary?"

"Who knows," said Duke. "She was always doodling in journals and stuff, but when it came time to try and find something with some writing in it, the cops came up empty. I would have sworn she had one, but my lawyers showed me pictures of the house after the pigs were done with it. A mouse couldn't have hidden a diary in there."

"I don't know," said Betty. "We were told the same thing, but they said you insisted there was one, and—"

"Sweetheart, if there ever was one, it's long gone," said Duke. His words didn't match the tone. Duke had meant them to sound cruel, and he'd succeeded. "Besides, even if Mandy had kept a little book of her hopes and dreams, do you think it would be worth reading? There's nothing in there that would exonerate me, there's nothing in there that will help you find Jason, and I highly doubt she was writing in it the day she got killed."

"I don't mean—"

"Listen," said Duke. He was pointing at them through the glass, but the glass wasn't enough. Betty had to force herself to stay in her chair. "I've been a good boy and put up with all your bullshit—and your creepy-ass friend—but I'm about out of time. Here's all you need to know. If Mandy had a diary, it's gone. You will not find Jason Lattrell, but it doesn't matter because he was just a silly little dope-dealing repressed homo. He didn't and doesn't know shit. Last, there was a man in a green coat there that day besides me, just like I always said. Of course, you're not going to find him, because it's been fifteen years and he's a ghost. There are your three answers, all right?"

"Yes," said Betty, and over Duke's shoulder she could see two guards coming to the table.

Duke leaned across the table, close to the glass, and said, "Money is what is going to make this go away, money and nothing else, and it certainly isn't going to be a couple of teenagers that figure out who killed Mandy and why the cops did such a shit job. All I know is that I'm going to die soon enough, and if I'm lucky I'll get to do it outside of this hellhole. It's been real." A hand clapped on his shoulder and Duke stood.

June said, "Thanks for talking to us."

"Christ, that fucking voice."

FORTY-ONE

Betty drove with the radio off but neither of them spoke because there was nothing to say. That they'd failed at the prison was an understatement, and what Betty couldn't figure out was why in the hell either of them had ever thought just talking to Duke would be enough. Cops, trained detectives, had spent hours with him, and had come to the same conclusion as a jury of twelve. The most likely assessment of the situation was exactly what Van Endel had told her: Duke was guilty but had managed to drum up a following due to some irregularities in his prosecution. Betty knew instinctively there had to be many convicted felons who could concoct the same type of story.

"He hated us," said June as they passed by Lansing. "I mean, he faked it well enough, but he was bored by our questions, he hated my voice and the way I looked, and he resented you for talking about things he didn't want to discuss. I hate to say it, Betty, but I'm not sure this little trip is even worth including in our report. Mr. Evans is not going to give us a higher grade just because we made a convicted murderer dislike us."

"It's true that Duke didn't tell us much we didn't already know," said Betty. "That said, we still have a few things to consider."

"Like what?" June asked, and Betty was certain June really did sound as much like Mandy as Duke had insisted. *Was her voice really similar enough to terrify him?* Duke didn't look like a man who scared easily, but that part of the interview had definitely not gone as Duke had planned. Unfortunately, the only result of his revulsion was that June had been unable to speak, and Betty had been forced to carry the interview by herself. Betty didn't blame June for the odd turn of events, but it still hadn't helped the situation any, especially with Betty so terrified over the identity fraud they were committing.

"First of all," said Betty, "we need to remember that just because Duke didn't know about a diary doesn't mean there wasn't one. It's even possible Duke destroyed it himself. That seems even more possible if Mandy talked about him beating her in it."

"You think he did that?"

"Beat her? Yeah, I definitely think so. Did he destroy the diary to cover it up? I don't have a clue about that. I do know this isn't the end, though. Mr. Evans told us this was going to be hard, and I think just because we had a little luck we forgot that. We can still search for Jason Lattrell, we can still go to the house, and we can keep looking around online."

"So what now?"

"Now we go home," said Betty. "I'll e-mail Nickel so I can meet up with him Monday, and I can see if he wants to come check out the house with us."

"That sounds OK," said June. "It's better than nothing, at least."

"Yeah, beggars can't be choosers."

"I have a bit of a confession, Betty," said June.

Betty turned to her friend, momentarily forgetting her place at the steering wheel. "What is it?"

"I don't think Duke did it. I think he was a rotten man, and he's still a rotten man, no matter how many famous friends he might have, but I don't think he did it."

"Neither do I."

"You know what that means, though, right?"

Betty shook her head at the question. She really had no clue what June meant.

"That means the guy who killed Mandy is still out there somewhere. The guy who killed my aunt is still free, and I want to change that."

"We're going to find him, June," said Betty. "I have no idea how, but we're going to do it. Even if it takes us longer than some dumb project, or even longer than high school. We're going to figure this out, and as soon as we do, we're going to call the police."

"We have to," confirmed June. "We have to do it for her."

FORTY-TWO

I told myself that by the time Paul called my pager I'd have the balls not to call him back. It would have been bad enough to just ignore the situation going on over there, but far worse to profit from it, regardless of my money troubles.

I am calling him back, though. My brain went on autopilot, and all of a sudden the phone is ringing and I'm holding it.

"Yeah? Hold on." There's deep breathing coming from the phone, and I hear Paul say, "Knock it off, girl. Damn." I wait, let the silence grow between us, and then he says, "Yo, Nickel?"

"Yeah, I'm here."

"I have to admit, my friends were pretty impressed, dude."

I grimace. I shouldn't be on the phone at all, I should never have lain down with this snake. I can still hang up the phone, but I'm not doing it.

"I'm glad," I say, my voice feeling like it's being controlled by a ventriloquist, but that would just let me off the hook. This is me compromising my morals, nothing more, and certainly nothing that can be blamed on anyone else.

"I bet you are, man," says Paul. "Would have been bad for you if they hadn't been. Best-case scenario, we wouldn't have been able to work together. But worst-case, shit. We don't need to talk about that." I want to remind him there is no worst case, or even a best one, not unless I allow it to happen. Paul can't find his own ass with both hands and a flashlight, much less find me in the webs of disinformation I leave lying around for just such an occasion. I don't remind him, though.

"How much are you going to want?" I ask. "I've got fifteen pounds, all dry and ready to go."

"I want it all." There's an edge to his voice now, no more joking around, apparently. "Every last bit of green you've got, and then I'd like to get on a sales schedule with you. This isn't the last batch, right?"

"There's always more coming," I say, and it's true. It's going to take longer than he might like for me to get the next batch going, but that news can wait. "What were you thinking you'd be able to pay for fifteen?"

"I don't know," says Paul. "We'll figure that out when the time comes. I mean, you know I can't pay street for that weight."

"Yeah, I know. I'm not expecting that."

"Well, don't expect me to get anywhere close. Fifteen pounds is massive, and there's a lot of people that are going to need to make money on down the line. What I'm saying is, don't get greedy."

Pulling the phone from my face, I take a deep breath, and then reply, "Nobody is getting greedy over here. I just want to sell some stuff, get my money, and then walk away to do it all again. It's just business for me, plain and simple."

"I feel the same way," says Paul. "I'll page you at seven, you call me back, we set up a drop. If we're both cool, this will be as smooth as silk." The phone goes dead and I stuff the burner into my pocket, then walk back out to the garage. All I can think of is the facedown woman in the kitchen, him calling the girl on his lap a bitch, and the little boy on the stairs. None of this feels good, and I have a bad feeling it might never feel right, not even when it's been in the rearview mirror for a few months.

The tow-behind-a-bike children's carrier I bought for twenty-five dollars from the yard sale I passed when I was leaving Paul's is coming along nicely. I've already hung black sheets over the breathable mesh on the inside, and I'm planning on coating the inside layer of those in more of those ridiculously useful dryer sheets. It won't exactly be stylish—my ratty bike and the trailer make for a particularly sad-looking combo—but the weed will fit inside just fine. Assuming everything goes well, so will the money.

The trailer affords me one other option as well: the idea of some sort of self-defense. Guys like Paul are typically pretty cowardly, but if he feels like he needs to impress someone, I have no doubt he'll off me, good source of weed or not. That's part of the game. As I look at the trailer, I think I can probably set up some measures, both on myself and in the vehicle, that will level the playing field a bit.

I'm not readying for war, at least I don't think so, but there's definitely a part of my mind that likes the idea of breaking some bones.

I give the trailer a final look and walk back into the house. There's only a few hours to go, and if I'm lucky, Betty will e-mail soon so we can set up a time to meet. Even with all this other crap going on, I still want to hear from her about the prison and Duke. And truth be told, I just want to hear from her.

FORTY-THREE

The rest of the week was boring in comparison to sneaking into a prison, but that was to be expected. The moms were out of the house constantly, busy setting up for a show at Ophelia's studio. On Sunday, Betty could have come along for the ride to help decorate, but she declined, a decision she regretted later when she realized she had nothing to do.

So the moms were out, June had to go to her dad's house, and Nickel hadn't returned her e-mail yet. The only person that was available was Jake. His texts had been picking up in frequency, and though Betty knew she had to stop brushing him off, she wasn't sure what to say after so long.

Nickel was the person Betty wanted to talk to the most. She knew if anyone could put a positive spin on what little information she'd gleaned from Duke, it would be that odd boy—assuming Nickel even still had interest in her or the murder of Mandy Reasoner. Betty figured he would, though, even if this was the longest he'd taken to respond to one of her e-mails. She'd even kept the message short, the way he seemed to like.

Betty found herself staring at the pictures of Duke and Mandy—obsessive behavior at its worst—and couldn't stop wondering what truths the still images were hiding, and how many of them would be lost forever. *You know something!* She could practically *see* the pictures screaming it at her, but there was no truth to be had there. Frustrated, confused, and bored out of her skull, Betty wandered down to the kitchen to find something to eat.

Returning to her room ten minutes later with a still-steaming bowl of ramen, Betty promised herself she was done being unproductive. The endless browsing and regurgitating of the same information over and over again had to stop, lest she descend into madness. The vow lasted as long as it took Betty to refresh her e-mail and see that Nickel's silence had continued. Seconds later, she was back on the Free Duke site, skipping around between the timeline and the trial sections. There was nothing new to be seen there, but when Betty went back to her e-mail a few head-splitting moments later, there was a message from Nickel.

Betty was dying for something new, something that could move everything forward, and though what she got was curt, it was exactly what she needed: "I can meet you tomorrow. Same time, same place. N."

Betty smiled as she closed the e-mail. It wasn't much, but it meant that tomorrow would be different. She didn't know for certain that Nickel could right the foundering ship their investigation had become, but she was sure that he could help them in some way or another.

With her sights set on the coming day, Betty clicked on Reddit and killed time. *At least here no one wants anything from me.* It was a welcome break from the pictures of Mandy and Duke, but it didn't last. Their eyes kept haunting her as they cried out for vengeance and freedom, and Betty felt sick wondering if everyone else working to free Duke had found themselves in a similar position. All the investigators were stymied. They needed new evidence, but where was it going to come from in a case this cold?

Betty flipped back to e-mail and scrolled down until she found the message Andrea had forwarded her from Van Endel and clicked it open. The address beckoned her like a siren, and despite the cop's request that she go no closer than the road, Betty knew she had to enter that house, and she had a pretty good idea of who would be willing to go with her.

June might go, but Nickel will be standing next to me with a crowbar.

There was an odd comfort in the thought.

FORTY-FOUR

The days are getting warmer, but the nights are still just as cold. Knowing that I'm too uncomfortable to fall asleep is small consolation for suffering outside, but at least I know I won't miss anything.

Not that I really have to worry. The GPS I attached to Jack's car will wake me up once he gets moving, but as it turns out the app on my phone is unnecessary. I'm awake as Jack leaves the house with a shadowy woman, and the two of them get in his car and take off.

I consider turning my bike around and tossing his house again now that I know he's safely away from it, but I decide against it. That particular oyster hadn't left me any pearls last time, and I don't think tonight will be any different. Nope. I want to watch Jack in his element, drinking, with all the territorial responsibilities of a drunken American male with a woman on his arm.

My head's telling me I'm wasting my time, that Jack is going to let me down. My gut tells a different tale, though, so here I am, pedaling in the cold. Claire's suspicions agree with my gut's. But then, how many ex-wives don't believe their husbands capable of dire deeds? My gut and his ex might like Jack for the death of Mandy, but my head knows there's nothing besides circumstantial evidence pointing toward him.

As it turns out, I really didn't need the GPS. I haven't reconned him at night yet, but I have my guesses about his habits, and they prove accurate. The closest bar on this end of town is the Shipwreck. Rolling into its unpaved lot, I see a few cars, all with varying body damage, and Jack's Impala happens to be among them.

I park the bike at the back of the lot, do my thing with the chain, and then walk on over to the car. I should have done this at the house when quiet streets would have made for easier work, but my curiosity is killing me, and the car is beckoning me like a Detroit siren. Jack's house didn't stand a chance against my lock-pick set, and neither will the Impala.

The tumblers roll like a bowling ball down a bumpered lane. There are a few slow spots, but I know I'm going to knock them all down. I'm inside in less than a minute.

Jack's car isn't the vehicle you'd expect a terrible husband, dangerous father, and possible murderer to drive. It's more boring than his house. The home itself was a mess, but the man's clothes were neat, the woodsheds out back had been well organized, and his projects well thought out to my eyes. And now here is his Impala, banged up but pretty much neat as a pin inside. Everything together does the opposite of setting off my warning bells. In fact, I'm downright calm. Jack's just a guy out on a date, and his car doesn't even have the typical stray fry to throw under the microscope.

I leave the vehicle after just a few minutes. I could've been more thorough, but cars keep pouring into the lot, and between their headlights and the door to the Shipwreck flashing open, I was having a hard time maintaining my calm.

It doesn't matter. Jack isn't hauling around rope and a buck knife, nor is the car covered in bloody handprints. The car is just that, a sedan owned by a lower-middle-class man, and nothing in it tells of anything else. I feel a little silly to have even fantasized it would, after all this time.

I'm not as disappointed as I ought to be, though, as I fade back into the darkness, slide into a small grove about a hundred feet from the parking lot, and flick on the night-vision monocular. I don't know why I'm not more discouraged. Yes, Jack is everything a good prosecutor would have been happy to find if he hadn't been handed a junkie's confession to run with. He was a relation by marriage, so he had to have known of the girl at least, and there was just no way he'd made it to that point in his life without falling afoul of the law at least once or twice. He was way too angry not to have a record.

But none of that matters. Even if Jack had killed her, the police already had that confession, already had an easy bust.

This is the talking-to my head is giving my gut as I huddle behind my monocular in that stand of trees, but my gut's ignoring it. It's too intent on waiting for Jack to leave the bar.

And then Jack does leave the bar, and everything changes.

Jack's only been in the Shipwreck with his date for a little over an hour, but the drinks must have been flowing pretty well, based on the lean they both carry into the parking lot. The woman stumbles, mutters something indecipherable, and then I can hear Jack ask her, "What the fuck did you just say to me?"

There's laughter after that—from the woman, not Jack—and then he hauls off and smacks her. It looks like an open palm strike from where I'm sitting, but that doesn't really matter if you connect well, and from the way she drops, I'd say Jack put his weight into it.

I'm moving across the span before I realize my legs are in motion. Jack is hurting her, and he's going to hurt her again, and my thoughts are pitch black.

Jack beats my pace across the field, though, giving the woman one more wallop—softer this time, but still audible—just as she regains her feet and then telling her, "Get in the fucking car."

I'm close then, close enough for him to see me if he's looking, but I stop dead in my tracks as the two of them get in the car like nothing's happened. There's no way Jack should be driving, but the woman—what in the hell is she doing, getting in there with him? Hasn't he just been beating on her?

This is obviously just another night out for these two.

It's disgusting and sad, but nothing I can do anything about, so I'm turning away when I'm stopped by something about the shape of the woman's head, or the way she moves as she checks the damage to her face in the mirror in the Impala's sun visor.

I know her.

She's my damn client.

FORTY-FIVE

School was every bit the drudgery Betty had become accustomed to. By the time she and June made it to the library, the day's sole bright point was that she'd only seen Jake once. She was starting to feel like officially breaking up with him might even be a bit redundant at this point; it couldn't have been much clearer to him that his request had had the opposite of its intended effect on her. Still, as Betty walked into the library she really doubted she was going to get off that easy. She was going to need to put Jake down, and she knew, after her meeting with Nickel, that today was going to be the perfect time to get the unfortunate task over with.

June walked into the library ahead of her, and they headed to the bank of computers near the back of the room, where they had been holding court during fourth period for the last few weeks. June had an impatient look on her face, and as she sat, she said, "About the only good thing to come of that trip was the fake IDs. That and the fact that, though Duke's a bitter piece of crap, we both left with the impression that he probably didn't kill her. Not that that's exactly a good thing."

"He's just angry," said Betty. "You find anything on the roommate?"

"Nope."

"Me neither," said Betty. "I'm hoping Nickel can help with that. And maybe he can convince us the trip to Jackson State wasn't a complete waste of time."

"Hey, it wasn't all bad," said June. "I was in prison, waiting to get arrested while I sat with the guy who knew my aunt, and maybe even killed her, and it was still better than spending time with my dad. I swear, the only reason he even has me over is so he can feel like he's getting a good return on the child support."

"That gives me a crazy thought," said Betty. "What would you think about us interviewing your dad?"

"No way," said June. "Not going to happen, not possible."

"Don't be so negative. Think about it. He had to have known Mandy. Maybe he has some inside information. Not about how she died, of course, but about what kind of person she was. For all we know your dad even knew Duke, or met Jason for some reason."

"No," said June.

"Why not? Seriously, we can't talk to your mom, and your dad is the only person we know of besides Duke and that cop that were even close to this case. What if he can give us a little piece of the puzzle we're missing?"

"Just drop it, OK?" June implored her. "My dad barely wants anything to do with me in general. He's not going to put up with us going over there and asking him questions."

"June."

"What?"

"Please?"

"Seriously? I don't think I can be much more clear. He's going to say no, and he's going to get pissed that I even asked."

Betty just looked at her. For a while June pretended not to notice, but finally she heaved a sigh and locked eyes with her.

"Just ask him," urged Betty. "It can't hurt to ask."

"I'll ask, fine," said June. "But you're wrong about the second part. Trust me. My dad's creative, and he'll find some way to make me feel like an absolute asshole for bringing this up. He always does."

FORTY-SIX

I'm furious, but I don't want Claire to see my anger. I'll just give her the chance to tell me why she was at the bar with Jack last night, and why she's having me investigate him in the death of her murdered sister if she's OK with going out with him for a few drinks and a beatdown. Jack was slipping off my radar, but now I'm fully focused on him, benign lifestyle or not. Mandy was beaten savagely before she died, and now that I've seen him in action, imagining Jack doling out that punishment is all too easy to imagine.

I see Claire waiting for me in her car, just as I instructed, and I climb into the passenger seat through the unlocked door.

Claire looks a little worse for wear. Not only is this the earliest in the day we've met, but she had a late night. To indicate this further—as well as the two solid shots I saw her take—Claire has on enormous sunglasses and is wearing thick liquid makeup. She looks like hell.

"Anything you want to tell me?"

"No," says Claire, taken a little aback. "You called me, so I thought you had some information."

"Where were you last night?"

"Home," she says, before pausing and asking, "Why? What does this have to do with me?"

"You were out with Jack last night," I say softly. "You were at his house, then the bar, and then the parking lot. After that, I stopped caring what else you did with him. Let's cut the crap: I need to know why you were with him, and I want to know why you're not at the police station filing a report right now."

"You saw me," she says, a statement, not a question. "How did you know—"

"I didn't know, I had to see it for myself. I was doing the job you hired me to do. I was following him, checking things out, just like you asked me to, and then I saw him beating you up in the parking lot. It was an eye-opener. He's got a talent for it. Seeing how much he enjoyed it, I think he's obviously—"

"Jack didn't hurt Mandy," says Claire, her voice subdued but solid. "I provoked him and he hit me. It's no excuse, but we were married for a long time, and I still know exactly how to push his buttons."

"You're damn right it's no excuse. He hit you, it shouldn't matter what you—"

"That should be true," Claire says, "but the world isn't black and white. I knew exactly what would happen when I said what I did."

I cock my head at her. "So you're saying you literally asked for it."

She doesn't respond to that.

"It doesn't matter," I say. Though of course it does—but that's not my job. "What matters is that if he has a history of abuse, if it's the kind of hobby for him it obviously seems to be, that could be his link to Mandy. Someone as vulnerable as she was, out on the streets, nobody but a junkie looking out for her—"

"Stop it. I don't want to hear that. This wasn't anything like that. I tricked Jack into taking me out so I could rag on him in front of his friends about child support. I know he's got unreported income, and some of that money should be mine. I'm raising our daughter, and I'll happily take a lump or two if it means that bastard will kick June a few more bucks every month. God knows the state won't help me out."

Again, all I can do is cock my head at her like a puzzled parrot. "Let me get this straight. You got just what you were after? This was your plan? What did you say to him?"

"Enough in the bar to make him look like the piece of shit he is in front of his idiot buddies, and just maybe enough to make them look at old Jack Derricks a little cross-eyed when he starts bragging about pulling in some extra money on side jobs." She smiled coldly, then said, "But I saved the good stuff for when we were alone."

I'd say this was the dumbest thing I've ever heard, but I'd be lying. It's a contender, though. All I can think to say is, "You can't expect me to investigate him for killing your sister if you're going to compromise your own safety with him."

"Then don't," she says. "Keep your eyes on June, just like you were doing before, and just let this Jack business go. He had nothing to do with my sister's death, and I was a fool for ever saying as much. I was with him then, we were still good, and there was nothing that happened back then that would make me think he had anything to do with Mandy's death."

"All right," I say, because there's nothing else to do. I step out of the car feeling cold, even though it's warmer out than it has been in days.

I'm not sure I should let Jack go so easily, but I'm not sure there's a point in doing anything else. Claire knows the man, says she knew what she said would get her smacked, and in a rough-and-tumble-looking bar like the Shipwreck, that seems about par for the course. I don't like that she got hurt, but it's clear it wasn't Claire's first rodeo.

I check my phone as she pulls out of the parking lot. I have hours until I need to meet Betty, and right now all I want to do is ride. Between this mess with Paul, the revelations from last night and now this morning, my ongoing investigation, and my still-healing wounds, I'm feeling overwhelmed and beaten down. Hopefully putting some miles under the tires will make me feel better, and even if it won't, there's no point in not trying. I need my head clear right now, so I jump on my bike and get moving.

FORTY-SEVEN

Betty sat on the bench at Riverside, convinced that Nickel wasn't going to show up. Then, as she scanned the area behind her, a voice of growing familiarity uttered a greeting.

"Hey," said Nickel.

When she spun to see him, her frustration must have been visible, because he followed up the greeting by saying, "Everything all right?"

"I'm good," said Betty, "so long as you discount the fact that I'm completely over school, I'm at a dead end in the Mandy thing, and everything else in my crappy life is driving me insane." Betty almost told him about Jake—the words had been about to slip out of her mouth—but she caught herself just in time.

But why do I care, if Nickel and I are just friends? It wasn't a question Betty was ready to deal with, at least not right then, and it was a blessing when Nickel spoke.

"Well, I can't help very much with school, but I would like to hear all about Duke, and about why you think you're at such a dead end."

Nickel sat next to her and she began to recount everything that had happened at the prison, starting with the fake IDs being accepted, the pained look on Duke's face whenever June would speak, Jason Lattrell, the man in the green jacket, and the diary. She finished by describing for Nickel exactly how she'd felt when Duke had left them, and how useless the whole thing had felt once he was gone.

"It was almost like he was getting off on it," said Betty. "Like he enjoyed the fact that we thought we might find some answers by speaking to him, but that we'd failed like everyone else. He said the only thing that was going to help him was money, and that we were just a couple of fools for wasting our time with him."

"Ouch," said Nickel. "That considered, though, there's really only one thing left to do."

"What's that?"

"We need to go through their old house," he said, making it sound about as exciting as going to buy groceries. "If Mandy kept a diary even Duke couldn't find, it had to have been spectacularly hidden, especially since the cops didn't find it, either. Are you sure he wasn't lying, and he didn't just dispose of it?"

"He wasn't lying," said Betty, "at least not about that. I do agree that we should go in the house, though, especially if you're game to come along."

"I'm in," he said. "My weekend was busy, but I've got some free time until tonight, and I'm always up for some urban spelunking."

"Isn't that what they call it when you go in a cave?"

"Yeah, that's why there's the urban part in front of it. It basically means exploring abandoned property somewhere, like Chernobyl, or that creepy Six Flags that got blasted by Katrina."

"Well, I've never done anything like that," said Betty, "but I'm up for looking through that house. It could be creepy, though. We'll need flashlights and maybe a baseball bat or something." When Nickel cocked his head as if to question the need for a bat, Betty said, "You know, in case there's, like, people that aren't supposed to be there."

"Fair enough," said Nickel. "If you want to give me a ride back to my house, we can grab everything we need."

"You have flashlights and stuff like that?"

"Sure."

Betty just shook her head. "Is there anything you're not ready to handle immediately?"

"I hope not," said Nickel as he stood.

Betty wasn't sure what to say to that, so she stood as well and the two of them began to walk to her car.

Betty would think later that she should have seen it all coming, that she should have been able to predict what was about to happen, but she didn't.

As Betty and Nickel crested the hill to leave the playground, Betty saw someone parked near her car but she thought nothing of it. As they came closer she realized that someone was standing by her car and staring at them, and when she shielded her eyes from the sun with her hand, she saw that the someone was Jake and that he was furious.

"Who are you with?" said Jake as they stepped onto the asphalt, and Betty wasn't sure what to say to him. Instead, she turned to Nickel.

"Let me handle this," she said, but Nickel didn't say anything back, and then Jake was walking quickly toward them.

"I asked who the fuck you were with."

Betty felt like she was being filmed for some stupid teenage soap opera. "He's a friend," she said as she took a step toward Jake, and then there was something buzzing toward her face, and she dropped to the ground as though she'd been shot, her mind dull and murky.

This wasn't supposed to happen. *We were supposed to go to the house.* That something else was wrong had yet to occur to her. Betty struggled to stand, but she felt drunk, felt like that time she'd taken a bong rip while she stood on Kevin Felman's kitchen table and then had to be helped down.

Someone yelled, "Fucker!" from some impossible distance away, and then Betty rolled over to see Jake stalking Nickel. Blood was dripping from Jake's nose, and Betty wanted to shout to Nickel to get away from him, that Jake was a good kid but that he was also strong as an ox and probably just as impossible to knock out. Jake did varsity wrestling, and he'd played lacrosse and hockey, but Nickel had said he knew her from Rhino's gym. Somewhere in the distance an adult was yelling as Jake closed on Nickel.

Betty watched Jake throw a haymaker, the kind of punch meant to devastate. The blow had been thrown from Jake's waist and would have ended the fight—*Is this a fight over me?*—as swiftly as it had begun. The problem was that Nickel wasn't there when the punch landed. He was feinting to his right and peppering a jab into Jake's face, staggering Jake slightly as the blow glanced off his ear. Jake shook the injury off immediately, though, launching another attic-clearing haymaker, but once again the punch missed as Nickel bounced away. Jake's hands came instinctively up as Nickel circled to his right, but Nickel kicked at Jake instead of punching, and even from where Betty was slowly trying to stand she could tell the kick had heat. Jake staggered as Nickel's shin and instep found purchase against the meat of his thigh.

Betty wanted to scream at them to stop, to make it end. A part of her wanted none of that, however. There was a slowly growing realization that somehow, impossibly, this fight hadn't started over a girl. It had started because Jake had punched her and Betty wanted to see him hurt.

Shit, be careful, thought Betty as she dragged the car keys from her pocket. The normally easy task was made arduous through the fog in her mind, and then she slipped and took a knee on the blacktop as her fingers finally found the key ring. She watched as Jake threw another frustrated haymaker at Nickel, and once again

Nickel was able to dodge the punch and kick Jake. This time the kick landed on Jake's inner thigh, and he howled and screamed, "You dirty-assed little chickenshit! Fight like a fucking man!"

Betty stood, sea legs coming back now, and saw Jake throw another punch that Nickel managed to avoid. The latest dodge was less clean than the last two, but this time the answering kick was better timed and caught Jake squarely in the crotch, making a sound like a mallet squashing plums. Jake shrieked and fell to the ground, his hands cupped over his groin and blood still pouring from his nose.

The adult yelling in the background was louder now, and Betty wobbled away across the parking lot to her car, turning to see Nickel wind up as if he were kicking a penalty shot in a World Cup match. Jake's head snapped backwards, launching a spray of blood, teeth, and misery as Nickel's Converse All Star found its target.

Jake was screaming now, and then Nickel was across the lot to Betty, grabbing her under her arm and half-carrying her into the passenger seat of her car and then taking the keys from her hand. Whoever the adult was hadn't gotten any closer, at least as far as Betty could tell, and then Nickel was in the seat next to her and flooring the gas as he pulled out of the parking lot.

"You can't drive," said Betty. Her voice sounded like it was coming from somewhere far away and from someone else's mouth. "You acted like you'd never even been in a car before, much less driven one."

Nickel's hands were wrapped so tightly around the wheel that Betty could see white skin stretched across his knuckles, along with blood. Blood that had come from Jake. Betty felt her own forehead, the sight of the blood on Nickel making her realize that she'd been doing some bleeding of her own.

"I can drive," he said. "At least I think I can." He turned to look at her, and terrifyingly, didn't seem to like what he saw. "We need to get you some help, Betty. That bastard really got you good." Betty smiled drunkenly at Nickel, and then the world went black.

FORTY-EIGHT

I tell her I can drive, and maybe it's true, but right now I feel like the only place I'll be driving us to is jail. Betty's head is lolling on the seat next to me, and it doesn't take an expert to see she's in bad shape. I turn on the ignition and look in the rearview mirror to see that asshole concussed on the pavement, and then there's someone running up the hill, probably the same do-gooder adult that was doing all the yelling.

I look to Betty for help in getting this vehicle moving, see that there's none coming, and then mash my foot on the brake and slide the shifter into reverse. I let off the brake and the car jerks backward, and then I stomp the brake again, move the shifter to drive, and smash the gas pedal. I've never done this before, but there's a hurt kid on the pavement, Betty probably has a concussion of her own, and it's time to go.

I drive without thinking, and that's probably for the best. I never considered that I might have to drive a car, at least not until I was eighteen, and now I'm driving under duress with an unconscious minor next to me. Sweat is pouring off my forehead, and memories from the fight start to trickle in. All I see are little flashes of it as I pilot the car, but I know I won, and that my friend Rhino would be proud of me. After all, I adhered to the basic rules of a street fight: keep moving, and don't stop hurting your opponent until you know they can't hurt you, or you can escape.

I'd feel bad for Jake—he wasn't planning on seeing Betty with me—but when I think of him hitting her I get mad all over again. It wasn't just Jake I saw in that parking lot, either. I was still reeling from talking to Claire and having seen her getting knocked to her knees, so it was easy to imagine Jack standing across from me as well. Visualizing the hospital, I take a too-fast left turn past a pair of honking and furious drivers. I give them a wave, and then hit the gas again. I want this to be over more than just about anything.

Betty is stirring as we take another left. I give her a look to see if she's responsive, and then her head rolls to the right and I know she's out again. There has to be something I can do, but there isn't. All I've got is going with what the world is throwing at me, and keeping in my back pocket the idea that if I crash this car Betty is not going to be OK. I barely know her, but the thought of losing her makes me feel sick. She's been the only thing making me feel human lately. I'm the one who's supposed to be doing the work she's doing. I'm the one Dad gave a mission to, but she's the one out trying to make things right while I'm mired in a drug deal, so I can hold on to my life. If I'm not careful, the house and everything else could just slip away, and to avoid that, I need a cash injection.

I whip a quick right. The car's controls are finally starting to make sense, and so is everything else. I resent myself for feeling good after a fight—it's too animalistic, too basic—but it's what I was born for. Dad wanted me to be a warrior, trained me up to be everything he dreamed a kid in my position could be. And it worked. He just died while school was still in session. That doesn't matter. I've been my own guide for years, seeking out men like Rhino to help me forge myself into iron, and now I need to get back to making good on what Dad wanted for me.

The hospital comes into sight, and at that exact moment, Betty comes around. I want to be happy—it's a huge release—but she grabs the wheel and gives me a drunken look. My gut says to knock her off the wheel, to get her the rest of the way there and let the pieces fall where they may, but her words have me nailing the brake instead.

"Get out," she says.

I pull the car to the curb and throw it into park.

"I have to finish," she says. "They have cameras everywhere."

I'm not arguing, but I do help pull her over the center console. I want to ask her if she's sure, if this is really what she wants, but I'm out of the car and Betty nails the gas before the door is even closed, and I watch as the road curves and she disappears.

FORTY-NINE

Betty woke in a white room. She was completely unsure of where she was, and then the moms were standing over her. Sure she was dreaming, Betty reached a hand up toward Andrea, and when her mother took it in hers, Betty knew this was no dream.

"What happened?" Betty asked, but as the words fell from her mouth she remembered everything. Nickel, the plan, Jake hitting her, and Nickel beating the shit out of Jake and then somehow driving her. Betty began to sit up—Nickel had to be in the room somewhere and she wanted to thank him—but strong arms pushed her back into place on the bed.

"You need to stay down, Betty," said Ophelia. "You have a concussion."

Betty turned to Andrea. Her other mother was nodding slowly. "You do. Nothing you won't recover from, but thank God you had the sense to get yourself to safety. I don't know quite how you did it in your condition, but I'm glad you did."

Betty opened her mouth to tell them that she didn't, that Nickel had, but the thought of telling her mothers about Nickel in that moment seemed like a horrible idea.

"I'm just glad that you and Jake are OK," said Ophelia. "We're not happy you were hanging out with him again, but we're glad you were able to get away from whoever attacked you."

"The police are going to want to discuss that when you're ready, Betty," said Andrea. "They're talking to Jake right now. He's in worse shape than you, I'm afraid."

Betty shook her aching head. This was all wrong. Everything that the moms and the cops thought had happened was wrong. There hadn't been some imaginary mugger who attacked them while Jake heroically defended her. Jake had punched her in the head and would have done who-knows-what if Nickel hadn't been there.

"We weren't mugged," she said, "and I wasn't hanging out with Jake."

The moms shared a look above her, their faces making it quite clear that neither of them believed her. "You don't need to try and get yourself out of trouble," said Andrea. "We can talk about that later, once you're feeling more yourself again."

"You need to listen to me." She pushed their hands aside and pulled herself into a sitting position. "I was talking to this guy I met in the park, and I never even caught his name. We were just talking about nonsense, and then I was walking back to my car and Jake must have been spying on me or something, because he was there waiting for me. He hit me hard, really hard on the side of my head, and then everything after that is really foggy. Jake hit me, not some mugger."

Ophelia looked shocked, but Andrea's face was pure rage, more mad than Betty could ever recall having seen her before.

"I'm going to talk to Van Endel," said Andrea to no one in particular. "You two stay here." Andrea was out of the room in a flash, the door banging shut after her, and then Ophelia was left to stare at Betty.

"Are you sure about this?" she asked.

Betty nodded. "Positive, Mom. That guy in the park might have saved my life."

"Jesus Christ." Ophelia crossed herself, the gesture a relic from a long-forgotten Catholic upbringing. Tears welled in her eyes. "We could have lost you. Good God, we could have lost you." Ophelia let her go and pulled back. "No more adventures, Betty. Just finish off the school year and make it nice and boring for us, all right?"

"OK," lied Betty. She already felt like she was escaping the fog that clouded her thinking, and judging by the clock on the wall, she'd been at the hospital for at least two hours. *As soon as I'm out of here I'm e-mailing Nickel to thank him, and as soon as I'm able to, we're going to that house. One more little adventure won't hurt anyone.* Betty smiled at Ophelia and her mother smiled back. *The only hard part is going to be insisting that I'm feeling better.*

The door to the room swung back open and a mean-mugged Andrea strode in with a harried-looking Detective Van Endel in tow.

"Tell him what happened," said Andrea.

Van Endel grabbed a chair and sat next to the bed. He still looked tired, or perhaps even a little hungover, but Betty could see that the kind look in his eyes from the day before had been replaced by something hard, even predatory.

"I want to know everything," said Van Endel. "Start at the beginning, and don't stop until I tell you I'm bored."

———

The questioning in the hospital room took a little over an hour, and though both Van Endel and the moms seemed distrustful about certain parts of Betty's account of the afternoon, by the time it was done the group agreed that Jake Norton was going to be in a world of hurt. Van Endel was unable to tell them exactly what he thought the district attorney might choose to charge Jake with, but he figured that assault with intent to do great bodily harm seemed a good starting point.

The other thing the three adults agreed upon was that Jake Norton was going to be pretty well fucked, physically as well as legally, as a result of the afternoon's activities. Betty wasn't quite sure why, but there was a part of her that found that to be very sad. Jake had done something unforgivable, Betty readily agreed, but the simple fact was that, as long as her condition remained the same, she would be going home in the morning. Van Endel assured her that would not be the case for Jake.

"Jake is going to be fine," he said, "but he'll probably be spending some time at the dentist, maybe even a plastic surgeon." Van Endel cocked his head. "I know we've been over this, Betty, but are you sure you don't remember anything about the person who helped you after Jake hit you?"

"Positive," said Betty. "The last thing I remember is Jake hitting me. Everything from then until the time I woke up here is gone."

"It might come back," he said, "and if it does I want you to let your mother know."

Andrea turned to him. "I'm not sure I'd call you even if she did remember, Dick. That boy may well have saved her life."

Van Endel opened his mouth as if to say something, and then closed it slowly. After a moment he said, "You just do what you think is best, Andrea. But the fact is, that boy in there is pretty profoundly messed up. That was one savage beating. I was talking to his doctor before you came to get me, and in addition to the facial injuries he suffered, there was a good deal of damage done to his—"

"Dick, I'm serious," said Andrea. "I don't care how hurt that kid might be. Betty can't remember who her savior is, and that's just going to have to be that."

Van Endel nodded. It was clear he was torn between his duty to his job and his loyalty to Andrea. "I guess that will be that," he said. He patted Betty's arm. "I hope you get to feeling better soon," he said and then left the room.

When the door was shut behind him, Andrea cracked her knuckles and said, "Oh, that kid is so screwed."

Betty didn't know why, but there was something about the words that made her feel as if a part of her was dying inside. Jake hadn't been perfect—and especially not earlier today—but he'd been a good boyfriend for the most part. She didn't want to attempt to excuse any part of his attack on her, but at the same time, all he'd wanted was to be with her, and she'd treated him like shit toward the end.

"Just let it be, Andrea," said Ophy softly. "He's already hurt, and you better than anyone know what dark paths can cause something like this to happen. We don't need to like that boy, but there's no need to gloat."

Andrea grunted in response, but Betty closed her eyes and lay back on the bed before she could hear what else her mothers had to say. She was sure that she'd just rest her eyes for a moment, but when she opened them again it was morning.

FIFTY

Acceptance is the key, I tell myself. I can accept that I'm going to sell marijuana for less than it's worth to a man I really don't like because I need money.

That only lasts a second. Because what I really can't accept is the memory of that coloring book and the child sitting on the stairs. I can't know that the facedown woman in the kitchen is his mother, but I *know* it all the same, just like I know to look for cracks if I'm buying eggs.

It's Nick and Eleanor from foster care all over again. It's Sam. That poor kid on the stairs is already learning how to be a victim.

That kid could be me. It's a lead weight in my guts, and it's eating me alive. He could be me, and in a lot of ways, he *is* me. But, of course, the chances of him finding a man like Dad are almost nonexistent. *You can help* is the mantra in my head, and all I can think of is Nick and Eleanor. *Nick-El.* They're still out there, somewhere, two people broken by the system and the monsters who abuse it. Monsters aren't just in fairy tales. I know that, and so do they. All of us do, all of us forgotten children with secrets, secrets that we're never, ever to tell anyone about. Secrets that will mold our entire lives.

I know what I should do, what I have to do, but my mind keeps coming back to it like a tongue over a missing tooth. There's what's right, and there's what's necessary, and both of them are pulling at my heart like a pair of wild horses.

I need a plan, so I make one, and then I remind myself about what's really important. I can't save every child, I know that, but something in me has awakened, and I'll be damned if I'm going to put it to bed before it can eat.

It was seeing Jack, talking to Claire, the fight, the ride in the car, having someone depend on me again. I know that probably sounds incredibly childish, but it's true. I think people can stand taller when someone needs them, and that was what happened today with Betty. I wanted to run away, just like I want to run away from this problem, but the easy road is rarely the right one.

I walk to the garage and load the dope into the bike trailer. Even full, the trailer is still light. The pot might be bulky, but it's only fifteen pounds, and the stroller can take far more weight than that.

I check my watch. It's five to seven, but I'm wired. My thoughts are on Betty and Duke and on that poor kid at Paul's house. They're two separate problems, but intertwined all the same, and I know Dad is out there watching to see if I do the right thing. *I can, I know I can. It's what I am.*

The page comes through a couple minutes later, but I have to shake myself out of the fog I was in. The zero is my safe place. It's dark, black, and bleak, but that's the best place to go when you're scared. Remembering you came from nothing and every day is a blessing is a fine place to be, especially in times like this. The buzzing in my pocket snaps me out of it, though, and I know I'm on the right path.

Paul answers on the first ring, there's silence, and then words out of a dream. "Riverside Park, right now, alone," says Paul.

He couldn't have picked a more perfect place. I say, "I'll be there," and then the phone goes dead. I shove it back in my pocket, then pat the trailer twice on the roof, like I'm rewarding a loyal dog. I need this plan to work, and if I'm lucky the rest will just fall into place. Giving it one last look, I climb atop my bike, hit the clicker on the garage, and roll onto dusky streets. This is my world.

I make the park in about twenty minutes, and I'm happy to see when I hit Riverside that not only is it deserted, but dusk has turned to full dark. I'm sure that this was what Paul wanted, too: a nice quiet place to lowball me on money and make threats, but I'm ready for him. I have threats of my own, and even though he can't see it, I've got a big hammer poised and ready.

Lights flicker in the parking lot where Lou picked me up four years ago with a gunshot wound in my arm, and it feels like a homecoming. I can see a van with two people standing by it. Paul said come alone, but I guess that rule didn't cover him.

I see the lumps in their clothing as I roll up—barely concealed guns. There's nothing I can do but ride right up to them.

"Look at this shit," says Paul. I think he figured his friend would laugh at the joke, but he doesn't and an uncomfortable silence fills the air. He knows there's no joke. I brought the stuff they want, and he's only messing around because somehow this kid rolling up on a bike for his deal makes him feel like less of a man. It's a small victory. He keeps flogging the joke: "What, you babysitting?"

I shake my head as I step off the bike. "Not yet. Everything's in the trailer."

Paul nods at his guy, and the dude comes over to give the stuff a look. He fiddles with the zippers on the trailer for a minute, finally figures it out, and then pulls the door open and sticks his head in.

"Four bales," says the guy, his voice muffled, and Paul smiles.

"Get it."

The buddy grabs some dope, walks it to the van, and then rolls on back. No one has mentioned money yet. He's just unloading my stuff and walking to the van, and I'm not sure if I should remind Paul this is a two-way street.

It's Paul who brings it up, though. "We never talked money," he says. "You know what that means?"

"It means we need a number."

"Yeah, we do," he says with a chuckle, and I want to punch him in the throat. I don't, though. I just stand pat, waiting for the bad news to drop.

"I can do $5,000 on this," says Paul, and I nod slowly. It's not a bad price, but he and I both know the pot's worth a lot more, especially once it's broken down to street prices. Still, it's a good lump sum, and I need the money for the house. "Go weigh that shit in the van," he calls to the other man, and Paul's crony disappears into the back of the vehicle.

"$5,000 will work," I say. "This time. Next time it's going to need to be more."

"We'll see how long this takes to move, Nickel. Might be less, might be more. Time will tell." We turn as the other man pops out of the van.

"Fifteen pounds, man, right on the money."

"Excellent," says Paul with a nod. He shoves his right hand into a pocket on his jacket, and when he takes it out there's a roll of money. Banded twenties have never looked so good. He hands it over, and I make the cash disappear without counting it. That will come later. "All right, Nickel. You let me know when you can do this again."

"One more thing," I say, and Paul turns to look at me, irritation visible in his eyes. "There was a kid staying at that house with you, and he didn't look good. Will you make sure—"

"I'm not staying there no more," says Paul. "We pulled out yesterday, as a matter of fact. Not that it's any of your goddamn business."

"So the kid—"

"What the hell?" Paul's getting annoyed. "Why the hell are we talking about this bitch and her kid?"

I keep my voice even. "Because the kid looked messed up to me. The mom, too, but that's not—"

"I'll say the mom's messed up," Paul says with a toxic laugh. "Likes the nose candy way too much. Caught a bad blow-cold. That was her laid up on the floor the last time you were there." He squints at me like he honestly can't imagine why I'd care about any of this. "Listen, don't worry your bleeding heart, Nickel. Either she'll come around or the kid will eventually catch wise and head to the neighbors. All I know is I wasn't going to stick around to hold her hand." He shakes his head, and I force myself to stay calm. "Dumb bitch, but hey, junkies are junkies." He's smiling that smile that makes me want to rip his throat out. "So hey, Nickel, if our little social services talk is over, I'm going to bounce. Let me know when you want to make some more money."

He's in the van and gone just a few moments later, and I'm left staring into the night. The money is a hard lump in my pocket, but I don't care about that right now.

I walk back to the bike and board it. My thoughts are on that little boy on the stairs, and on Sam and the small hole in the snowy ground. I start pedaling, the trailer behind me fifteen pounds lighter, and I'm rolling without looking back. The night is here now, but I still have one more thing to do before I can go home.

———

I make it to the house where I'd met up with Paul in a little under a half hour. Not bad for biking in the dark, but I'm already tired of the trailer.

I park in the driveway. It does look like Paul and all his buddies have pulled out, just like he said—at least, all of the showy cars from before are gone. I tell myself all I need to do is knock. A good, simple ending. Knock, find the little guy and his mom, either get them to go for some help or make sure some help goes to them. The hairs on the back of my neck are standing up, though.

Enough negativity. Enough paranoia. I knock on the door three times, try the bell, and then give the knob a spin.

The door opens, and I slide inside and walk down the same hallway Rio led me down last time I was here, doing my best to be quiet. The house is still and silent, but I'm beyond paranoid that trouble is going to roar out of the darkness. I slip into the space between the kitchen and the living room. The TV, Xbox, and everything but the mess has disappeared from the living room. When I look into the kitchen I sigh, like I really expected that woman would still be lying there.

I head to the stairs. They're dark, but I can see the coloring book is still on the landing. My nerves feel electric, and as I head up the stairs my optimism for a happy ending is sinking. I'm just some dumb kid, I shouldn't even be here, but I am and that's all that matters.

There're no lights on upstairs, either. I want to pull the flashlight from my pocket but I don't. I'm still not convinced I'm alone. There are three doors off the upstairs hall, but only one of them is closed and that's the one I go to, giving only the most cursory looks into the other two.

As I try the knob, I know it won't spin, but it does, and the door swings open. It's dark, but I can see shapes. A bed with a lump on it, a dark mass on the floor that I don't want to look at. My heart feels like it's going to explode when the lump on the bed stirs. The darkness makes it impossible to tell what it is, but then it all makes sense.

I take a step into the room and say, "It's OK, buddy. Come here."

The boy does, the boy from the steps. He's shaking, probably starved half to death on top of everything else that's happened.

He slips off the bed and skirts the shadowy mass on the floor, and when I pick him up it feels like picking up a bunch of sticks. This is what real skin and bones feels like. I leave the room with him in my arms, and the boy is crying against my chest.

"It's OK," I say, but I know it isn't. The boy's mother is dead in that room, and he's been sitting in there with her, probably praying that she'd wake up. I know that was her on the floor. I couldn't help but look at her when I bent down to pick him up. Even in the darkness I can see the bruises on her face and on her throat, black ones, along with a mask of blood on the lower half of her face. I take a deep breath, absorb the rage, and then say, "I'm Nickel, what's your name?"

"Ben," he says, and we go down the stairs together, and then leave the house.

I'm not going to tell you what I said to Ben when I put him in the trailer, because that's for us, the lost children, but I think he understood.

I was a kid like that, and Dad found me. I have a place where Ben can go, to a friend of mine who would be even harsher to Paul and his friends than I want to be. I get pedaling and head there. I know he'll be there—he always is when I need him—and I know what he'll say when I introduce him to Ben. *"Vou encontrar-lhe um lugar."* I'll find him a place.

Just as important, this business with Paul is now a lot bigger than money. I could have taken care of him when we made the deal, I know that, but I'll find another way. I have to. It's bad for business for another doper to disappear, bad for me to be attached to it, but none of that matters anymore. Sam in the snow, Ben in my arms, Dad teaching me what was right and wrong. Paul has a debt, and I'm going to collect on it.

FIFTY-ONE

The day after Betty's discharge from the hospital was hell. Ophelia took the day off of painting, and Andrea even took a personal day from her job. The moms crowded her like they never had before, too much for her to do even as much as e-mail Nickel or text her friends to let them know what had happened. Not that Betty had much doubt about their knowledge of what had taken place. It would have been impossible to think the story hadn't raged through the high school like a midsummer wildfire.

People are going to know about it, and you're going to have to accept that.

Betty had rolled the words over and over in her head, but by the time she was actually driving to school two days after the attack, the advice no longer seemed relevant.

She knew people were going to talk, and she knew she was going to hate it. Not that stories like hers didn't turn out a lot worse on a pretty frequent basis. She'd have known that even if Andrea hadn't drilled it into her head. It was hard to feel lucky, though, knowing that her name was going to be in everyone's mouth. Her head didn't look that bad, but she did have a wicked black eye, along with a few scrapes from landing on the pavement.

Betty let these thoughts tumble through her mind like clothes in the spin cycle as she drove to school, but it wasn't until she was pulling into the lot that she had the revelation that this was exactly the sort of abuse Mandy had gone through. It had all turned out worse for June's aunt, of course, but had it started with just a random act of cruelty? The conclusions Betty had settled on at the prison now seemed childish. Duke had cared for Mandy, but what did that have to do with anything? After all, Jake had cared for *her*, and he could have easily killed her if she'd fallen on her head wrong. Or if Nickel hadn't been there.

Betty parked and walked into the school. She could see a gaggle of freshman girls talking behind their hands, but she paid them no mind. Even if they hadn't been freshmen, Betty had bigger fish to fry, but that would have to wait until fourth period. Right now all she had to do was survive and not make a spectacle of herself.

The halls didn't become quiet as Betty walked into the school, but there was a lull in the cacophony typically present by the junior lockers. Betty tried to ignore the drop in noise and was comfortable enough to lock eyes with anyone who stared at her too intently. In every case but one, the owner of the too-curious eyes pulled her gaze away. The last one was June.

"Oh my God," said June as she grabbed Betty's arm and dragged her through the packed hallway.

Somehow her friend's interest had lessened their peers' interest in the high school spectacle, and Betty felt so thankful for June grabbing her that she wanted to burst into tears. Instead of crying, she said, "Thanks for coming to get me. They're like a bunch of piranha that smell blood."

"Nothing new about that," said June. "C'mon, I'll walk you to first period and you can fill me in on what exactly happened."

"Oh God," said Betty, "I'm not sure I want to tell you or anyone else. But anyway, I can't tell you jack until fourth period."

"I knew it," said June, her grin more appropriate for a shark than a best friend. "I totally guessed it. I wish I had some money riding on him."

"What do you mean?"

"I've been thinking about who could have given Jake Norton a run for his money," June explained, "and there was only one name that came to mind. How bad was it?"

"Well, my head still hurts," said Betty, "but it hasn't been long enough for—"

"I don't mean that," June interrupted. "I mean the ass whipping Nickel put on Jake. How bad are we talking? Like, I get that it was hospital bad, but—"

"Oh my God," said Betty after recovering enough from what June was saying in front of all of these people to speak. "You need to shut up immediately. We can't talk about him, and we can never talk about him like this."

"But—"

"Fourth period. Not another word about this until fourth period."

June nodded, and then mimed zipping her lips, fastening them with a key, and pitching the imaginary key over her shoulder.

Betty smiled at the purse-lipped June, and the two of them burst into laughter as the bell rang to signal the beginning of first period.

———

"I've been waiting all day," said June, "so spill."

They were sitting at their usual place at the back of the library. Two of the library's recently-updated-but-still-outdated desktop computers were fired up to various pages littered with information on the Duke case, but neither of them was looking at the computers.

"I don't suppose I have a choice in the matter?"

"Oh, hell no," said June. "I want to hear about the knight in shining armor, so make with the goods."

Betty shook her head, unsure whether she wanted to laugh or cry. She'd gotten a concussion, Jake had been badly beaten, and Nickel could've gotten into some really serious trouble. And, weirdly, the idea of Nickel getting in trouble was even scarier than any injury she herself could have incurred without his timely interruption.

"I met Nickel in the park to talk about going to the house where Mandy died," she said. "We were walking back up from the bench, and then I saw Jake in the parking lot. He was waiting by my car, pacing back and forth, and when he saw Nickel and me he raced over to us. I tried to get between them, mostly so I could talk some sense into Jake, but before I could even really say anything, Jake punched me in the side of the head."

"What a piece of shit," said June. "Seriously."

"Pretty much," said Betty, "but what happened next was crazy. Nickel basically ruined Jake. He was kicking his legs and dancing around him, and then he kicked him right in the balls and Jake fell over and started screaming. I was almost to my car, and when I looked back, I turned to see Nickel kick Jake in the mouth really hard." Betty swallowed thickly. "It was pretty gross."

"So are the cops looking for Nickel?"

Betty shook her head. "No. I told them I didn't know who helped me, and Andrea pressured the cop to let it go. It blew away the detective I talked to the other day. Jake had been telling him a story about how we had been hanging out and got mugged. I think Jake thought I would be too messed up to remember anything."

"That's horrible," said June, and the look on her face made it clear she meant it.

"Yeah, pretty much. The only positive thing to take away from it is that because the moms both had to take a day off to see me at the hospital, and then another one to stay with me at home, they're going to be superbusy at work. I promised them I was done with adventures, but all I've been able to think about since Jake hit me is the house where Mandy died, and about Duke."

"What about Duke?"

"You know how we both came away from the prison thinking he was innocent? I think I might have changed my mind. Just because Duke loved Mandy doesn't mean he didn't hurt her. In fact, that could just provide even more evidence it *was* him. There probably isn't much left of Duke and Mandy in that house, but I still want to look inside. Are you still game?"

"Yes, all the way."

"Good," said Betty with a smile, the grin causing a ripple of pain to flow through her face. *Even now I can't be happy because of Jake.* In that moment Betty hated him more than any person she'd ever met, but she still felt sympathy for him. Jake had let his temper destroy his foreseeable future, and even though she had been hurt, Jake was going to be the one to feel the real pain. The physical wounds would heal quickly, but if he happened to be charged as an adult, the rest of his life was going to wear an asterisk next to it. Betty frowned, making the pain flare up again, and then said, "June, did you ever talk to your dad?"

"No. Maybe tonight."

"But probably not, right?"

"Yeah, probably not," said June. "Besides, my dad is going to be useless compared to what could be in the house. He might not know anything at all about what happened, or like most things with my dad, he'll have some awful theory or tell us about how Mandy deserved it, and that he still thinks so."

The bell rang, making both of them jump, and as they gathered their things and signed out of the library desktop computers,

Betty shouldered her bag and said, "I'll e-mail Nickel after school. If he's up for it and I can get out of the house, I want to go to that house tonight. Are you in?"

FIFTY-TWO

Betty had been prepared to e-mail Nickel and ask if he wanted to go on exactly the sort of adventure she had assured her mothers that she was over, but there was a pair of messages from him waiting for her in her inbox. The first one said simply, "Let me know if you still want to go to the house. Hope you're feeling better. N." Betty responded, "Yes!" and asked him if she could meet him at the gas station by his house.

The second of the two, a few hours older, said, "Think this is him?" followed by a masked hyperlink that said, "Hmmmm." Betty clicked the link, which led to the Facebook page of someone named Anne Lattrell. There were numerous pictures of this Anne and what appeared to be members of her family, as well as a man—presumably her husband—with whom she was shown going to amusement parks and posing for cheesy portraits. This man—balding, at least semi-well-off, happy—looked nothing like the image conjured up in Betty's mind of how an aged Jason Lattrell would look.

Betty wasn't quite sure why this profile was on Nickel's radar, and then she got to the bottom end of the photo gallery and saw pictures of a tired-looking, skinnier, hairier, long-ago version of Anne's husband, a maybe-Jason posing in front of a brick wall with a group of other punk rock kids. Duke and Mandy were nowhere to be seen, but the manner of dress was correct for the time period. Betty wondered if current-day Jason even knew the picture was on here. He looked like hell. The picture was surrounded by shots of Anne with braces, Anne wearing a figure-skating dress, and Anne with her parents in a graduation robe, but the picture of the maybe-Jason was posed in front of a very familiar address: 4527. Betty knew without a doubt the house had to be on Lincoln, and if Duke was telling the truth, had probably been taken around the time Mandy was killed.

It's not a smoking gun or a confession, or even proof of a man in a green jacket, but it's something.

Betty flipped back to her e-mail and saw that Nickel had responded to her, saying simply, "Gas station, as soon as possible." Betty snapped her computer closed, left the room, and bounced down the steps. She walked to the closed basement door, funk rock again pouring through the seams, and called to Ophelia, saying, "I'm going to June's house, to study, OK?"

"All right," said Ophelia. "Call me if anything changes or if your head hurts too much to drive."

"OK, thanks," shouted Betty, the lump of guilt in her throat almost too much to swallow. Lying had been bad enough before Jake had attacked her, but now that she'd made her other promise, everything about their research was just a further extension of the same lie.

It's too late to worry about that. This is more important than a lie and more important than school.

Betty dialed June as she drove, but was forced to leave a message when there was no answer. Leaving her phone on her knee so she wouldn't miss anything—every parent's worst fear: a teenager far more in tune with the phone than the road—Betty and her car made it unscathed to a waiting Nickel at the gas station. Nickel got in just as the phone began to ring, and Betty waved at Nickel as she answered it.

"Hey," said June. "What's up?"

"I'm driving to that house with Nickel. Are you in?"

"I wish. I have to go to my dad's again. Some insurance forms he needs to sign so Mom can fax them in, and then he's going to work on my car. I might try to talk to him about Mandy, but honestly, I don't think I'll actually do it. It seems bad enough before I'm in front of him, but it's impossible once I'm actually there."

"Sorry," said Betty. "Well, hopefully I can get a hold of you later and we can fill each other in."

"Yeah, well, much later, maybe. I'm going to be stuck there for a few hours at least. Today is over already, as far as I can tell."

"That sucks," said Betty.

"Totes," said June. "But I have to get over there. He can keep me waiting for hours at a time, but if I'm ten minutes late with him, I'm dead meat. I'll let you know how it goes."

When they'd said good-bye, Betty turned to Nickel. "Well, looks like it's just the two of us."

"Fine by me," he said, then cracked a thin smile. "Unless you have any other angry admirers that have set off after you for revenge. If so, I'd really like to know ahead of time."

"Yeah, sorry about that," said Betty, but instead of blushing, she was smiling. "He was a pretty good guy for a long time, and now, well, you saw what happened."

"He must have cared about you a lot," said Nickel. "People can be funny when they're hurt like that, or scared for a loved one. That's why moms can lift cars off of toddlers and why defense attorneys use terms like *crime of passion*."

"Yeah," said Betty, "he loved me so much he punched me in the head."

"It's not as strange as it sounds. I bet if you asked most people who killed a loved one, they'd be confused, remorseful, and possibly even in denial when they were confronted with what they'd done."

"People are crazy," said Betty. "Jake was telling the cops all about how someone mugged us and beat him up when he was trying to protect me. I thought he'd just lied through his teeth, but hell, maybe he really believed it. That actually makes some sense." Betty paused and then said, "Well, as much sense as getting beaten up by your ex-boyfriend can."

"So what did you tell the police about me?" Nickel asked as Betty turned out of the gas station, and Betty smiled.

"Do you really think I would tell them anything?"

"I don't know," he said with a shrug. "I mean, I know what my threshold is for lying during something like that, but I don't know yours."

"Well, I didn't say anything," said Betty. "I told the cops I made a friend at the park, Jake just came out of nowhere and attacked us, and that was the last thing I remember."

"Did you give them a description? It's OK if you did, I just need to know if I need a haircut and some new clothes."

"No, I couldn't do that," she said. "My mom let the cop know that everything was OK, and that was the end of it."

"You're just lucky they believed you," said Nickel. "Me in that same situation, I'd be completely fucked."

"You'd be OK," said Betty. "It's not like it would be your fault you got hurt, and eventually your dad would have made everything all right with the cops, no matter what they decided to believe."

After a beat of silence, Nickel asked, "Do you think Jake's parents are making everything OK for him?"

"No," Betty allowed. There was a flinty look in Nickel's eyes, not a cruel one, but something cold and impermeable. Not for the first time, it occurred to Betty that she really never was going to know all there was to know about this boy, and perhaps no one on earth really did. "I'm sorry," she said. "I wasn't trying to presume anything."

"I know," said Nickel. "It's just hard for me to think in shades of gray. Everything in my life is either peachy or a complete disaster, and it's a razor's edge that separates them. I could tell you stories that you'd never believe, but there's no point. I'd just look like a fool."

"No, you wouldn't. I'd never want you to feel like that on my account, especially not if you promised me you were telling the truth."

Betty was inching her right hand closer to Nickel's on the console when Nickel said, "Hold up," and she jerked her hand away as if it had been scalded.

Nickel was just looking at her with a grin. "We're here."

Betty smiled at him and then parked the car.

FIFTY-THREE

The neighborhood was a ruin, exactly the sort of place a girl like Mandy would have been killed in. It was the sort of post-apocalyptic suburb that moistened movie producers' panties at the thought of the money they'd be saving, the kind of neighborhood that made its way onto placards telling people that something had to be done.

This was the sort of place Betty and her friends had been warned away from their whole lives, but now here she was, feeling as out of place and vulnerable as a newborn child.

She stood next to her car, staring at a house. The door and windows were boarded shut, black gaps showing through the missing boards like the spaces between knocked-out teeth. To Betty, it seemed impossible that ten minutes in a car could take her to such a place. She knew there were people who lived with less than she did, but this was an unimaginable level of poverty and desolation.

Mandy lived here. Mandy died here.

"C'mon," said Nickel as he walked toward the house with a duffel bag in his hands.

Betty wanted to follow him, but her feet felt nailed to the street. Finally she began to move toward him, not entirely sure if her feet were moving under her own power or if something far worse was beckoning her to the house, a siren song that Nickel was too brave to see for what it was. *Death.* That was what the house cried to Betty. As she moved toward it, she decided that was just as it should be. *I am here because of death, so what else did I expect?*

Nickel grinned back at her, his smile an odd joke under the circumstances. *He smiles because he's afraid,* thought Betty, *but for him, there is joy in being afraid. What fire forges someone like this?* There was time to wonder but not to solve the bizarre puzzle.

Nickel was happy here, so why shouldn't she be?

Betty smiled as well as she was able, took an offered flashlight from Nickel's open bag, and looked over her shoulder to make certain they weren't being watched. The neighborhood was as quiet as Nickel's, but in a far more sinister way. There, curtains had been closed, but she knew the houses were lived in. Here, everything appeared abandoned, but it was impossible to tell how many pairs of eyes were set upon them.

Nickel walked to where the front door of the house had once been. Attached to the door were several signs warning against entry, a faded and cracked strip of police tape, and a barely legible notice marking the house as condemned. Ignoring all of it, Nickel began peeling boards from the entryway as if he owned the place. Once the way was clear enough to slip through, he took his own light from the duffel and flicked it on. "Are you ready?" he asked, and when Betty nodded, he slipped inside.

Betty shuddered, gave a last look to the suddenly-no-longer-as-forbidding neighborhood—she could now imagine happily having a picnic on that weed-choked lawn, so long as she didn't have to go inside this house—then flicked on her own light and slid into the gloom.

There was more light in the abandoned house than their flashlights cast. Thin beams of illumination cut through boards in the hastily sealed windows, as well as through the rotting ceiling above them. Yellow police tape littered the inside of the house, "Police

Line" and "Do Not Cross" far less faded than they had been outside the door.

Betty watched Nickel slowly traverse the floor ahead of her, letting his beam guide his eyes while he checked the wood below for rot before trusting it with his full weight. Mimicking him, she started after him, the wood creaking and barking at her as she made her way over it.

Then Nickel stopped a few feet from the front door, at a spot in the hallway that sat at an intersection between the kitchen and living room. "Look."

If there had ever been an effort to clean up the mess made from Mandy's passing, the task had been short-lived and handled lazily. The boards in the hallway were stained a dark blackish brown. Neither Betty nor Nickel spoke as they stood shoulder-to-shoulder and let their flashlights dance over the permanently stained wood.

This is where Duke found her, thought Betty. *Or where he killed her.*

As if to confirm her thinking, Nickel said, "It feels like all of this has been waiting for us to walk in and find it, the place where she died."

Betty nodded, not sure how to answer. The house was exactly as she had figured it would be, but she hadn't been prepared for seeing the dried blood on the floor. That was worse than anything she could have imagined. There wasn't going to be a ghost or some rotting Mandy zombie rushing down the stairs at them, but that stain was worse. It was Mandy's last and only mark on this world, and it had been dismissed and forgotten in the wake of her murder, just like everything else about her. Only Duke, her lover and possible killer, persevered as the last living artifact of her death, and Betty thought that might have been the most unfair thing she'd ever heard.

"Let's go," said Nickel as he stepped gingerly over the stained floor, and then used the beam from his flashlight to point down the hallway. At the end of it Betty could see another boarded-over doorway, but just to their right was a staircase leading up. Nickel headed straight for the steps and then began to ascend them.

Once again Betty followed his lead, but she wanted to shout at him to stop, to tell him they'd made a mistake. *There might not be secrets or bodies buried here, but this sure feels like we're robbing a grave.*

Nickel stopped at the top of the steps and let his light play on the floor, and then Betty slid into the doorway beside him. "Hold up," he said, not that she had any intention of continuing past him. "The floor up here is bad. Look." He toed a shoe onto the floor and Betty watched it sink through the rotten board without a sound. "Broken leg territory."

Betty nodded and let her light twitch over the room's exterior walls. If there'd ever been interior walls, they'd been cleared out to make the upstairs one giant room. Bleached-out flyers hung from the walls, and trash and what could've been smashed bits of furniture (or, really, anything at all) littered the floor.

And there, across the room from them, a barely discernible shape that had been either painted or pressed into the wall. Even with her flashlight, Betty couldn't quite make out what it was, but she was strongly drawn to it.

Feeling the floor with her own foot, Betty found none of the squishy wood Nickel had showed her. Looking down, she could tell why.

"I'm going over there," she said, pointing with the flashlight to the shape and then, lowering the light to the beam she now perceived to be stretching out from her to her goal, she skipped around Nickel's outstretched arm as he tried to block her.

"It's OK," said Betty in answer to Nickel's sputtering, "I'm on a crossbeam. See? Look at the nails." Nickel's beam joined hers at her feet, doubly illuminating the neat line of nail heads she was walking along.

She slid one foot in front of the other, making sure to stay atop the crossbeam, which felt rock-solid under her weight. *Eight years of gymnastics is finally paying off.* Thin rays of light were blasting up from the bottom floor, and Betty smiled as she crossed the ruined room.

I figured it out before Nickel, thought Betty as she made the halfway point across the upper floor. She paused to look back and give him a grin.

Nickel returned her grin with one that was both hopeful and terrified, and then Betty continued her journey.

Her last glance at Nickel had confirmed that she was most definitely on her own. Betty considered whistling as a distraction, when her foot edged just a few inches away from the beam, and the board under her misstep promptly cracked like a rifle shot under her shoe. Without thinking, she simply stepped on past it. Anything else would have turned out poorly.

"Are you OK?" Nickel yelled from what felt like a million miles away.

Betty nodded her flashlight in answer before continuing, shocked that she wasn't panicking. *Is this how a stage and a microphone feel? Is this being alive?* Betty didn't know, she couldn't know, but now she could see what was waiting for her on the wall ahead.

She slid the last fifteen feet without lifting so much as a toe from the line of nail-heads, and when she finally made her way to the wall she let out a sigh she was unaware she'd been holding in.

"It's a heart," she called behind her. "She painted a giant heart on the wall!"

"OK," said Nickel in return. He might not know what it meant, but Betty did. This had been Mandy's heart. This was her private spot, where she cried and fantasized and wished for a way out, but also where she got high and dreamt her opium dreams.

This was her prison and her honeymoon suite.

Betty knew that knowing such a thing was impossible, but she knew it all the same. This was Mandy's spot, it was sacred, and she had earned her way in.

The only problem now was what to do next. As usual, Nickel knew exactly what was required.

"Do you have a knife?" he called to her, and Betty shook her head. "Tap the wall, down by the bottom of the heart," he said. "Give it a good hard knock, but don't lose your balance."

Betty did as she was told, rapping her right knuckle hard against the wall, and the sound that came back wasn't drywall. When she looked at Nickel, she saw he'd heard it, too.

"It's plaster," said Nickel. "You're not going to be able to kick your way through, at least not without falling over. I've got a blade, but I'm not sure I can bring it to you. You've got me beat as far as weight is concerned."

Betty chuckled into her fist despite the perilousness of her position on the beam. Nickel didn't look any bigger than her at all. But then again, she'd seen the fight with Jake. He had to be carrying some heavy muscles around.

"Throw it to me," said Betty.

"No."

"I'm serious. I don't want to waste time dragging my ass back there, so just throw it to me, OK?"

"All right," said Nickel, but Betty saw he was already disagreeing with himself as he dug through the duffel bag. He did something with his fingers and then a knife appeared in them, the wan light from the holes in the ceiling giving it an almost magical glow. "Duck low," he said, holding it by the tip and winding up like a freaking circus knife-thrower. Betty dove to the floor atop her magic crossbeam, then felt and heard something hit the wall above her.

"I think I did it," called Nickel. "Which is weird, because I've never really thrown a knife before."

"You threw it?" asked Betty breathlessly as she stood. The knife was buried halfway down the heart, and Betty gave it a yank to free the thing from the plaster. "I meant toss it to me, or slide it. You know, closed."

She could see Nickel's grin from across the room, despite the dim light. "Oh yeah," he said. "I could've done that. Crap." He laughed a choked-sounding laugh. "I guess I just heard 'throw the knife,' and then I was doing it. I was just following orders. And it worked out pretty well."

Betty wasn't sure what to say to that. "Hang on," she said, happy to change the subject. "I'm going to start cutting the wall."

It was far easier to sink the knife in than it had been to remove it, and after a couple hacks at the heart painted on the wall, Betty understood why. The back inch or so of the blade was serrated, and though the whole blade was sharp, the serrations grabbed on to the plaster and shredded dust onto her forearms. Betty used the thing as carefully as she could, holding the flashlight between the crook of her neck and her shoulder, making sure to keep her fingers away from the blade. When she had carved an outline around half of the heart, Betty began slicing at the other half, forced, finally, to sidle close to the wall to move to the next crossbeam, an exercise she accomplished so quickly it never even occurred to her that she should have been nervous.

Tracing the second half of the heart went far faster. Not only was Betty cutting better, but the new beam was holding her weight as steadily as the one she'd crossed on. Betty ran the knife down the outermost lobe of the heart, and then brought it down to the point at the bottom, finishing with a flourish that was as much for her own ego as it was for Nickel's eyes.

She wasn't sure what to expect now that the tracing was done, but she had figured that something might just magically happen. Instead, the wall was cut, the heart molested, but there was still no reveal. Frustrated, she pulled the knife free from the heart and smacked the wall, and then the heart broke and fell between the floor and the beams . . . and then came a deeper rumble within the wall, and a sound like a small rock slide inside the house.

Nickel whistled, and Betty felt her own thudding heart rise high in her chest as the building continued its complaints, sounding as if it might collapse. And then the noise was gone—save for the occasional screaming of displaced rodents and still-falling crumbs of plaster—and Betty knelt on the crossbeam until her pulse stopped thundering in her ears, and began to search the hole she'd made in the wall.

She shoved the knife into her pocket and used the flashlight to help her look for the diary she was convinced was there. Some of the floor of the revealed space within the wall had fallen away, and all that remained were bits of plaster and loose nails. *It has to be here*, thought Betty. *There's nowhere else that would have been safe enough for her to hide her thoughts from Duke, and for the police to have missed it in their search.* No matter how sure Betty was of its placement, however, the diary still eluded her. She leaned further into the hole and went from methodical searching of the detritus there to frantic scratching and banging.

"Calm down!" called Nickel across the span, and the sound of his voice made Betty nearly teeter off the beam. "You need to look more gently. We don't know what condition anything in there might be in, and you don't want to ruin it by rushing."

"All right," she said, but she only slowed her pace for a moment, then redoubled her efforts. *There's nothing here.* The idea of having to cross the room and its rotten floor empty-handed made her feel like she could throw up. But at last she had to pull herself out of the hole in the wall and face facts.

"There's nothing here," she admitted.

Across the room, she could see Nickel nodding with a half smile on his face. "It's not your fault, Betty," he said. "Come on back, but remember to go slowly. Concentrate."

Betty nodded, and then she began the walk across the beam.

FIFTY-FOUR

Betty slowly slid atop the crossbeam. Her heart was roaring in her chest as she moved, especially as the beam began moving underneath her, swaying ever so slightly as she crossed the span. Then, suddenly, the beam went from a slight bounce to a full-on funhouse wobble, accompanied by exactly the sort of wooden groans she didn't want to hear.

It will hold, just keep moving.

Nickel seemed much further away than he had when she'd been at the heart, even though he was getting closer every second. The bravado she'd exhibited over what felt like a sure thing was gone, replaced by a growing terror over the new beam's swaying misbehavior and a deepening despair over the futility of her efforts to date. There had been no diary, and once again the sands of truth were slipping through her fingers. *We did everything right, but it still didn't matter*, thought Betty, and for the first time she understood Duke's frustration.

If Duke really was innocent, then the trial, fallout, and eventual Free Duke movement had to have seemed equal parts horrible and impossible. And even worse, Mandy was still dead, regardless of his fate. Betty had seen such a small part of it, felt such a small measure of the frustration, that it remained impossible for her to even properly empathize with a person who had been locked up for most of his life. *What happened in this house is either the truth Duke has been hoping for over the past decade and a half, or something he wishes desperately would just go away.*

Flushing the thoughts from her mind, Betty tried to focus solely on her return slide across the beam, but her mind kept offering useless and pointlessly dangerous ideas about which of the remaining walls she should carve into. She knew she wouldn't, though, no matter how many harebrained ideas offered themselves up. If there had been a diary, it would have been behind that wall. Since it wasn't there, either it had never existed at all or it had been stolen away years earlier. Whichever it was, the lack of a diary meant there might never be an answer. Even if Duke were released, the real truth would probably always stay buried.

With maybe ten feet still to go, the floor below Betty now erupted in bursts of what sounded like screaming. Even as Nickel began to shout at her that she needed to hurry, Betty ignored him, ignored the noise, concentrating on the floor. Every step brought more wood screams, every move she made was the possible catalyst for the ruined floor's collapse, but Betty knew that sitting and waiting for help would see her falling through it just as surely as a misstep would.

You wanted to show off and get to that wall. But that didn't work, so now you just need to get back to the stairs.

Nickel was silent now, but he was shining his light on the floor before her, just away from her own unsteady light but close enough so she could see further than with just the lone flashlight. Some of the nails connecting the floorboards to the beam were popping up, dancing free from the wood, and the sight of them bouncing about in the dust was hypnotic. Stepping over the lifted nail heads, she felt herself losing her balance and tried to recover but her next step strayed. Feeling a floorboard give beneath her, she drove her weight off her foot and heard the board snap behind her, but it didn't matter. She was already on her front foot then and driving off that one, too scared to slide or hold her line anymore.

She began to sprint.

The boards snapping in her wake sounded like a television gunfight. Betty was watching her feet so intently that when she felt arms wrapped around her a scream burst from her mouth, and then a hand curled over her mouth and a kind voice said, "Betty, it's Nickel. You're OK, all right? You made it, so please don't scream anymore."

Nickel slowly took his hand from her mouth, but he held on to her as she looked out over the room. Aside from the ruined wall and a few extra nails on the floor, it still looked exactly as it had before Betty had traveled across it, a booby trap in the purest sense.

"I want to go," she said.

"Don't blame you in the least."

"But we can't go. We can't."

"Betty," he said. "The house is a bust. There's nothing here to be found but trouble and old blood. We can still look into Jason Lattrell and see if there's anything else there, but I have a feeling that's going to be another dead end, too. Not that I don't think we should explore it, of course. I mean, we have to look in the darkest and least likely places if we're going to find anything out."

"We've been looking in those places." Betty broke free from him and walked down the stairs. His arms had felt wonderful around her, but solid ground under her feet would feel even better. "I've been to prison, the hospital, and now a murder house, trying to get information on a fifteen-year-old crime," she whined over her shoulder at him, "but there's nothing left. Whoever was panning this case for information before must have gotten all the pieces worth getting, and when the people that want Duke free came along, they took everything else."

"If it's so hopeless, then why are you still at it?"

They were standing at the bottom of the stairs now. Not solid earth, but an improvement.

"Because I don't want to give up," said Betty. "This was June's aunt—my best friend's aunt—who maybe never even knew June was alive. If we don't try and really find out who hurt her, then who will?"

"That's it, all right."

He'd spoken in just over a whisper, as though he was talking more to himself than to her. "What do you mean?" she asked him.

Nickel looked at her gravely then, and this time he was definitely talking to her. "That's why I do what I do," he said. "I try and do the things regular people won't do, see things they refuse to see."

Betty had turned to face him, her feet finally planted on something solid and the shaking feeling in her calves fading. "You sound like . . ." She trailed off, but he knew what she was going to say.

"I don't think I'm some superhero, believe me," he said. "Sometimes I wish to hell I was, but I'm not." He was still looking further into her eyes than anyone ever had. "Do you remember that day in the park when we met?" Betty nodded. "I was there because I had a meeting with a client. She hired me because she was worried about her daughter. June."

"No." Betty was too shocked by the admission to say anything else, even though her tongue was burdened with questions she was desperate to ask.

"She wanted this all to stay a secret," said Nickel. "If not forever, then for just a little longer." He swallowed, then took a matchstick, tucked it into a small gap between his left incisors, and sighed. "There's more. I said I'd help, and then I met you and everything changed." He grinned—a sardonic and sad grin—and Betty wanted to grab him the same way Nickel had latched on to her when she was finally off the collapsing floor.

"There's more than that, even," said Nickel. "June's mom had me look into her ex-husband. She thought maybe he was the one that killed Mandy. I broke into his house, followed him around, but there was nothing there. I stopped looking when I saw him out with June's mom—divorced or not, they still have some sort of a relationship going. I never meant to get this far into this situation." He worked his matchstick to the other side of his mouth and looked away. "And I never thought I'd meet someone like you on a job."

"Does your dad know what you do?"

"My dad is dead, Betty," said Nickel. "He's been dead for years, and this is my life, this work. Helping people that need me, and punishing people that manage to avoid the police. That's what I do. This work we've been doing has practically been a vacation compared to my last job."

"Why are you telling me this?"

"Because I want to," said Nickel. "Because I think there's a small possibility you might not think I'm some creepo liar. And because . . . because I think you're the same as me. There are terrible people out there, and more often than not they do awful things for years before they're caught. Even worse, their victims fall through the cracks, too. I live my life because of them, and I see that in you, too. I think it's been there all along, but what happened upstairs let me see it for what it is. This isn't just some project for you, and I don't think it's ever been."

Betty did grab Nickel then, hooking her arms around his body, and then finding her mouth on his. The kiss was electric, a fire in her belly that made every other stolen kiss seem childlike. It was over in seconds, and then the embrace faltered and they were two teenagers again, staring at one another as if they weren't entirely sure what had just happened or what they were going to do about it.

"I'm sorry," said Betty. "I know that's not what you're looking for, and—" The first kiss was fire but the second was better still. Nickel pulled her toward him by the hand, and in that broken house, with its bad death and bad living, they fell into each other's arms. Betty felt the heat rising in her face, and could never recall having been so happy. It was the adrenaline from the floor above, the impossible admission from Nickel moments earlier, the strength in his arms. He was exactly the fractured person she longed for, and he didn't need a guitar to find a song.

"Don't be sorry," said Nickel when he pulled away. "Please don't be sorry for that."

Looking down, Betty could see the dried blood on the ground, but what they were doing felt like the furthest thing from desecration.

"All right," said Betty, flashing Nickel a grin. "I'm not sorry at all."

But Nickel wasn't looking at her. "Betty," he said, nodding off the way he was looking, "I don't want to spoil the moment, but what the hell is that?"

Betty turned to look over her shoulder and then she followed Nickel's gaze to the foyer. The floor there was covered in rubble from the collapsed wall. Bits of plaster and pieces of heart had been flung across the already filthy floor, and then Betty's eyes fell on the same thing Nickel's had. At the center of the rubble, sitting there as if it had been placed there for them by Mandy herself, was a spiral-bound Mead notebook. What looked like dental floss was wrapped around the leather cover, and strings of it trailed off into the filth.

Betty and Nickel fell away from one another to walk to the notebook. Betty felt almost as if she were in a trance. She'd given up all hope of finding a diary, and she was so scared to pick it up and have it amount to nothing that she wasn't sure she wanted anything to do with it. The fear of it being empty was simply too much to deal with, but she was only able to hold out for a moment. Her hands found the notebook, stripped it of the floss that had clearly been used to lower and retrieve it from its secret space in the wall, and then opened it greedily.

"Let me see, too," said Nickel, and with shaking hands Betty held the notebook open so Nickel could see and shine his flashlight on the pages.

"She wrote this," said Betty after a moment, and Nickel said, "Turn to the last page. That's the important part." Betty nodded, then flipped to the end. There were several blank pages at the back of the book, and then Betty found writing. She flipped back a few more pages, and then found the beginning of the last entry in Mandy Reasoner's diary.

I know who beat me up, because it happened again, but this time I saw his face. I thought it would be a good thing to know, but it's not, it made everything worse. I didn't think it was possible for anything worse to happen, but this makes all the drugs, the hooking, all the shit look like nothing by comparison. All I want to do is get high and forget any of this ever happened, but that's not how it works.

I can't hook right now, not as ugly as I look, and even if I weren't hurt I'm not sure I'd ever be able to again. He knows where to find me. I don't know why he wants to fuck with me when all I want to do is be left alone, but that's what he wants, and I know if I go back out there he's going to be waiting for me. Stupid motherfucker. Asshole. Fucking rapist piece of shit.

This is my punishment, my penance for all of the horrible things I've done to get off. Why did I have to know him? Why can't I just tell D. and then wait for this asshole with him and let D. kill him? Because I know he'd kill D. Bad as D. is, he'd kill him and like it. If I thought anything different, we'd already be doing it. D. would be stomping his face into grape jelly, but instead I'm sitting here with a busted-up face, feeling sorry for myself. I feel so low I even miss Jason, and I'd grown to hate him. At least he was someone else to talk to, someone who could sort of understand what was happening to me, but D. told him to leave and there's no way Jason would disobey D.

I don't know what to do, but for the first time in a long time I'm serious about calling my sister. I need to just tell her I need help. I

*need to own up to so many things so I can start to get better, but I
just can't do it.*

*There's a place in this world for me, I know there is, I just need to
accept what I am and get past it.*

*The first step is going to be telling my sister everything. Claire
needs to know about Jack. She needs to know about what happened
five years ago, when he raped me. She needs to know that he's been
watching me, stalking me for whatever psycho-ass reason. She needs
to know that he's attacked me twice and I'm scared that if he sees me
on the street again he's going to kill me.*

*I should never have put myself in that position that first time,
but I was practically a kid and didn't know the type of man he was.
We were just flirting, and then the next thing I knew I was dizzy
from the wine and we were alone. He raped me and made me feel
like such a piece of shit, and nothing's ever been the same since.*

*Nothing is ever going to be the same, but it can still be better
than it is now. I can call my sister and tell her the truth. If he's been
beating me and attacking me, I'm sure he's been beating her, too. I
can throw her a life preserver at the same time I'm reaching for one,
and maybe then Jack can go away. He can leave Claire alone, leave
me alone, and hopefully leave June alone. I've never even seen her,
but I think about her growing up in that house with that poisonous
man and I feel sick to my guts.*

*D. will be back soon, and he's going to want to get high. That's
OK, I can get high, but when it's over I'm going to tell him I'm leaving
and he needs to come with me. I'm not even sure if I'm going to take
this journal with me. I don't know what good it would ever do me. It
might be better here in this house, a ghost destined to just fade into
nothing.*

*I can hear D. on the stairs, so it's time to hide this, and then get to
the rest of it. If things go well, you and I are never going to speak again.*

Kiss kiss,

Mandy

FIFTY-FIVE

"Oh crap," said Betty as the words sank in, and then the book tumbled from her hands as if it were on fire. "Oh shit, oh crap. We have to help her, we have to go now."

Nickel picked up the diary and tucked it under his arm, and then Betty had his arm and began to shake him. "She's at her dad's. She's at Jack's right now. She's going to talk to him about Mandy."

Nickel opened his mouth to speak, but Betty pushed past him out the door and across the lawn at a run and then all but threw herself into the driver's seat. Nickel was in the passenger side just after her, and then Betty had the keys in the ignition, the car in drive, and her foot on the gas.

They exploded from the broken neighborhood onto a main drag. Betty was dialing her phone while she drove the car, her fingers fumbling but finally managing to pick June out of her contacts list and hit the "Call" button. Finally the phone began to ring and Betty pushed it to the side of her face. After ten rings and no pickup, the phone went to June's aggravating automated message, and when it was done, Betty said, "June, you need to get a hold of me right away, OK? We made a mistake, so as soon as you get this you need to give me a call, OK?"

Betty hung up the phone and set it on her knee. She felt sick. There was no way they could possibly get there fast enough. Whatever was going to happen, they were going to be too late. June was there, babysitting the time bomb that was her father. Betty wiped the tears she had just noticed were streaming from her cheeks with the back of her hand, and only then, as she turned to Nickel, did she realize just how screwed they really were.

"I don't know where I'm going," she said. "I've never been to her dad's house. I'm just driving like an idiot! I don't know what to do!"

"This way, take a right." A furious look had taken over Nickel's face.

Betty swung the wheel, making the tires screech.

"Dammit," said Nickel. "He was my only suspect in this thing. I screwed up, bad. Really bad. He didn't fit the profile right, and the only things he had going were that he was alive at the time of Mandy's death, he had a history of violence, and he was related to her by marriage. I was wrong. Take a left. Not there, at the light."

"He's in this end of town?" He lived just outside the city, not even a fifteen-minute drive from their school.

Betty turned at the light.

They had the journal, they knew the truth about June's dad, and nothing was going to stop it from getting out now. They just needed to get June away from him.

Betty screeched around a corner, then whipped around another at Nickel's direction. And there, so close to the slum Mandy died in, was June's car sitting in front of her father's house, and Betty just missed it as she ripped onto the gravel driveway. She could hear a neighbor yelling at her to slow down as she left the car, and then she and Nickel were sprinting across the lawn.

Nickel was at the door and rearing back to kick it in. Betty had time to wonder if he shouldn't have just knocked first, but that thought was tempered by the knowledge of the monster June was alone with. Betty cringed as Nickel's Chuck Taylor slammed into the door and blew it open, and then the two of them were rushing in.

The last thing Betty saw as she entered the house was Nickel pulling something from his bag ahead of her, something black and mean-looking.

FIFTY-SIX

"What in the fuck?" June's dad said to no one and everyone. He was seated at a battered Formica table, across from a sobbing June, and between them was a stack of yellowed newspapers.

Jack stood to face Nickel and Betty, then turned to June. "Your friends are going to pay to fix that door, just so we're clear," he said, and then he turned again to stare at his guests.

The words Jack said made no sense to Betty, nor did June's tears or the fact that her friend appeared to be in the furthest thing from a life-or-death situation. *It looks like they're just talking about Mandy.* When Betty turned to Nickel, she could see by the sheepish look on his face that he was thinking the same thing.

"I'm serious, you little freaks," said Jack. "You're going to be paying to fix that fucking door." He grinned, a sickening expression made worse by the situation and the way the skin surrounding his over-tanned mouth drew away from his teeth. Jack waved them to the two empty chairs at the table and said, "You must be here for the show. I've been telling June all about it."

"Let's go, June," said Betty. "We can talk about this later."

"We're going to talk about it right now," said Jack. "Right fucking now."

Betty saw Nickel fidgeting with something behind his back, and though she didn't know exactly what he was doing, she found herself hoping he had some answer. *Do something*, thought Betty, but instead, Nickel took one of the seats offered by Jack, and she followed suit.

Jack plopped himself back down in his chair. He was drunk. Betty could see it in the lazy-lizard way his eyes rolled up slightly as he spoke. "We are settling up," said Jack. "You two retards and this queer think I was up to something, I can see that, but you got it all wrong." Jack smirked. "Dead wrong, as far as I can tell."

"You killed Mandy," Betty heard herself say, and she could tell from the way June stiffened that she wasn't alone in her thinking.

"Now that's funny," said Jack. "We were just talking about that very thing. In fact, I was just telling June here about how I seen that idiot the day she died, right before that maniac killed her."

"You killed her," said Betty, less sure of herself than before. *He's lying. Mandy all but stood up and pointed him out in her diary. June's dad hurt her, and he decided to make her go away so she couldn't tell anyone.*

"No, I didn't," said Jack. "I may have roughed up the girl a couple of times after I saw her selling her ass." He turned to June. "But that had as much to do with your mother as it did with my own feelings about whores."

"Mom would never have asked you to do something like that," said June. "Never."

"Sure, you're right," said Jack, "except of course for that time she did. You, your mother, and I were driving somewhere, I can't remember where to save my life, not that it much matters, and then your mother saw Mandy standing there on Division Avenue. She wasn't holding no sign saying what she was doing, but you didn't need to be a rocket scientist to figure it out. The little junkie was out there peddling her twat, and I know that part's true, because I saw it myself."

"Mom wouldn't have cared about that," said June. "She loved Mandy, I know it, and—"

"You need to slow down and listen up. All three of you do, especially you two that kicked my fucking door in looking to act like Batman or something." Jack leveled a pointed finger at June. "Your mother asked me to do it, June. She said it made her sick to see family out there doing something like that, and I asked her what she thought we should do about it, figuring she'd tell me to call the police."

"So why didn't you?" Betty asked. "She'd still be alive if you had."

"She was a junkie and a whore," he said, with exaggerated patience. "There's no telling what might have happened if we had done that. Maybe she'd be alive, but I doubt it. It's a hell of a lot more likely she just would have found some other way to get herself killed. Not that it matters, because we didn't call the police. I got out, told my wife to circle the block, and then I pulled my hood over my head and I went over there and tarred the hell out of her."

"You raped her," said Betty and out of the corner of her eye saw June flinch at that. Betty shot a glance at Nickel to try to make the now-mute boy speak, but Nickel didn't say a word. "We found her diary," Betty said. "It's all in there. You raped her. You started doing it when she was young, and you couldn't help yourself when you saw her on the street."

That awful smile of Jack's was back. "You might be a looker without that purple shit in your hair," he said, "but there ain't a man on this earth that would ever confuse you with a smart person. You think I raped that whore on the side of the road with my wife and baby and God only knows who else watching? It was dangerous enough just to paste her a couple of times, but I took the risk on that. Rape her? Never. Her line of business, I expect she caught a lot of beatings. Maybe she was charging too much for her ass. No way to know for sure. All I know is my wife said she felt sick and she asked me to put a whooping on that whore, so that's what I did."

"That wasn't enough, though," said Betty. "You went back and did it again."

"You're damn right I did. I told her to stop whoring herself out, and when I saw her out there again that was the same as her telling me to fuck off. This wasn't just about her, this was about her dragging her family's name through the mud. I was just trying to teach her a lesson, but that crazy bastard they caught killing her was the one that taught her the last lesson. Bad end to bad trash, that's what I say."

"I don't believe you," said June. "I don't believe Mom would ask you to do that."

"Shit, you can call and ask her yourself." Jack pulled a cell phone from his pocket and threw it on the table. "I guarantee you the second you mention that slut's name, ol' Claire will tell you exactly what she thinks about what happened to her." He grinned. "Mom could tell you some stories, you can trust me on that."

He rocked back in his chair, locked his arms over his chest, and looked from one to the other of them, grinning that awful grin. "You need to understand something, all of you do, but especially June. We didn't want you to know about any of this. It's all deep, dark, nasty family shit, and there isn't a single person in this family that's proud of what happened to that poor girl, but that don't make it anyone's fault but her own.

"Mandy was living the way she wanted to, selling herself to get high, and catching a few beatings a week from that psycho she was living with to boot. That's no way to live, and—"

"How do you know Duke was beating her?" Nickel asked, the first words he'd said since they'd entered the house.

Jack turned to him with a smile. "I didn't think you had the balls to open your mouth, but you fooled me. I'll answer the question, though. I know he was beating on that bitch because when I saw her the last time she was already covered in bruises. That and the fact that he wound up beating and stabbing her to death. I consider that last part to be pretty important. It does show character, after all."

"So you're saying you were the last person besides Duke to see her alive, is that correct?" Betty asked the question slowly. There was something she was missing, something Jack was skirting around. June could see it, too. Betty could tell by the way her friend was staring at her father.

"I want to know, too," said June. "You said earlier you saw her before she died. Do you mean you saw her at their house?"

"Of course. I went by to check on her to make sure she was staying in, and when I left she was doing just fine."

"You raped her again, didn't you?" Betty asked, and Jack shook his head.

"Nope, never raped her. You're going to have to let that one go, little miss. I'm starting to get pissed off as it is. Looking at my door right now does that to me, and you asking questions like that, questions I already answered, is getting to be a bit much."

"How did you know where she lived?" Nickel asked.

"It was easy to find," said Jack. "I followed her home once, and—"

"Dad, first you said you beat her twice," said June. "You never mentioned anything about following her or knowing where she lived. You never said any of that, but now you admit you followed her? How many times did you see Mandy without Mom?"

"Everything I did was done because your mother asked it of me." He was less sure of himself now, and more pumped up and indignant to cover it. "You can think what you want of me, but don't for one second think I did any of this without your mother knowing about it, June. If you're going to blame me, you have to blame her, too."

"Did you own a green jacket back then?" Betty asked.

He just sneered and said, "I sure did. Is that it? Anything else?" Jack stood and flipped the table over, sending silverware and cell phones flying. Betty leapt to her feet, but not as fast as Nickel. June still sat in her chair, an enraged look on her face, but Jack was rushing away from all of them into the next room.

"You guys need to go now," said Nickel. Betty could see the thing in his hand now. It was black with two metal prongs at the top and a buzzing bolt of blue electricity humming between them. "Now," said Nickel.

From the back of the house came the sounds of a shotgun being racked, and then a growing, animal bellowing that became Jack yelling, "Get on the ground and cover your ears, June!"

Nickel had run toward the doorway Jack had gone through and stepped behind the opened door just as Jack filled the door frame. Betty was frozen next to the upended table with June, who hadn't followed her father's order to get on the floor.

"Accuse me of this shit in my house," Jack seethed as he stepped into the room, lowering the shotgun at Betty as he came. Betty watched Nickel move quickly and silently from behind the door and plunge the Taser into the center of Jack's back. The shotgun roared in his hands, sending metal hurtling into the ceiling above him, and then Jack fell flopping like a fish and Nickel dropped with him. The Taser was probably still buzzing, but Betty couldn't hear it. She was deafened by the shotgun blast and only knew that Nickel was still shocking June's father because of the crackling blue light coming from the weapon. Jack was writhing on the floor with Nickel next to him, the Taser the only thing keeping him on the ground. Betty had June in her arms then, and though she could feel her friend saying something against her chest, it was impossible to know what it was.

Nickel left Jack on the floor, and then the three of them were in Betty's car and driving away.

Muffled sirens could be heard in the air, but there was no one outside wondering about the disturbance at Jack Derricks's house. June was bawling in the backseat, and Nickel said, "Just drive. We need to get me home, and then you need to call the police so you can tell them you were here." Betty nodded, pushed the gas pedal down, and blasted out of the suburbs.

FIFTY-SEVEN

It was three days later before the police finally caught up with Jack Derricks. He was holed up in a friend's hunting cabin, and he surrendered like a meek kitten when the Department of Natural Resources and State Police finally came knocking.

All Jack wanted to do was talk about the teenagers who had screwed him over, but he could never find a cop that cared all that much. Betty and June learned about everything through the slow filters of the television and the Internet, and the slower filter of what Andrea was willing to share with them after work.

In the days after the arrest Betty and June worked nonstop to bind together all of the loose ends in their project, telling the truth not only about what had really happened to Mandy, but also—mostly—about their own investigation. The cops knew there had been a boy in Jack's house with them, or at least they suspected it after hearing Jack's description of what had gone down there and interviewing the neighbors. That was unavoidable, but Betty and June remained mute on the subject. Both girls were insistent to the police that despite what Jack and the neighbors may have had to say, they had been there alone. Eventually, the questions stopped, even the ones about the small burn on Jack's back.

Duke would have been released from Jackson with the new revelations of the true nature of Mandy's death, but he died before the case against Jack Derricks could be finalized and the process to release him could be completed. A combination of liver damage from substance abuse, hepatitis C, and AIDS saw to his end in prison.

With his impending release the concert was delayed, and then canceled altogether after his passing. The girls couldn't have cared less. A concert seemed boring by comparison, a useless endeavor, especially to June. Instead, they enjoyed their time at school, heroes in a way that none of them had ever imagined, but with a sheen of guilt for the lie at the center of it all that was Nickel.

Betty checked her e-mail obsessively in the hopes that he might get hold of her, but for two weeks, no message came. She also found herself regularly accompanying Andrea to Rhino's to work out, at first just thinking she might see Nickel again, and then just because it felt good to train. She felt her body transforming swiftly. She'd already been fit, but as she pounded mitts and rolled with her mother and other students, she felt like she was coming into her own, and she liked the feeling.

The question of whether or not Nickel would ever contact her was answered finally by a typically terse request to meet at his bench in Riverside Park: "I have a job if you want to help. N."

Betty nearly screamed with excitement when she read the message, but managed to keep her joy inside. Nickel was her secret, the only part of her that wasn't in the public eye, and she wanted it to stay that way. And she wanted to know what other mysteries he might be hiding. Betty deleted the mail, closed the browser, and then headed downstairs.

FIFTY-EIGHT

I know honesty is the only policy in this case, so I tell Betty everything. Dad. Arrow. Sam. Ben. Paul. When I'm done, she does the last thing I ever would have expected: she throws her arms around me.

"How can I help?" Betty asks, and I just shake my head. I'm about to ask her to assist me in the commission of multiple felonies, and just sharing this stuff could be the end of both us, but she's acting like I asked her to dance. This shouldn't matter, but it does. I can't do this alone, and I do need her help, but I never could have predicted her enthusiasm.

It's Duke and Jack and June all over again, a problem begging to be solved, but this time I'm the one who needs help, not Betty. That's OK, I've told myself over and over again, but now that I'm really asking it's just as scary as launching myself after Jack Derricks and pushing a lightning storm into his back.

"If we do it right, it's going to be simple," I tell her.

"And what happens if we don't do it right?"

"We could end up in a lot of trouble, or maybe even worse."

"I don't care," says Betty, and I believe her. There's beauty in her eyes, but there's a coldness there as well, and it's been growing since we talked about Ben and his dead mother.

"I'm serious," I say, but she just shakes her head.

"What do I need to do?"

I explain, but she doesn't like what I have to say.

I wasn't expecting opposition, but Betty hates the plan. I suppose I shouldn't be shocked, but I am anyway, and we're right back to not having a plan at all.

We're already crumbling and the job hasn't even begun.

It's a good and just plan, I'm sure of it. I'll be planting a bomb in Paul's car, an IED that will blow him to hell where he belongs, and I need Betty's help to make the job safe.

By the time we're through, the ice in her eyes is back. She knows about Ben, she knows about his dead mother, and she knows I need her help to get to Paul. We work it together, and finally everything clicks.

———

I'm breaking into Paul's van to place a small package in the trunk under the spare tire. There's no question that if this thing doesn't work I'm going to be a mess, but I can be confident at least that if Paul comes out to the van while I'm still working, I can handle myself. Betty has the burner with one number on autodial, and she knows if he comes out to check his ride, she needs to hit "Send" immediately. That way, no matter what else might happen, he'll still get taken care of.

It's hard to work with a cool head when you're fired by angry, urgent retribution, but I do OK, and by the time the trunk is closed the butterflies in my stomach seem to have found a place to roost. I walk from the van, beelining for Betty and the safety of the trees and forcing myself not to look back. This plan only really works if Paul doesn't see me and just gets in his van and leaves. I part the thick curtain of tree boughs and disappear behind it, grinning as I see Betty.

"Did you do it?" she asks, and I nod. "Will it work?" she asks, and I nod again. It will, there's no doubt about that. When I put something together to hurt someone, I make sure to be very thorough, and that is most definitely the case with the package in Paul's van.

I sit next to her, and Betty settles down as well. We're ready for the fireworks.

It's two more hours before Paul leaves the house, climbs into the van alone, and takes off. Betty doesn't ask me if she should still make the call. She punches "Send," and I watch Paul's van roll off down the street.

"I need to report a drunk driver," says Betty into the burner, before rattling off the van's plate number.

Paul might not be drunk, but he does have a couple ounces of blow in his trunk, along with a flash drive with a couple gigs of some really sad child pornography. I hated compiling it, but at least it's being used to pound the final nail in a coffin that sorely needs closing.

"They're dispatching a car right now," says Betty as she stands, and I nod before following her lead.

As it turned out, Betty thought killing this particular roach with a sledgehammer might have been a little too much, and too dangerous for the attention it might bring my way, especially in light of the recent fire and mess left at Gary's. I didn't want to agree with her, but I know she was right, and that just gives me one more reason to be glad I called her.

Still, it's a strain acclimating to this less direct, less violent course of action. "Think they'll check the trunk?" I ask.

Betty smiles and shakes her head. "Yes, dummy. You heard me tell them he was drinking when he left the party and how he kept bragging about all the coke he was holding." She pats my hand and smiles. Everything about this moment, about these last few hours, is so beautiful and surreal it feels fake. "He's going to go down hard, and you have nothing to worry about."

"I still kind of feel like we should have blown up the van."

"You can think whatever you want, but if you want me to keep helping you, you need to think around both sides of a problem." Betty leans over and kisses my cheek as we walk out of the woods, and I can feel my face catch fire as her lips brush against it. I never want to get used to that feeling, to take it for granted and act like it isn't a miracle.

I can't say anything like this, of course. Instead, I stammer, "I do think around problems," and Betty laughs.

"No, you decide whether you should blow a guy up or just beat him into a coma," says Betty, and I shake my head.

"I'm just used to nuking my problems."

"'Don't get caught,' remember? That's rule number one."

I nod. She's right, that was always the number one rule, but I never had a reason other than fear to want to avoid capture before now. If being with Betty means taking my work down a slightly safer path, then that's fine with me, just as long as I still get to crack some heads once in a while.

"You want to go to Rhino's?"

"Sure thing," says Betty as we approach her car and she walks to the driver's side, and for the first time I realize I might not need Lou anymore. "You think Ben will still be there?"

"No, Rhino will have moved him, either somewhere else, or with extended family if he could. Ben and his mom have been on the news way too much lately," I say as I get in the car. There was some hubbub about the missing boy after his slain mother was found, but it didn't last long. Without crying family members around to keep the fires hot, the press had moved on to the next tragedy. I know from experience that without some serious media heat, lost kids are far too common to keep on generating PR on their own. That's why I'm in the business I'm in.

Everything feels like it's changing, and I usually hate change, but this is different. I'm scarred for life, I know that, but right now I'm happier than I can remember being since Dad was alive. I can't bring Dad back, or Sam, or Ben's mother, but I can be happy, at least once in a while.

Betty starts the car and I lean back in the seat. I'm still adjusting to being in the front of a car, but that's OK. The view's actually better up here.

ACKNOWLEDGMENTS

It's so easy as an author to wax poetic about the trials and tribulations of one project or another, always forgetting as we do so that we are the blessed ones, sharing our dreams—and, all too often, our nightmares—with our friends. I felt like I was in that situation with this very book, in fact, and I could tell you in vast expanses of text how hard this one was for me, how the edits stretched on and on, and about how the words struggled from my fingertips. But I won't. Instead, I want to tell you about Anne.

When I first began dating my wife, I realized I was going to be in for a bit of culture shock if our relationship had legs. I was raised in a very small family, while she grew up with an army of aunts, uncles, cousins, and the occasional hangers-on, all of whom were very friendly, if a little scary for me at first. It's hard to blame them in retrospect. After all, I was dating one of the young women from their so-called tribe, and having a daughter of my own now, I consider myself lucky that I wasn't clubbed, tarred and feathered, and then sent packing. However, as polite as they were—and they all were, despite my nervousness and difficulty with names—Anne stood out.

Just a few months before my wife and I began dating, her aunt, Anne, had lost her husband, Carl, far too early in life. Despite the obvious pain she was suffering, not to mention the fear any parent would have upon losing their life partner, Anne was immediately welcoming. I think she saw me as the same sort of outsider she had once been before receiving full tribal status. It was a kindness that wouldn't have been a shock to anyone who knew her. Anne was that outgoing woman who always had a smile on her face. Despite the loss of her husband, and despite the loss of her father when she was just a girl, she always wore a grin.

On December 3, 2013, we received the news that Anne had died in her sleep; it didn't—and still doesn't—seem possible. She was young still at forty-seven, had recently remarried, and was very happy. It seemed a cruel twist that nearly fifteen years after Carl had passed Anne would find love again, only to die, and it sure did suck the wind out of any complaints I might have had about entering another round of edits. Anne was one of those irreplaceable people, the kind of woman who lights up a room, and I know everyone who knew her will miss her like I do.

First and foremost, I need to thank my wife and daughter for sticking by this writer as he occupies the kitchen table and battles enemies of his own design, all the while swinging from mood to mood like some yet-to-be-housebroken chimp. I love you both so much, and I can never thank you enough for the constant anchor you both provide for my well-being and my occasionally fragile mental health. I could never do this without you both and desperately hope I never have to try.

A wild round of applause for my parents, who continue to offer rock-solid support for my literary career, but especially to my mother, who has been asking for another Nickel novel since before the first one went to print. If you have been clamoring for more Nickel, trust me, my mom is the person you want to thank.

A massive thank you goes to my new editor, Anh, who found herself in the unenviable position of dealing with neurotic little me shortly after I decided to do this writing thing full-time. Anh, thank you so much for your support of this book, and for the tons of help you gave me as we built this thing up from the skeleton I passed along to you last year, help that got us where we sit today. This book is better because of you, and I can't wait to work on another one with you.

The other person who made sure this book was as good as it could be is my long-suffering creative editor, David, who, upon reading one particular passage—I believe I described a room as smelling like "ass and bad breath"—wondered whether Max Perkins ever had to wrangle phrases like that while editing Hemingway or Fitzgerald. Probably not, David. Probably not.

Thanks to my good buddy Greg, who always offers a sunny disposition to all things literary, and who got married to Maggie this past year. Much love to you both.

Thank you to Sarah Burningham of Little Bird Publicity, who always manages to get a hold of me when I most need a shoulder to complain on, or to field questions about this wild world of writing.

Thank you to Jacque, for your help in the early edits of this novel. As it turned out, just about everything you suggested last fall wound its way into the final copy. As usual, I could save myself a lot of trouble if I always just listened to the people I work with, instead of waiting four edits down the road to make things right.

Big-time thanks to Laurel and Pete, who met my wife and me at Founders Brewing Co., shared a sandwich and a beer, and then got to work. By the end of our lunch my wife and Pete were discussing Michigan beer, and Laurel and I were discussing the film rights of my work. I can't wait to see what the future brings, Laurel. Thanks again for working with me.

Of course, I need to thank everyone else from Amazon Publishing, and though you are far too many to name, I need to be sure to thank Jeff, Terry, Jon, Sarah, Gracie, Tiffany, Andrew, Alex, Caroline, Jodi, Alan, Justin, David, Jessica, Ashley, Luke, and every other gosh-darn person there who is making this work for us lucky authors. You guys are the backbone that allows all of this to happen, and I appreciate you all so much.

One last thing: thanks to every single one of my readers. I think I'd write this stuff either way, but it sure is fun sharing it with all of you. You guys are the best, and I appreciate everything you've done for me. I hope to see you again soon.

ABOUT THE AUTHOR

Born in Ithaca, New York, Aric Davis has lived most of his life in Grand Rapids, Michigan. He is the author of *The Fort* and the acclaimed YA novel *Nickel Plated*, called by Gillian Flynn a "dark but humane, chilling and sometimes heart-breaking work of noir" and given a "Top 10" Booklist designation in 2011. An aficionado of punk rock and other music, Davis worked as a body piercer for seventeen years before putting down the needles to write full-time. He and his wife and daughter live in the chilly Midwest, where they enjoy roller coasters, hockey, and cold weather.